THE SNOW WHITE EFFECT

a novel

A.K. Mills

Dark Wolf

Publications

"No." Mickey shook his head. "That chick was hot."

"Careful," Dale cautioned.

"Nah, Cindy's not bad either. That's not what I'm saying. She's cute and looks familiar." Mickey paused.

Dale waited patiently.

"Dude, is that the waitress?"

"Sure is."

"But you sent a sundae to the other girl."

"Sure did," Dale replied.

"I don't get it," Mickey said as Cindy returned to the table.

Dale stood up, allowing Cindy to slide into the booth. "I gave the girl the sundae so I had an excuse to write something for Cindy."

"What did you write?" Mickey asked.

"It said Happy Birthday. Enjoy the sundae," Cindy answered. "Can you give this number to the waitress and tell her I think she's beautiful?"

Mickey nodded in approval. "Nice."

Their courtship was short, a little too short for their parents' liking. But it was hard to deny their love. It radiated so brightly, illuminating everything within a mile of where they were. Lord knows they fought, but they also made up, growing closer with each argument.

After six short months, Dale proposed. He was working construction for his uncle's company, with dreams of building his own house one day. Cindy, still working at the diner, answered with an emphatic "absolutely!" They were married eight months later, neither one of them looking back except to smile.

Dale shook his head as the elevator chimed on the third floor and the doors opened. *This isn't happening.*

EMMA AND RUSSELL

"What time is your appointment?" Russell asked, stepping onto the elevator and glancing at his watch.

"Twelve-fifteen," Emma answered, sliding between her husband and a somber-looking gentleman.

Russell looked at her, panicked. "It's quarter after now. This is an important appointment. We can't be late."

"It's fine." Emma smiled. "She's never on time anyway."

"It's not fine," Russell replied. "I don't like how this is presenting."

Emma looked at the man to her right. The wilted stem sticking out of the pink ceramic pot in his hands, coupled with his red-rimmed eyes and hunched shoulders conveyed the severity of what he was dealing with. She wasn't about to get into a public discussion with Russell about her vaginal bleeding and increased pain during intercourse.

"Make sure you tell her about the ice chips," Russell continued. "I don't like that either."

"Yes, doctor."

"I'm serious Em," he said, practically jumping from the elevator into the hallway when the doors opened on the second floor. He turned, waiting for Emma, who took her time stepping off the elevator. She smiled, taunting her husband.

She'd put off seeing Nicole Stein for a while. But after having Jocelyn, her menstrual bleeding had increased dramatically and the pain from what she was told was a benign uterine fibroid was not resolving. Originally, the fibroid presented as a textbook case. Emma had heavy periods her entire life, but it wasn't until she became pregnant with Hope that she noticed the mass in her uterus. Even so, her gynecologist wasn't concerned. Neither were she and Russell. However, during her pregnancy with Jocelyn, the fibroid grew.

At twelve thirty-seven, Emma was called from the waiting room. She pulled back the sleeve from her wrist to expose her watch and showed Russell the time. He rolled his eyes as he stood up and followed Emma through the doors to the exam room.

"Sorry for the wait," Dr. Nicole Stein began as she walked through the door. "Crazy day. So, what brings you in today, Emma?"

"I have concerns about my fibroid," Emma began. "The bleeding has continued, and I feel more pressure. I'm pretty sure it's grown."

"She chews on ice chips all day," Russell interjected. "She's clearly anemic."

"I see," Nicole said.

"It needs to come out," Russell said.

"Surgery is definitely an option," Nicole said.

"It's the only option," Russell replied. "Emma has waited to see if this was going to resolve. It hasn't. I'm not comfortable with her level of discomfort."

"I know the symptoms can be concerning, unnerving even. But fibroids do this."

"They don't grow like this," Russell pointed out. "And the bleeding? That seems a bit irregular."

"I've seen it before," she said. "Emma, you're young and healthy. This is clearly a benign condition. However, if you want to go the surgical route, I suggest a total laparoscopic hysterectomy. The recovery is quicker, less blood loss. You should be able to go home the same day."

Emma laughed, thinking that a longer hospital stay might not be the worst thing in the world. One or two nights alone in a bed to sleep soundly without little hands in her face and feet in her sides. A traditional hysterectomy sounded better the more she thought about it.

"I'm not concerned about going home the same day," Emma replied. "If an open procedure is best given the size of the fibroid, I'm okay with staying in the hospital overnight."

"You'd have a bigger scar," Nicole said.

"I've had four children," Emma said. "A scar isn't going to effect the appearance of my stomach."

"It's more invasive," Nicole replied. "TLH is safer."

Emma didn't need Nicole to explain the risks and benefits of laparoscopic versus open procedures. She was a doctor who'd seen both procedures performed many times. And yes, while laparoscopic procedures were better in some situations, others required a more invasive approach.

"I told you, you didn't have to come," Emma said as she and Russell exited Nicole Stein's office.

"I wanted to be there," Russell replied.

"So, what do you think?"

"I'm not as confident as Nicole is that it's nothing to worry about," he answered. "The changes aren't normal."

"She ordered a biopsy, bloodwork," Emma said. "I'll have them done and we'll go from there."

Russell looked at his watch. "I'm late for my case." He kissed Emma on the cheek and hurried off.

Emma, realizing the time, quickened her pace as well. She also had a case coming up and really needed it to finish on time, though the likelihood of that happening was rare. Unlike many other professions, medicine didn't run on schedule. The human element often required more time and explanation than what was planned for.

As Emma made her way to the operating room, she was called in on a gunshot victim which meant her original case would be postponed.

"No, no, no," Emma cried, pulling her phone from her pocket.

"I'm about to scrub in," Russell said quickly.

"Is there any chance you'll be out in time to meet Kaitlin's teacher tonight?" Emma practically begged.

Russell laughed. "The OR is booked for eight hours, Em. There's no way."

Emma sighed. "I promised Kaitlin I'd make it."

"You can meet her teacher another day. I'm sure he'll understand."

"Jacob's teacher is the guy," Emma replied. "Kaitlin's teacher is Mrs. Kind who, according to Kaitlin, is anything but. Kaitlin made me promise I'd be there."

"She'll understand," Russell said. "I have to go."

"There's no way she's going to understand," Emma said. "I have to find a way to make it to the school."

Russell had already hung up

Four hours. The surgery to remove the bullet took four freaking hours and the guy didn't even make it. Sometimes it was obvious her attempts would prove futile, but this time she thought there was a chance she could stop the bleeding. Unfortunately, the bullet had pierced an artery and nothing anyone did could combat the excessive blood loss.

Emma had become immune to the sight and smell of blood, so much so she barely even noticed it anymore. The entire time the surgical team dug around in the patient's leg, searching for the source of the bleeding, all she could think about was how disappointed Kaitlin would be and how she was going to make it up to her. Jacob, she knew, would be fine. He didn't care nearly as much about school.

Being a firstborn herself, Emma empathized with Kaitlin's oldest-child plight. Kaitlin, eight going on forty, was well-versed in having doctor-parents. One of her first sentences was "Mommy on call." Kaitlin sometimes went days without seeing Emma. Oh, how Emma looked forward to the days of leisure when her schedule would become somewhat normalized. She and Russell could start climbing out of their mountain of debt, and life could really begin.

RICHARD

"The elevator's almost here," Richard said into his phone. "So, I'm probably going to lose you in a minute. I'll call you when I'm on my way home tonight."

"And what time is that going to be?" his wife asked.

"I don't know." He sighed, irritated by the slowly descending elevator. "Don't wait on me for dinner."

The elevator chimed and the doors opened as Elaine yelled something about a semblance of family life. Richard, in no mood for yet another rant about how the hospital took precedence over everything in his life, including his family, stepped onto the elevator and ended the call.

"Poor reception." He smiled smugly at the forlorn man who just stood there staring at him. He looked familiar, though Richard couldn't place him. As department chair of surgery at Kendal Slate Memorial Hospital, he came into contact with more faces than he had the memory for. "You going up?" he asked, selecting the button for the seventh floor.

The man shook his head and stepped off the elevator without saying a word. Richard was too busy tapping away on his phone, which had perfect reception, to see the man turn and scowl at him as the doors slid closed. Elaine had already sent two heated text messages. The first about being hung up on and the second about the importance of family dinners.

It was a constant battle with Elaine and one Richard didn't think she fought fair. She never complained about the luxuries his salary afforded them: the house, the lawn service, the cleaning lady, the cars and country club. Yet, she was always the first to criticize the hours and dedication it took to maintain his position.

"This isn't what I signed up for," she'd made the mistake of saying during one of their weekly battles.

"This is exactly what you signed up for," he laughed. "You met me during residency. You knew what my hours were like."

"You told me you worked because you didn't want to go home to your wife," she corrected.

When Richard remained silent, she glared at him. "Do you not want to come home to your family, Richard? Is that what this is about?"

"Don't be ridiculous," he replied, though her attitude didn't especially make him hurry home. Admittedly, there had been times he could have put a case review off until the following morning but lagged behind instead.

Medicine was his life. He'd devoted countless hours to obtain the title of chair of surgery and what Elaine failed to understand was that he loved what he did. Few people would ever understand the excitement of cutting into a human body. The control and focus it took to keep his hands steady, the expertise required to remove and repair organs within the human cavity. All these years later, surgery still elicited the same rush. It was something he would never grow tired of. Marriages, as evidenced by his first to Janine, could come and go, be hot and cold. Surgery would always remain.

He hadn't felt the gradual shift in his happiness, his discontent growing with his first marriage until he found himself teetering on the verge of an affair. Richard hadn't fallen out of love with Janine as much as he'd fallen out of love with their life. The chipped linoleum floors and stained laminate countertops of their one-bedroom apartment had only felt more claustrophobic with the addition of an unplanned baby.

"It's Richard now," he'd said when Janine pleaded with him to give their marriage another chance. "Not Ricky, not Ritchie, Richard."

"Well that's fitting," she'd replied, going cold. "Because Richard sounds like an uptight asshole, which is exactly what you've become."

"I'm sorry, Janine."

They both knew he didn't mean it.

"For what, exactly? Tell me, Ri-chard," she spat his name. "How is it we were good enough to get you through medical school and part of your residency but not anymore? Are you ashamed of us?"

"Don't be ridiculous," he'd answered, knowing it was true.

He wasn't ashamed that his girlfriend was a bartender while he was still in college. Not knowing what Janine wanted to do with her life, she'd taken some time to figure it out. That was one of the things Richard liked the most about her. She wasn't in a rush for anything. Her main goal was to enjoy life. And when he was with her, he forgot about the pressures of being a biology major and studying for the MCATs. She was his own personal escape.

The only time Janine panicked was when she found out she was pregnant. Even then, she remained cool and collected, taking on a dayshift job as a waitress and tending bar at night so they would have enough to scrape by.

"You can make it up to me when you're a rich doctor," she'd often joke.

"I will," he promised.

At the time, he'd meant it. At the time he wasn't aware of the hidden evil lurking within the hospital, with its on-call rooms and overnight shifts. The high-stress environment alone was a breeding ground for infidelity. Dealing with life and death on a daily basis made even the toughest people crack. It also left the weak, like Richard, hopeless.

Richard, enduring the emergent care rotation in his training, was the lucky resident in the ER when Elaine hobbled in.

"I hurt my ankle doing a sirsasana," she explained.

It was lust at first sight and Richard had a hard time focusing on Elaine's foot. "Excuse me?" he asked.

Elaine giggled. "A headstand, in yoga. It's usually one of my best poses, but I lost my concentration for one second and ended up falling back and hurt my ankle when I tried to catch myself."

"I see," Richard replied, struggling not to compare his wife, at home with their daughter in sweats and a t-shirt, to the energetic blonde smiling at him. Her breasts were perky, not having deflated like Janine's after a year of breastfeeding. Her thighs still tight, her hips thin, not rounded or soft. And her abdomen flashed skin from where her tank top barely touched the top of her pants.

He ordered an x-ray and returned with the diagnosis of a severe sprain.

"Rest, ice, compression and elevation," he instructed. "Keep off of it, and your head, until the swelling goes down and you can put your weight on it. I'll write you a prescription for naproxen to help keep the swelling down. But rest is going to be the best thing for you."

"That's a lot to remember," she said, feigning confusion. "Do you make house calls?"

Richard's cheeks warmed. "Just remember RICE."

"How is eating rice going to help my ankle?"

He chuckled. "It's an acronym. Rest, ice, compression and elevation."

"Right," she smiled.

Richard hadn't done what a loyal, faithful husband would have done when Elaine slipped him her number while she was being discharged. He didn't politely refuse, noting that he was happily married. Instead, he slid her number into his pocket. When he got home the following day, he made love to Janine picturing Elaine the entire time.

The elevator chimed and opened on the seventh floor. Richard stepped off and made his way to his office.

"Mom, it's fine," Addison groaned on the phone, watching the number on the display change as the elevator descended from the seventh floor. "I'm not worried about it and neither should you."

"What if you decide you want to try again? You're still so young," her mother said.

"I can't do it again, Mom." Addison fought back the tears. "This last time almost killed me."

"It's still fresh, Addy. Just take some time. Talk it over a little more with Keith. Make sure it's really what you want to do."

"It is what I want to do. I've made up my mind."

"Just think about it," her mom persisted.

"What's there to think about? For the past four years, I've tried to get pregnant and for the past four years I've failed. I've had three miscarriages and an ectopic pregnancy to top it all off. Endometriosis might rob me of the opportunity to carry a child full-term, but I'm not going to let it rob me of my life."

"Addison—"

"The elevator's here. I'll call you later."

"Don't make any final decisions today," her mom pleaded.

"I love you," Addison said and hung up. In the elevator, she shook her head to rid her mind of her mother's doubt. Sometimes she thought her mother didn't believe that the years of internal scarring had left her barren.

My mom wants me to think about it some more, Addison texted her husband while she waited to be seen. *She wants to make sure we're sure this is what we want.*

Keith responded immediately. *She really wants a grandchild, doesn't she?*

I think surgery makes her nervous.

Didn't the doctor say it wasn't that big of a deal? Minimally invasive, low chance of bleeding, quick recovery?

Addison sighed before responding to her husband. *I know. But they still have to put me under. There are risks.*

Did she talk you into changing your mind? Addison could sense the tension in her husband's response.

No, not at all, Addison texted quickly. *I just thought it was better to tell her I'd think about it some more instead of debating the issue. You know how she feels about the medical community."*

Yes I do. Did you tell her you picked a date?

I think I'm gonna wait until it's done.

Yeah…, Keith responded. *We know that will never happen.*

Addison laughed when she read Keith's text. *What??? I could do it.*

You can't even go a day without talking to her, Addy. There's a better chance of you having the surgery without telling me than your mom.

As ridiculous as it sounded, Keith was right. Having grown up without a father, Addison and her mom had an undeniably tight bond.

I'm being called back. Addison replied. *I'll see you tonight. Love you.*

Love you. Keith responded. *Be strong!*

DALE

The house had been quiet for a while now. Cindy had been in and out of the hospital so much since her surgery that he'd grown used to being home alone, stuck in the silence of his tormenting thoughts. Now that the battle was over, what was he supposed to do? Would the thoughts go away or morph into constant memories and never-ending regrets?

"If that's what you want," he'd said when Cindy suggested the surgery.

"It's quicker," she smiled. "We'll be back on the trails in half the time."

"Sounds good." He smiled back, confident she was in good hands. But now he second guessed everything.

Should he have asked more questions? Done some more research? While he didn't know the first thing about using the internet, he could've asked around or at least gone to the library. He'd failed Cindy and their three girls.

Watching as they sat vigil by their mother's bedside in the hospital, talking to her, holding her hand, pained him. If it were up to them, they would've moved into Cindy's hospital room until she was discharged. But they had lives of their own and needed to tend to their own families. The grands, as Cindy affectionately called their grandchildren. What would they do without her sugar cookies and kisses? Dale often pleaded with whichever God was listening to take him instead. His presence, he bartered, would not be as devastatingly missed as Cindy's.

Though grown, the girls still needed their mother. Rebecca called almost daily, even before the diagnosis, to check in and say hello. Gail made it a point to come over every Sunday for dinner. And Carmen, the baby who'd just had a baby of her own, was at their house more often than not. But now the house was silent. Even the refrigerator had stopped humming.

Dale walked around aimlessly, not wanting to sit or stay in one room for too long. Every inch of the house contained a memory that pulled at his heart. She was his soul mate. Without her, he was hollow.

He'd made the assumption that seeing his wife take her last breath was the hardest thing he'd ever do. But far worse than watching his soulmate surrender to the terrorist who'd seized her body was telling his three precious girls.

"She's gone," Rebecca had said, so matter-of-factly, she could have been the one telling Dale Cindy had died.

Gail had dropped the phone. At first Dale had been scared she'd fainted, but then he heard mournful sobbing on the other end of line.

Dale didn't know if he had the strength to call Carmen—she'd melt for sure. So, in "typical fashion" (as Rebecca would accuse, she and Gail both convinced he babied Carmen) he went to his youngest daughter in person.

Carmen was their "oh my," baby. Cindy refused to call her a mistake—Yes, Carmen had come along nine years after Gail, an even ten after Rebecca, but Cindy said, "she was created in love and would be received in love." Though he'd never admitted it, Dale had hoped for a boy, someone to carry on the Reichter name. All hopes for seeing the family name into the future were shattered when the doctor announced, "It's a girl!" But all it took was one look in his daughter's wide blue eyes and he was wrapped around her tiny pinky.

Dale slowly made his way to the car. Throughout their nearly four decades together, Dale had joked about going first. Cindy refused to entertain the notion of existing without him for even a second.

"Nope," she'd shaken her head adamantly. "If you go, I'll be right behind you."

"Yeah right," Dale had laughed. "You know you'll be back on the market in no time, looking for a younger man like all those other cat ladies."

"You mean cougars? My prowling days ended the day I took your order."

Dale's stomach tightened as he pulled into Carmen's driveway. As soon as she answered the door to her father standing on the porch, Carmen's hand went to her mouth and the color drained from her cheeks.

While Rebecca and Gail had accepted that death had become a matter of when and not if, Dale had seen the hope Carmen clung to. Even with the words "metastasized" and "unresponsive" thrown about, Carmen refused to give up on her mother. Dale greatly respected his youngest daughter while pitying her at the same time.

An hour later Rebecca showed up at Carmen's front door.

"Yep, I found him," she said into the phone, her face tear-streaked. "He's at C's house."

"How did you know I'd be here?"

"I went by your place first," she said. "When you weren't there, I knew the only other place you'd be."

Thirty minutes later Gail knocked on Carmen's door, walking in with the same grief-ridden eyes as her siblings. Together, they sat in silence in the living room while Carmen rocked her daughter Lois—Cindy's middle name—to sleep.

Around nine o'clock, Rebecca placed her hand on Dale's. "Come on, Dad. Let's take you home."

EMMA AND RUSSELL

"Thank you so much, Sara" Emma said as she received a sleeping Jocelyn into her arms.

"No problem," her nanny replied. "See you tomorrow." Sara didn't stay to talk. She'd been at the house since before six that morning and it was close to seven-thirty.

"Mommy's home!" Hope shrieked, running to greet Emma at the door, waking Jocelyn in the process.

"Hi baby," Emma said to Hope, stroking the back of her head.

"Did you talk to her?" Kaitlin appeared, arms crossed.

"Kay—"

"I knew it," Kaitlin huffed and stormed out of the room.

She hadn't even made it past the foyer and she'd already let one of her children down.

"What did you have for dinner?" Emma asked Hope.

"Nu-nu's and brocwi," Hope yelled, her three-year-old pitch unable to whisper.

"It wasn't even good," Jacob said, his eyes fixed on the television. "I'm still hungry."

"That's because you didn't eat your dinner," Kaitlin, wasting no opportunity to rat out her brother, yelled from the kitchen.

Emma often couldn't decide whether life was more hectic at home or at the hospital. Working in the emergency room often offered her more peace than being at home.

"Is Dad coming home tonight?" Jacob asked.

"He'll be home in the morning," Emma answered.

"Donuts!" Hope yelled.

"Nonuts!" Jocelyn matched her sister's excitement.

Russell had made it a habit to bring the kids donuts when he returned home post-call. It was his way of making peace with his hectic schedule.

An hour and a half later, when homework was done, baths were complete, and the kids were in bed, Emma sat for the first time all day. Well, she actually was lying in bed. With the exception of sitting across from Nicole Stein and discussing her surgical options, Emma had been on her feet all day.

She didn't want the surgery. She didn't want to eliminate the ability to have more children. Emma loved her babies. She loved being pregnant. But Russell was right. The fibroid had to come out. She was more in favor of a myomectomy versus the total hysterectomy. Removing the fibroid while leaving the uterus intact would allow the potential for more children. Not that they were planning on having more children. Emma just didn't want to be without the option.

A knock on her bedroom door interrupted Emma from her thoughts on the surgery.

"It's okay if you didn't go tonight," Kaitlin walked in the room. "But can you at least try to meet her?"

"I'm going to call first thing tomorrow," Emma said and patted the mattress next to her.

Kaitlin walked over to the bed, crawling in next to Emma. "She's not nice, Mom. She's probably going to be angry you didn't go tonight."

Emma kissed the top of Kaitlin's head. "I'll take care of it."

At five-thirty a.m., Emma's alarm sounded and she awoke to Kaitlin on her left, Jacob on her right, and Hope across her head. She was pretty sure that if Jocelyn wasn't in a crib, she would have found a way into Emma's bed as well.

Emma carefully reached over Jacob and silenced the alarm. She carried Hope back to her own bed before jumping in the shower. Five-thirty hurt, no matter how much sleep she'd gotten.

"I didn't sleep at all," Russell yawned into the phone. "Crazy night. Are the kids up?"

"Kaitlin was just getting up when I left," Emma said. "Sara should have the rest up and ready by the time you get home. Don't let Jacob forget his homework. He hasn't handed it in the last two days."

It was pointless reminding him about Jacob's homework. Russell was running on fumes—he'd probably already forgotten, if he'd been listening in the first place, which he often wasn't. She knew the only things on her husband's mind were a shower and sleep.

Russell's eyes might have blinked a little too long on the drive home and he may have even fallen asleep in the drive-through line at Dunkin Donuts and been rudely awoken by honking and yelling, but he made it home, a dozen donuts in hand.

RICHARD

It was too dark to appreciate the professionally manicured exit of his six-acre estate, the solar lights only illuminating the path of the driveway, as Richard pulled out. But the gentle vibration of his car on the cobblestone drive made Richard smile. He'd come a long way from the apartment he'd shared with his first wife and daughter during medical school. Some days he longed for the simplicity of that life, although everything from gas to groceries had been a struggle.

At five forty-five a.m., Richard pulled into his dedicated parking spot on the first floor of the garage at Kendal Slate Memorial Hospital. He enjoyed the quietness of the early morning.

"Good morning," a nurse passed him in the lobby.

Richard nodded as he continued to the elevators. He had a busy day ahead of him and Elaine had made him promise he would meet her at the twins' school for their conference. If there was any chance of that happening, he had to hit the ground running and couldn't afford any distractions.

With a warm cup of coffee in hand, he stepped off the elevator and made for his office. First on his towering to-do list was a review of resumes for a new plastic surgeon. Dr. Raymer, the current go-to-guy for plastics, had decided to start his own practice. While the plastics department had other competent surgeons, Raymer was the best. If Richard couldn't find another set of magical hands, the hospital would lose reconstructive revenue, which would lead the board directly to him.

As Richard turned the corner to the hall where his office was located, he noticed a man hunched over in front of his door. Initially Richard thought he was drunk. He wasn't disheveled enough to be one of the many transients that found their way into the emergency room every night. Still, he could've been looking to score some pain medication.

Richard addressed him briskly. "The emergency room is downstairs."

The man looked up. "Are you in charge?"

Richard vaguely remembered seeing him around the hospital. "Yes," he said. He didn't stop to introduce himself. Rather he unlocked his door and walked in the office.

The man followed him in.

"I'd like to talk to you," the man said as Richard flipped on the lights and removed his jacket.

"Listen," Richard said with zero patience. "There is an information desk downstairs in the lobby. I'm sure you passed it on your way in. They can assist you with anything you need. Now if you don't mind."

The man continued as though Richard hadn't spoken. "You're responsible for patient complaints, right?"

"Ultimately," Richard said with a sigh. "But there's a process if you have a complaint with the hospital or one of our personnel."

"I see," the man said. "The thing is, I don't care about processes."

"Well, I do," Richard said. He reached for the phone. "I'm sorry you have a complaint. If you make your way back downstairs to the information desk, they can direct you on how to file it. If not, I'm going to have to call security and have you removed from the hospital."

"Is this what they refer to as bedside manner?" the man scoffed at Richard.

"I am a very busy man," Richard replied.

"I used to be busy," the man spoke. "I used to have to care for my wife as she suffered on the tenth floor, rub cold ice chips over her dried, chapped lips. I held the buckets as she vomited."

Richard exhaled loudly. Like many, many other surviving spouses, this man blamed the hospital.

"Look, Mr.—" He put the phone back down in its cradle.

"Reichter," Dale said. "Dale Reichter."

"I'm sorry for your loss, Mr. Reichter. Losing a loved one is never an easy thing to witness. I watched my own mother succumb to cancer. And while I wanted to blame the world for her death, I realized after a good time of mourning that these things just happen."

"I understand that. But my wife didn't have cancer when she came in here three months ago for surgery. She didn't have cancer when she left the same day feeling good. The cancer came so quick after her surgery, it just doesn't make sense. I'm not a doctor, but even I know something isn't right here."

"I'll tell you what I can do. Leave me your wife's information. I'll take a look at her medical file and see if I can make sense of what happened."

"That's all I'm asking," Dale replied. "I just need some answers."

"I'm sure you do." Richard offered Dale a pen and piece of paper. "I'll be in touch."

ADDISON

As the alarm sounded, Addison fought the urge to shut it off and drift back to sweet sleep. She dreaded what was going to be a long day. Her days were usually done by three thirty, but today she had parent-teacher conferences—the bane of her existence as an educator.

Addison had been so excited to meet the parents of her students her first year of teaching, even the difficult ones. She wanted to make a difference, impact each one of her students. Addison had actually been naïve enough to think the parents would care what she had to say. But after the third mother started a defensive rebuttal with "no offense," and repeated reminders of how the parents knew their children better than Addison, she saw that parents hated attending the conferences as much as her students did school.

"Do you want to call out sick?" Keith asked, walking in the room with a cup of coffee.

Addison sat up, graciously accepting the cup her husband held out for her. "I'll tell you what," she said after a sip. "I'll go to the bank and help people with their mortgages and you can talk with the parents tonight."

Keith let out a laugh that conveyed both his admiration and pity for her. "What do you think is easier? Telling people they can't afford their dream house or telling parents their children aren't working up to their potential?"

"You haven't met these parents. You can't tell them anything without them thinking you're criticizing them. They hate me."

"I'm sure they don't hate you," Keith said, leaning in and kissing Addison on the cheek. "You're shaping their children. How could they hate you?"

"They judge me."

"They judge you?"

"Because I don't have any kids of my own," Addison answered, her voice trembling. "What could I possibly know about raising a child when I get to say good-bye at the end of the day?"

"Addy…" Keith sat beside her on the bed and wrapped his arm around her.

"I'm sorry." She sniffled, feeling stupid for getting upset.

"I'm sure they don't think that," Keith said softly. "And even if they do, it's just because they're jealous that you're more of an influential presence in their child's life than they are."

Addison wiped her eyes. "I doubt that."

"It's true." Keith pulled her in tighter. "You're a great teacher. Everyone knows it." He paused, choosing his next words wisely. "Not having children doesn't make you any less of a great teacher. Anyone who thinks differently is an idiot."

"Maybe I should call in sick." Addison curled into her husband's side. "Maybe we both should. We could spend all day in bed watching movies."

"You know I would." He kissed her. "Just say the word."

Addison considered it, the allure of hiding from the world and cruel reality that she would never carry a child of her own.

"I'll be fine," she squeaked.

Keith looked deep in her eyes. "You're going to be great."

Addison forced her best smile and rose from the bed, taking the coffee with her into the bathroom and started the shower. Standing in the warm water, she refused to shed another tear. She was stronger than this. There were worse things in life than not being able to have children of her own.

In fact, she had children. She had fifteen children relying on her to pull it together. Granted she only had them for a portion of the day, but it was an important portion and she wasn't going to let them down. Students like Taylor Forrest who lived to be praised would clearly be disappointed if Addison didn't talk to her parents. Or Robbie Opel who did well in Addison's classroom, despite his reputation. She needed to be there to let his parents know he was excelling, that she'd reached him.

Keith knocked on the bathroom door and walked in. "So, I take it we're not playing hooky?"

"Sorry," she said. "I can't do it."

"Didn't think you would. I'll see you tonight."

"Can't wait," she replied, so thankful to have a man like Keith in her life.

Keith smiled, grabbed his jacket from the closet, and made his way downstairs. He was worried for Addison. Yes, they'd endured everything together. But it wasn't his body rejecting life. It was hers. His sperm count and motility were just fine, though he wished he were the one preventing their family. He shared her feelings of sadness and disappointment, but he couldn't begin to understand how Addison was going to come to peace with her situation, if she ever could.

"You did what?" Rebecca stared at her father in disbelief. She'd shown up at his door, 'coincidentally' around lunchtime with two hoagies, claiming to be between errands.

"I went to get answers," Dale replied. "I owe it to your mother."

"She had cancer, Dad," Rebecca said with a parental tone. "It was aggressive and untreatable. What answers do you want?"

"She was healthy, Becca," he refuted. "She chose to have surgery. It doesn't make sense."

"Nothing about cancer makes sense." She reached across the table and patted his hand. "That's why there's no cure."

Dale shook his head. "No, something doesn't add up. I know I'm not a doctor with a fancy degree, but I know we're missing something."

"You're missing Mom." Rebecca's eyes filled with tears. "We're all grieving. It would be so much easier if we could point a finger and blame someone. But no one gave her cancer. We just didn't know she had it."

"How could they have missed it?" Dale looked down at the table. "She had scans. They took her blood. Everything came back 'normal,' 'benign.' Your mother was so confident that everything would be okay because her doctor was so confident."

"No doctor wants to see their patient die," Rebecca said.

"No," Dale agreed. "But it happens and they get used to it. It's just part of the job to them."

"You need to let this go, Dad," Rebecca said. "This is the type of thing that can consume you. We've already lost Mom. We can't lose you too."

"Sorry, Becca, but I'm lost without her."

Rebecca inhaled to fight the mounting tears. Her father had always been so strong and unbreakable. The unraveled man sobbing across from her became more of a stranger with each tear.

"We need to discuss the funeral," Rebecca said. It wasn't a great time to bring it up, but it had to be done. As the oldest sibling, it was her job to broach the subject with her father.

"I'm going to have her cremated," Dale said. "So, there will be no viewing. Just a funeral. No burial."

"What?" Rebecca gasped. "What about the people who want to say good-bye?"

"Let them come and say good-bye," he replied, looking at her through scarlet eyes.

Rebecca couldn't remember ever seeing a time when her father cried. She'd seen him angry, his eyes dark and brows furrowed. She'd seen him happy, eyes wide and relaxed. But in her thirty-eight years of life, she'd never seen her father cry.

"But Gail and I thought she could wear her blue dress, the one you bought—"

"She's being cremated," Dale interjected with a stern voice that shocked Rebecca. "You saw what she looked like at the end, a skeleton with flesh hanging off of her bones. I won't put her on display like that. Let her rest with dignity. Let people remember how beautiful she was."

OCTOBER

EMMA AND RUSSELL

Dr. Stein came in to see Emma as she was prepped for surgery. "Ready to do this?"

Emma smiled. "As ready as I'll ever be."

"Good," Dr. Stein replied, smiling at her and Russell. "I have no doubt you'll be able to take the kids trick-or-treating next week."

"We know she's in good hands," Russell said. "Our children appreciate you taking such good care of their mother."

Both Emma and Russell had been in and out of the operating room more times than they could count, with no anxiety. But today was different. Today was Emma's surgery. She was the one on the operating table. The doctor now the patient with more at risk than a malpractice lawsuit. If something unforeseen happened, her children would grow up motherless. Russell wouldn't know how to cope. He was a doctor first and everything else second. It worked for them because Emma was a mother first. What would he do without her?

Russell fidgeted in the chair next to Emma's bed. "Have I shown you a recent picture of the kids?" he asked, producing his phone.

Dr. Stein smiled courteously at the picture. "Beautiful."

A nurse walked in with the anesthesiologist, Dr. Weisman, and Russell turned, showing them the family shot on his phone. "Four kids," he said. "Eight to two. They need their mother so please take good care of her."

Both the nurse and anesthesiologist acknowledged the picture briefly and turned to Emma.

"You know the drill," Dr. Weisman said. "No surprises here. How are you feeling?"

"Ready to get this over with," she said.

"Well then, let's get started," Dr. Stein said. "I'll see you in there."

Russell leaned over and kissed Emma on the forehead. "I love you," he said.

"I love you," she whispered, unease building.

Russell put a hand on her shaking arm. "You're going to be fine. Quick and painless," he said. "You've given birth four times. Think of Hope. This will be nothing."

Emma smiled and winced at the same time, thinking of Hope, her ten-pound baby. All of her kids were healthy sizes. Kaitlin, the runt, was eight pounds nine ounces. Jacob was an even nine pounds. Then came Hope. No one, not even the doctors, expected her to be as big as she was.

When she came out, after an hour and a half of pushing and screaming, the whole room widened their eyes when they saw her size. In the nursery, Hope looked like a toddler compared to the tiny newborns around her. Emma required a lot of stitches after that delivery. She should've had a C-section. When she found out she was pregnant a quick six months later, her labor wounds only barley healed, she was petrified. Thankfully, Jocelyn wasn't as large.

Emma didn't know why she was so nervous. She had the utmost faith in her profession, in Nicole Stein. This surgery was a good thing, necessary. She looked forward to no more bleeding, no more discomfort. Most importantly, she looked forward to having pain-free sex.

While she and Russell were pretty sure Jocelyn was going to be their last, Emma was saddened to know that after today there would be no option of another child. There was something unnatural about it all. Granted, there was also something unnatural about the mass growing in her uterus. Regardless of the tests and Dr. Stein's reassurances, Emma would be happier knowing it was gone.

RICHARD

The hospital was decorated for Halloween with buckets of candy on just about every counter he passed. Spiders and pumpkins hung from the ceiling in the cafeteria, dancing dangerously close to the top of Richard's head as he paid for his coffee. Fall and winter were his least favorite seasons. With back-to-school, Halloween, Thanksgiving, and Christmas all in a row, Richard was engaged in a constant battle between Elaine and the hospital. She didn't get that the hospital didn't celebrate holidays the ways she and the boys did.

"People get sick every day of the year," Richard had explained. "And the holidays don't help, either. People are just as stupid, if not more, around the holidays."

Last Halloween, Richard had missed trick-or-treating with the twins because a man came into the emergency room swollen beyond recognition and barely breathing. The emergency responders had to cut the mask of an orange and yellow chicken from his face.

"It kept sliding down," one of the other two chickens accompanying the unknown patient had said. "So, he super-glued it to his face."

"Super-glued it?" the ER resident had asked, suppressing the urge to laugh.

"Yep," his friend replied. "We were going to do it too, but then Mike started wheezing."

"Does your friend have any known allergies?"

"I don't think so," he replied.

"Nah, dude," the third chicken chimed in. "I think he's allergic to condoms. Remember, he said something about his junk swelling up after he had sex."

"Yeah, that's right."

"So, he's allergic to latex?" the resident pressed.

Both chickens shrugged and nodded in unison.

It wasn't hard to treat Mike, the chicken with his mask cut off, once they knew what was wrong with him. The problem came in removing the parts of the mask that were glued on. Made entirely of latex, the cheap chicken mask had practically melted to his skin when he applied the glue. And until they removed all of the allergen, his skin continued to react.

"Why did the chicken cross the road?" Richard had asked the resident after word reached him of a swollen chicken in the ER.

The resident shrugged.

"To get me out of trick-or-treating."

Richard took a picture to show the boys when he got home. It wouldn't make his absence better with Elaine, but he knew Eli and Ethan would forget all about him not being there to walk them around the block when they got a look at the puffy chicken.

ADDISON

"Halloween can't come soon enough," Addison ranted to her mom on the way home from work. "The kids are already bouncing off the walls."

"Have you thought about what you're going to be?" her mom asked.

"I don't know. The kids aren't into the same thing this year. It was easier when they all loved *Harry Potter*."

"What about the poll?"

"Standard witch, ghost, pumpkin," Addison replied. In an attempt to get her students to focus, she'd put up a poll for what she should be for Halloween. If they behaved, they got a gold star. If they were able to keep the star until the end of the day, they could vote on what Addison would dress up as. "Though the leader right now is Mrs. Fletcher."

"The principal?" Addison's mom laughed.

"Yes," Addison said. "They even have costume suggestions."

"Oh, Addy," her Mom said. "That could be dangerous."

"If it keeps the kids in line, I'm all for it. Besides, just because she doesn't smile often doesn't mean Mrs. Fletcher doesn't have a sense of humor."

"I don't know," her mom replied.

"I'll figure it out," Addison said. "Don't worry. Keith's salary can hold us for a while if I lose my job."

"Don't ever rely on a man for your financial well-being," her mom shot back. "Ever."

Addison should've known better than to suggest dependence on her spouse. Her mother had raised her to be independent and self-sufficient. When things got serious with Keith, Addison's mom had been very reluctant to accept him. Although he'd treated Addison with nothing but respect from day one, it took a lot of convincing for her mother to see that they belonged together.

"He's my husband, Mom," Addison said, feeling the need to defend Keith. "He's not my father. But I was just kidding anyway. I won't get fired. I'll find a costume more entertaining than Mrs. Fletcher."

She'd made a promise to her students. If they were good enough to earn the votes, they deserved to see her dress up as what they wanted. Otherwise, they'd never listen to her again. The only thing she needed to do was suggest something better. Either that or she would have to ask Mrs. Fletcher if she could borrow her black floral cardigan.

There was enough sunlight remaining when Addison got home to allow for a long walk. Being cooped up in the classroom all day with sneezing and coughing kids made her crave the fresh air. As she sat on the couch lacing her sneakers, she decided to call her best friend Rachel to see if she had any costume ideas.

Rachel had such an amazing eye for detail. Costumes were always more fun when Rachel was involved because she thought of everything, from hair accessories to footwear. It was one of the things that led her to being such a successful event planner. Rachel knew where to go for everything, if she didn't have it already. Need tinsel at midnight? Rachel could dig some out of her closet. A single red balloon? She probably had one in her trunk. Rachel was the most resourceful and quick-on-her feet person that Addison had ever met.

"Shouldn't you be at the gym?" Rachel asked when she answered the phone. Rachel didn't understand exercise, claiming her body got all it needed from sex.

"I'm about to head out," Addison replied, crouched over her left sneaker. "I just wanted to call real quick before I forgot."

"So, you heard," Rachel said solemnly.

"Heard what?" Addison sat up.

"Nothing," Rachel said a little too quickly. "You go first."

"Yours sounds more interesting," Addison said. "What's up?"

"It's nothing, really," Rachel said. "It's just that. Well, I heard that."

"Just say it," Addison demanded.

"Tina's pregnant," Rachel blurted out regretfully.

Addison exhaled and fell back into the couch. One big perk or downfall of Rachel's job was the gossip she picked up along the way. Goodnoe was a small town and Rachel did her best to keep abreast of the current events. "How else will I know who to hit up for business?" she'd admitted to Addison after dishing an especially juicy bit about a local grocery bagger and a well-known lonely housewife.

Tina, a client of Rachel's, also happened to be Keith's ex. They'd lived together for two and a half years. According to Keith, she'd been so committed to being a lawyer that she didn't have time for him or talks of a family. But Addison always felt he was holding something back.

"Really?" Addison asked, trying to pretend the thought of Tina pregnant didn't pull the air directly from her lungs.

"Yeah," Rachel said. "Her friend Tracy wants me to help organize the shower."

"I see." Addison untied her sneaker and tied it again.

"I can say no," Rachel offered.

"Why?" Addison asked.

"If it's weird for you."

"As long as you don't ask me to help," Addison said, trying to make the conversation light. "I'm sure it'll be good money for you."

"You know Tina," Rachel exhaled. "Nothing but the best."

"Thankfully I don't," Addison replied.

The only things Addison knew about her husband's former lover had come from his disclosure of their relationship and Rachel's rants over Tina's wedding. "A hundred thousand dollars!" she'd exclaimed on the phone to Addison. "It's not the biggest budget I've seen, but it's certainly up there."

While she was completely going against client confidentiality, Rachel didn't care. She told Addison everything. Addison laughed out loud at the thought of having a hundred thousand dollars to spend on a wedding, but privately wished Rachel hadn't told her. She'd already had a bit of a complex when it came to Tina. Tina was tall and thin. Addison considered herself average. Tina was a successful lawyer, with money to throw at a wedding. Addison was a teacher who had to work part-time on the weekends to save for her and Keith's dream wedding, which apparently cost the same as Tina's cocktail hour. And now, she was pregnant.

Apparently, the entire world was fertile except Addison.

"Fuck it," Addison said when she hung up with Rachel. They'd never gotten around to discussing the whole costume thing.

Addison never cursed but those two words felt so good to say. "It makes you sound trashy," her mom had said the first time Addison said "shit" in front of her. "And trash is not a word you want associated with yourself."

"FUCK IT!" Addison yelled louder and fell into the couch, sobbing hysterically.

DALE

One month.

One month and Dale felt no better. The memorial service was beautiful. Cindy would've appreciated the job the girls had done. And the community. It amazed Dale how much Cindy had touched other people's lives. So many friends and neighbors came to say good-bye, to offer their condolences, provide a meal.

Dale didn't understand the pairing of death and food. The last thing he wanted to do was eat. Yet his freezer was stocked with lasagnas, casseroles, soups. Dale had lost weight. Nothing like the drastic weight Cindy had lost, but he could tell and so could the girls.

"You're not taking care of yourself," Gail had said.

"I'm fine," Dale defended.

"Dad," she replied, giving him a knowing eye. "What have you eaten today?"

"I eat when I'm hungry," he snapped.

He hadn't meant to be short with her. But since Cindy had passed, the three of them were hovering. Gail, on more than one occasion, had asked him to come live with her. He'd considered it. But in the end, he wasn't ready to let go of the memories his house kept. The memories that pained him so much were the same ones that kept him going. Though it was hard—especially after the blow-off that doctor at the hospital, Richard Oakley, had given him.

"Mr. Reichter," he'd said on the phone. "I've done a thorough review of your wife's case. I've read the surgical notes, the post-op notes. Your wife had an occult cancer masquerading as a benign fibroid. There was no way to detect it preoperatively. Leiomyosarcoma is a quick spreading disease with a grim prognosis. I am very sorry for your loss, but I am confident that Dr. Clayton and the rest of the staff here did everything they could for your wife."

"Cindy," Dale spoke for the first time since answering the phone.

"I'm sorry?" Dr. Oakley asked.

"She had a name. You keep referring to her as my wife. Her name was Cindy."

Dr. Oakley cleared his throat. "Cindy had a very rare and aggressive form of cancer. There was nothing else this hospital could have done for her. I know you wanted more, but I'm sorry. Cases like this are what they are. Inexplicable and horrible."

Inexplicable and horrible. Those two words played back in Dale's head over and over again every time he looked at the urn on the mantel under the picture of Dale and Cindy with their girls and their families. The more time passed, the more he refused to leave Cindy's death as inexplicable. One night, in a fit of mournful rage, he banged away on Cindy's computer trying to get some answers but had no clue how to work the damn thing.

He successfully turned the computer on, but immediately got stuck at the log-in screen. "Password?" he said aloud. "Who needs a password?" Dale had rejected the technological advances of the twentieth century and refused to even consider learning as they progressed into the twenty-first century. Online banking? That was even more ridiculous than an ATM card. He went to the bank to cash his checks and get his money. Cindy laughed at his stubbornness.

"You'll see," he'd warned her. "All this technology is going to crash one day and the world will be up a creek."

"Not us," Cindy joked. "We'll be perfectly fine with our money between the mattresses and rabbit-eared television."

They didn't have a rabbit-eared television. He enjoyed his sports too much. Cindy was just poking fun at her "crabby old man."

"Password," Dale said again. *This is ridiculous.* He tried his name, their anniversary, birthdays, the girls' names. Nothing worked. If only he hadn't been so stubborn, such a…he paused and then entered the words one at a time…crabby old man.

The computer granted Dale access and he began to cry. Cindy had loved him so much, regardless of his crabby old ways. In moments like these, he was ready for death, ready to be with her again.

The internet was apparently full of information that could be delivered in seconds. And if he'd only paid enough attention to Cindy, the girls, the world, he'd know how to use it. But it was hopeless, Dale didn't have the slightest idea what he was doing. He could've easily called one of the girls, but they, like Dr. Oakley, had told him to move on. Instead, he pulled the phone book out and looked up the number for the library. Surely someone there could help him get the answers he knew were waiting to be found.

EMMA AND RUSSELL

"Hi there." Russell was smiling at Emma as he came into focus. "How are you feeling?"

"Perfect," Emma answered sarcastically. "How did it go?"

"Nicole said everything went as planned. There were no complications, nothing suspicious. She'll be back a little later to check on you."

"Do I have to stay overnight?"

"Not unless you want to. She said as long as you woke up feeling okay, she didn't see the need to keep you overnight unless you wanted the extra rest."

"I want to go home. I want my babies."

"I thought so," Russell replied. "Your mom is relieving Sara after school so there's no rush to get back."

Emma nodded and closed her eyes. She was tired. There was an aching in her abdomen, but nothing she couldn't tolerate.

"Go back to sleep," Russell encouraged. "Enjoy the silence."

"Is it strange that it's harder for me to sleep when it's quiet?" she asked, accustomed to drifting off to sleep with children whining and hands in her face.

Two hours later, Emma was up and ready to go home. She didn't live a sedentary life, she didn't like lying in a hospital bed with nothing to do. She was used to being the doctor, visiting the patients, leaving them to sleep.

"Knock, knock," Dr. Stein announced as she tapped on the door, opening it at the same time. "How are we feeling?"

"Great." Emma sat up to prove she was capable of going home.

Dr. Stein approached the bed. "Any pain? Tenderness?"

"Nothing more than expected." Emma lay back to be examined.

"I'm not going to bore you with all the post-operative instructions you've heard and delivered a million times." Dr. Stein looked at the incisions on Emma's abdomen and pressed lightly on her stomach. "You're going to be tender, especially around the incision sites. Bruising is completely normal. You can take acetaminophen or ibuprofen for pain as needed, just nothing with aspirin."

Emma nodded along. She knew the drill.

"Any excessive bleeding or high fever, come in right away. Swelling is normal, but keep an eye out for symptoms of a clot. You can walk around, but no driving, no exercise, and no heavy lifting. Not even for those cute little children."

"I'll keep an eye on her," Russell said.

"Enjoy your recovery." Dr. Stein stepped away from the bed. "I don't foresee any complications. Everything went great. But don't hesitate to call me if you have any questions or concerns."

"Thank you, Nicole," Emma said. "For everything."

"It was my pleasure," Dr. Stein said with a smile and walked out.

Emma had never felt more relief leaving the hospital as she did that evening. She always had anxiety being the patient. Even things as natural as childbirth could turn into a catastrophe in an instant. Each delivery brought stress and worry. Each discharge quelled the nervousness and she always made sure to say a quiet prayer, thanking God for her health. Emma wasn't foolish enough to think that bad things couldn't happen to her, she saw them happen to perfectly good people every day. So, when Nicole and Russell said the surgery had gone routinely, again she prayed, expressing her gratitude.

When she and Russell walked through their front door, the house was quiet and clean. They both looked around to make sure they were in the right place.

"Mommy!" Jocelyn came barreling toward them.

"Easy, Joce," Russell stepped in front of Emma. "Mommy is very sore and can't hold you right now."

"Mommy!" Hope screeched.

"Am I chopped liver?" Russell asked.

"Chop liver?" Hope twisted her face.

"We told them you were staying at the hospital." Emma's mom walked in the room drying her hands on a dish towel. "That way they wouldn't be let down if you didn't come home."

"Where are the other two?" Emma asked, sitting gingerly on the couch. The longer she stood, the more the aching grew.

"Your father took them to the movies. Their homework is done and they ate their dinner."

Emma exhaled. "Thank you."

"How are you?" her mom asked. "Can I get you anything?"

"Water would be great," Emma said. "And some Motrin."

Emma's mom disappeared into the kitchen, leaving her with the two little ones and Russell. Hope wasted no time in trying to jump on Emma's lap.

"No, no baby," Emma shielded herself. "Mommy's belly hurts. Can you get a book and sit next to me so we can read it?"

"I wan boo," Jocelyn demanded.

"You can sit next to me, too." Emma said.

Emma's mom walked in with a glass of water and two white pills. "Can I get you anything else?"

Emma shook her head and smiled, wrapping her arms around Hope and Jocelyn who'd snuggled up next to her. "I have everything I need right here."

"How are you feeling?"

"Glad it's over," Emma admitted.

"Me too," her mom said, letting out a large breath.

"Come on, Mom," Russell said, taking a seat on the recliner opposite the couch. "She was at one of the best hospitals in the country. They wouldn't mess up one of their own."

"That's comforting," Emma's mother replied.

"You know what I mean," Russell offered, realizing what he'd just said. "We take care of everyone that comes in. It's just that when we're operating on our own..." he struggled to find the right words.

"You take extra precautions," Emma's mom finished for him.

"Yes," Russell said. "I mean no." He turned to Emma for explanation. Emma just laughed.

RICHARD

"Yes?" Richard replied to the gentle tap on his door without looking up from the proposed newsletter welcoming Dr. Mason, the new plastic surgeon, to Kendal Slate.

Nancy, Richard's assistant, walked in his office and took her usual seat across from his desk. She sat, back straight and legs crossed, waiting for him to acknowledge her. Richard finished reading and looked up.

"You don't like it," she said.

"This?" He held up the paper and tossed it off to the side of his desk. "It's fine. You read one, you read them all."

"Then what is it?" Nancy asked, knowing Richard well enough to tell he wasn't happy about something.

"It's Hailey Mason," he replied.

"What's wrong with her?"

"Nothing," Richard admitted. "On paper, she's great. In practice, she's near perfection."

"So?"

"She's not Jackson Ervan." Richard shook his head.

The replacement for their star plastic surgeon had come down to two doctors with two very different specialties. Jackson was considered one of the best when it came to birth defects and deformities. His name attached to Kendal Slate would have attracted a new group of patients and notoriety. Jackson Ervan was Richard's choice, but the board pushed for Hailey Mason, a reconstructive and implant wizard. Breasts were the bread and butter of plastics at the hospital and the board was hesitant to move in another direction.

"Mason might surprise you," Nancy said. "She's got quite the impressive resume."

"At this stage, they all do. Innovation is what fuels success at this level. You can't just be great. You have to be better than great."

"You don't think Mason is?"

Richard shrugged. "I know Ervan is."

He initialed the draft lying on his desk and handed it to Nancy. "Print it, distribute it. Make sure everyone here makes Dr. Mason feel welcome."

"Including you?" Nancy smiled.

Richard grinned. "I'll do my best."

ADDISON

After hanging up with Rachel and once her meltdown subsided, Addison decided to forget about Halloween costumes, being a teacher, and infertility. Instead, she indulged in a bottle of wine and talk-show television. It was nice to get wrapped up in the drama of complete strangers for the two hours before Keith got home.

"Rough day?" Keith asked after Addison stumbled to greet him as he walked in.

"You could say that," she replied. "But it's been a fun afternoon."

"Looks that way." Keith kissed the top of her head. "Have you had any food with that?" He gestured to the empty bottle, on its side on the coffee table. Addison shook her head.

"Want to order a pizza?"

She shrugged. "Sure."

"Do you want to tell me what this is all about?" he asked.

"Halloween," Addison said and fell into the couch. She lifted the empty wine bottle and shook it into her wine glass, hopeful for a few more drops.

"Halloween?" Keith repeated, skeptically.

"Well, it started with Hallween," Addison slurred slightly.

"I see." Keith said, sitting across from her.

"Did you know Tina's pregnant?" Addison asked.

"Tina?" Keith said, assuming Addison meant one of her co-workers. There were so many teachers and assistants and student-teachers, he had a hard time keeping everyone straight. "That's great."

"Is it?" Addison spat.

"Isn't it?" he asked.

"I'm sure for her and her perfect little life it is," she replied.

"Who's Tina, again?" Keith asked, completely lost.

"You're cute," Addison replied.

"No, seriously—" then it hit him. "Tina Attleson?"

"The one and only," Addison confirmed.

"And you know this how?"

"Because Tracy wants to throw her the most spectacular baby shower."

"Rachel," Keith said, understanding the connection.

"You know I think they use Rachel just to spite me."

"Maybe." Keith shrugged. "But what does Tina have to do with Halloween?"

It had hurt when Rachel had told her Tina was pregnant. It hurt every time Addison thought about it. But it killed her to tell Keith.

"So, you regretting your choice in a spouse yet?" Addison asked.

"What?" Keith furrowed his eyebrows. "Addy, you can't be serious. Tina's crazy. Everyone knows that. I'm surprised she found someone to put up with her. If anything, I feel bad for that baby."

"At least she can have a baby."

"So what?" Keith asked.

"So what?" Addison shot back. "So that's the one thing I want in this world and the one thing I can't have. She probably got pregnant on the first try."

"Why are you letting her in your mind? In our house?"

"I'm so tired of hearing everyone's great news. You know, at first I was always so excited for everyone else, figuring our time would come. But our time isn't going to come, ever, and I'm going to be stuck for the rest of my life hearing how happy everyone else is."

"Are you not happy?" Keith asked.

"No." Addison shook her head and looked down at her feet.

"Am I not enough?"

Addison looked up at him angrily. "This has nothing to do with you."

"It has everything to do with me, Addy," Keith barked. "You're telling me that I'm not enough to complete your life. That we're not enough for each other."

"That's not what I'm saying." Addison started crying.

"Then what are you saying?" Keith demanded.

"You asked me if I'm happy," Addison said. "And I'm not. I'm not going to lie to you. I'm sorry if it hurts. But I hurt every day and I don't know how to feel better."

"Talk to me," Keith said. "Don't let it build up and explode. Don't drink it away. Talk to me. That's what we do. We figure things out together."

Addison cried even harder. "I'm sorry."

Keith patted his lap, signaling for her to come sit with him. Addison got up and sunk into his embrace.

"I love you, Addy. Children or not."

"I love you," she sniffled. She didn't say anything about children or not. He didn't push the issue. Instead he squeezed her tight and let her sob into his chest. When she was good and cried out they ordered pizza with a side of large cheese fries. Over dinner they brainstormed costume ideas.

"I got it," Keith said when a commercial for Dairy Queen ice cream came on the television later that night. "Have the kids vote on their favorite candy and go dressed as that."

"That's too plain for them," Addison said.

"Tell them you'll cover your costume in that candy and for every correct answer or good behavior, they'll get a piece."

"That could work," Addison thought of her student's reactions. They'd do anything for candy. "But do I want to deal with the sugar high?"

"Tell them they can't eat it until they get home," Keith answered.

"So I can have the parents after me?" Addison asked.

"Would you rather have the principal after you?"

The costume didn't take long to construct. Two pieces of felt, one pink, one purple, on top of a black t-shirt and yoga pants made it one of the most comfortable costumes she'd ever worn. "Happy Halloween," Addison welcomed her class. As the kids filtered in, their eyes grew wide when they caught sight of the boxes of Nerds candy pinned to the felt. It was going to be an interesting day.

DALE

"Are you coming trick-or-treating with us tonight?" Gail asked. "It would mean a lot to the boys. To us all."

Dale shrugged, then realized she couldn't see him over the phone. "I don't know. I was thinking of staying at the house and passing out candy."

"Leave a bowl," Gail said.

"So one selfish kid can take it all?" Dale huffed. "I don't think so."

"Then don't leave a bowl and shut your lights off."

"We've never shut our lights off," Dale replied. "Before you and your sisters were born, your mother and I sat on the front porch with hot cider and passed out candy to the neighborhood children. She always made such a big deal of every costume that came by. It didn't matter whether it was the first princess she'd seen or the thirtieth. She always made it seem like it was the best costume she'd ever seen. We didn't stop when you and your sisters had kids. I'm not going to stop now."

"I think it would be good for you," Gail pushed. "I know Dominic and Dean would love it."

"I'm going to stick to our tradition," Dale managed through the lump forming in his throat. "Your mother made me promise."

"Dad—"

"Thank you for the offer," Dale said. "But I'm going to pass out candy here like every year. Tell the boys I'll be by around five to see their costumes."

Every Halloween, Dale and Cindy would make the rounds to each of their daughters' houses, bringing a little Halloween bag for each of the grands before returning home to pass out candy. Dale looked at the six orange bags on his kitchen table. Even they looked sad. Cindy had always put the bags together, knowing what special trinket to include to make it personal to each grandchild, along with their favorite candy. Dale could never keep it straight. He cursed his lack of attention as he wandered the candy aisle at the grocery store, trying to remember things Cindy had said. In the end, he bought a couple bags of assorted candy, baseball cards for the boys and stickers for the girls. There was no sense in trying to fake it. The kids would know Cindy was behind their bags, their birthday and Christmas presents. She was what made the family flow and her presence would be missed in every celebration, every interaction, every day.

Dale appreciated the concern his daughters had for him, but if he heard one more time what would be "good for him," he'd go insane. Everyone, even his bank teller, knew what was good for him. Get out, go hiking, take a road trip. Apparently, what was good for him was anything that didn't keep him at home. But what if he wanted to be home? What if he took comfort in being home? Maybe what was good for him was for everyone to leave him the hell alone so he could grieve his wife and find out exactly what happened to her.

While he hadn't made much progress on that front, he was learning as much as he could about the cancer that ravaged her body. Even that was frustrating, as little was known about leiomyosarcoma. What information he could find was garbled with so much medical talk he needed a translator. Half his time at the library was spent trying to find information on LMS, the other half deciphering what it meant.

"Do you have a doctor in the family?" Sophia, the kind librarian who'd taken pity on him had asked. "Someone who can help make sense of this?"

Dale shook his head. "We're not that type of family. That's why these doctors think they can brush me off. What do I know, right? I'm just a blue-collar guy with not much education and a bunch of suspicion."

Emma and Russell

The phone rang at seven thirty-three a.m. While they should've been getting their shoes on to catch the bus, Jacob and Kaitlin raced to answer it. Jacob won.

"No, this is Jacob." Emma, who was in the middle of changing Jocelyn from her wet pajamas into dry clothes, heard him say. "Who's calling?"

Emma smiled at Jacob's politeness. He'd come a long way from answering the phone, "Who is this?" She'd worked with him, telling him only polite people were allowed to use the phone. If he wanted to answer it and be a big kid like Kaitlin, he would have to be nicer to the people calling. The only thing she didn't like was that he always identified himself. She didn't want him giving his name to everyone who called.

"Mom," Jacob walked into the family room with the phone by his side. "Dr., hold on," he put the phone back up to his ear. "What's your name?" He nodded. "Dr. Stein is on the phone."

Dr. Stein? Emma thought it strange she was calling so early, but she could just be checking in before her day started. It had been a week since the surgery and Emma hadn't had a reason to call. She took the phone and motioned to Jacob to get his coat on. The bus would be pulling up to the corner across the street in less than five minutes.

"Hello?" Emma said, pulling a shirt over Jocelyn's head.

"Emma," Dr. Stein said, regretfully.

Immediately Emma's mouth went dry, her heart stopped, and her hands began trembling.

"Yes," Emma said hoarsely.

"It's Nicole Stein."

"Yes," Emma repeated.

Kaitlin ran over to give Emma a kiss before sauntering out the front door. Emma walked over to the door, hugging Jacob good-bye and stepping out on the porch so she could watch them until the bus came.

"Emma, is there anyone home with you right now?"

Emma's heart beat faster. "Just me and the kids. Why?"

"The pathology reports came back," Nicole Stein said, "as leiomyosarcoma."

"Cancer?" Emma's knees went weak and she grabbed the railing of their wrap-around porch for support. Her mind raced, repeating the word over and over. She didn't know anything about leiomyosarcoma. The bus approached and Emma forced a smile when Kaitlin waved from across the street.

"I'm really sorry," Nicole offered.

Emma barely heard a word Nicole said as she walked back into the house and collapsed on the couch. The word *oncologist* filtered through the noise in Emma's mind, then *follow-up*. Emma hadn't realized Nicole had hung up until the phone started buzzing on the other end. Did she say good-bye? She couldn't remember. She had cancer. That's all she could focus on.

"Nana?" Hope appeared. "Nana, Momma?"

Emma broke down, crying hysterically into the locks of her two-year old daughter. She couldn't have cancer. She had four babies to take care of. She was a doctor. They'd done tests, biopsies and scans. Nothing to worry about, she'd been told. There had to be a mistake. This wasn't right. The tests must've gotten switched. There had to be a plausible explanation for this all. She was only thirty-eight years old.

Refusing to forget about her hunger, Hope pulled Emma into the kitchen to the counter where the bananas hung above the fruit basket filled with red shiny apples. She peeled the banana, handed it to Hope, walked over to the kitchen table and dropped into one of the seats. The table, still sticky with syrup from breakfast, was cluttered with half-eaten pancakes, cereal bowls and cups. Since she'd been home after the surgery, Emma had allowed mornings to be less stressed, less structured. Unable to drive, the only thing she had to make sure of was that the older two made the bus. Apart from that, the kitchen could be left messy, she'd get around to it. It was a nice transition from rushing out the door while the house still slept or creeping in just as it was waking up. For the first time in a long time, she was well-rested and refreshed. She couldn't have cancer. Things were going too well.

With a shaking hand holding her cell phone, she dialed Russell's number. It came as no surprise that he didn't answer. He was probably elbow-deep in someone's chest. She could page him, but what would that accomplish? She'd still have cancer when the surgery was done. She left a message for him to call her back as soon as possible. If he couldn't tell by the sound of her voice that it was serious, he'd have to know because she never left him voicemails. She'd usually just text him with whatever she needed. Neither one of them ever really had time to stop and talk during the day.

She ended the call and immediately selected another contact from her phone. This time, her call was answered on the second ring.

"Hello?" the voice answered.

"Mom," Emma choked out before she broke down sobbing.

"What does today look like for you?" Elaine asked as they left the school auditorium. Somehow, she'd managed to get Richard to go in late so that he could attend the costume parade at the boys' school.

"I won't know until I get in," Richard said, scrolling through his phone.

Elaine, annoyed at not being the focus of Richard's attention, sighed. "With all those highly qualified doctors, it's amazing that place manages to function without you."

Richard ignored her comment and responded to a lunch invitation.

"Are you going to make it home for trick-or-treating?"

"I won't know until I get in," he repeated.

"You promised the boys," she replied. "You know how much they enjoy when you take them." Elaine reached out and took Richard's hand. "This doesn't have to be a thing. I'm just asking if you can come home."

It was Richard's turn to sigh. "I know," he softened. "It's just that I'm going in late and to be home by six, I'm going to have to leave early."

She offered a smile. "What's the point of being department chair if you can't arrange your own schedule?"

"I'll do my best," he replied, bringing her hand to his lips and kissing it gently. "I have to go."

They walked in silence to their cars, his BMW, her Mercedes SUV, and drove in two different directions. Richard remembered seeing the cars, the clothes, the watches of the attendings in the hospital while he worked his way up. Unless you came from money, medical students and interns struggled for years to get by, living paycheck to paycheck while racking up huge amounts of debt. He laughed when he realized his first six-figure contract didn't cover his six-figure debt. In his opinion, most doctors weren't showy, they were just enjoying the fruits of their labor. To many he probably appeared extravagant, but he'd put in the time. He still did.

Elaine, too, had put in her time. She might enjoy many comforts, but those made up for practically raising the boys as a single mother. Richard knew he was harsh with her sometimes, giving her an attitude she didn't deserve when all she wanted was him. But that was the problem. Everyone wanted him. Her, the boys, the hospital. He was constantly pulled in all directions and he couldn't blame his profession. That was his first love.

ADDISON

"How bad was it?" Keith asked, walking in the door with a warm pizza.

"Bad," Addison said. "They promised not to eat the candy until they got home. They lied."

Keith set the pizza on their kitchen table and walked to the refrigerator for a beer. "I don't believe it. They ate the candy?" He feigned surprise with a grin.

"I know I should've known better." Addison couldn't help but smile. "But I had no idea they were going to act that way. They were pure monsters."

"What do you expect? You gave them pure sugar."

"They were the worst they've ever been. I'm sure I'm going to hear about it on Monday."

"Or maybe they'll crash when they get home and their parents will be happy."

Addison opened the pizza box and removed a slice. "No." She nodded vehemently. "It was like they got a taste for sugar and couldn't let it go. They wanted more. I was actually scared of being assaulted for my candy."

"Do you have any candy left for me?" Keith asked, drinking from his beer.

"That depends," Addison replied, reaching for the bottle as it left his lips. "Are you going to behave if I do?"

Twenty minutes later, Addison and Keith lay naked on their bed with two beers and the box of pizza open between them. Neither of them moved when the doorbell rang.

"Jesus," Keith said, glancing at his watch. "What time do they start?"

Addison laughed. "I told you, once they get the taste, they're like addicts."

"Well those addicts will have to get their fix somewhere else."

Normally Addison would've protested shutting the children out, but she'd had more than enough interaction for one day and was enjoying the intimacy of adult time. For a fleeting second, the thought of not having children seemed almost acceptable. She truly loved Keith and the time they spent together. The freedom with which they could come and go, do as they pleased was a nice way to live.

They had friends with kids who couldn't stay out past ten, whether it was too late for the babysitter or they themselves were tired. Addison witnessed the exhaustion on their faces and didn't envy them on those nights. However, when they were invited for barbeques or birthday parties and she witnessed the reason for the exhaustion, the love of children, she found herself envious.

"Where'd you go?" Keith waved a hand in front of Addison's face.

"Sorry." She snapped to. "Just thinking of how perfect this is."

"Really?"

"Really," Addison answered. "After today, this is exactly what I needed."

"How can I keep this perfection going?"

"How about we stay in bed all night stuffing our faces and watching scary movies?"

"You know me so well." Keith leaned over and kissed Addison.

Despite having the lights off, the doorbell rang constantly, tapering off as night fell. Keith and Addison remained in bed, tuning out the running feet and excited murmurs of children, enjoying the candy Addison had purchased for the kids.

Addison appreciated the genuine happiness children possessed. It wasn't faked or forced. When children were happy, you knew. When they weren't, you could tell. They were so much more honest than adults. More honest than her.

She rolled away from the sounds of the children and faced Keith. "Are you going to leave me if we never have children?"

"What?" he asked through a mouthful of chocolate and what appeared to be caramel.

"If I have the surgery and don't want to adopt. Will you leave me?"

"Addy, where is this coming from? I thought everything was perfect."

"You and Tina broke up because she didn't want a baby."

"Tina didn't want a commitment," Keith said with a sigh.

"But if she did, you would've married her. She'd be pregnant with your baby right now."

"No." Keith shook his head. "If, and that's a big if, we'd gotten engaged, it would've never lasted."

"How do you know that?" Addison challenged.

"Because I wasn't happy."

"You weren't happy?"

"I wasn't *us* happy."

"But you thought you were happy."

"I always knew something was missing."

Addison rolled her eyes.

"What?" Keith sat up.

"You loved her, Keith. You told me yourself. I don't know why you're not being honest about it."

"Just because I loved her didn't mean we were right for each other. Why does it even matter?"

"Because she's living the life you two were meant to have."

"She is living her life," Keith corrected. "I am living the life I was meant to have with you. A life which may or may not include children. And I'm okay with that because I know we are meant to be together. Do you remember what you said right before they wheeled you off to surgery?"

Addison's eyes moistened as a chill ran down her spine at the thought of the pain that ripped through her body when the ectopic pregnancy ruptured. "I said 'no more'."

"You said, 'no more,' and I thought, thank God," Keith said.

"You never told me that."

"Because I didn't want to upset you."

"Do you still feel that way?" Addison asked.

"Yes," Keith replied without hesitation.

"Wow." Addison unwrapped a miniature candy bar and put the whole thing in her mouth.

"We tried everything. I was tested, you were tested. We made love according to calendars, moon cycles. Even when we both were too exhausted, we forced ourselves. I know you think all guys ever want to do is have sex, but not like that. Not to a clock or schedule that can't be broken. It was too much stress. And that was all I had to do.

"You took hormones that put you into temporary menopause with the hope that when you stopped, you'd be able to conceive. We hoped, we prayed, we wished. And each time we thought our prayers were answered, it seemed like it was all worth it. But with each miscarriage, I realized it wasn't. When you almost died—" Keith inhaled. "I don't know what life is like with children, but I know what life is like with you and that is all I need. So yes, when you said no more I was happy. We could go back to being us."

Keith had never been so open and honest with Addison about what he'd been going through the past couple of years. He was right. She'd naively assumed he loved the amount of sex they'd had each month. Yes, there were times she had to beg him, which made her certain she wouldn't conceive. But she persisted and they'd had sex anyway. Temporary menopause wasn't a joke either. But it was a way people like her had had success in getting pregnant. Her body didn't appreciate the shock. When she'd started bleeding the last time, she was faced with her own mortality and had finally seen things clearly. Yet as she healed, the clarity faded and she was confused again. But it wasn't just about her. Keith had very clear opinions, she'd just never bothered to really ask.

"Spring break it is," she said, unwrapping another candy bar.

"What?" Keith asked.

"I'll have the surgery then."

"Addy…"

Addison shook her head. "I need to close this chapter of senseless hope and move on."

"Whatever you want to do," Keith said just as a woman screamed on the television, running from a knife-wielding, masked lunatic. "I just want you to be happy."

Addison moved the bags of candy out from between her and Keith and curled up along his body. "Me too."

NOVEMBER

DALE

"What do you have so far?" Carmen asked. She'd asked Dale over for lunch during the baby's nap. When he told her he had plans to meet Sophia at the library, she offered to help instead.

"It's a nasty disease," Dale began. "It's resistant to normal treatments and quick to spread."

Carmen looked pained. "We already knew that."

Dale referenced his notes. "Best chance of survival is if the tumor is found early and removed en bloc."

"En bloc?" Carmen asked.

"In one piece," Dale explained. "I don't get why they need these fancy words. If you ask me, they do it to keep people like me from knowing too much."

"The words are a bit much, but I doubt they're doing it to be exclusive."

"I wouldn't know," Dale said. "They could admit to just about anything and disguise it with their five dollar words and I'd have no idea."

"Have you found anything promising?"

Dale shook his head. "For all the great things I've heard about the internet, I'm not getting anywhere. There's some information about leiomyosarcoma, fibroids, and uterine cancer, but not what I'm looking for."

"What are you looking for?"

"I don't know," Dale said, defeated. "But I'll know when I find it."

"Ok." Carmen exhaled. Out of his daughters, she was definitely the most patient. "What can I try to help you find?"

He handed her his notebook. "I have the information of two families who lost women to LMS. Start with this website."

Carmen navigated to a page dedicated to "Pauline Harris." It pained Dale to see the image of a woman tortured by the same disease as Cindy.

"She was even younger than Mom," Carmen said.

"Do you know how to make one of these?" he asked.

"What?"

"A website, on the internet, where we could tell Mom's story."

She turned to him. "I know you want answers, Dad, but I don't think it's a good idea to put Mom's or your information out there. There are a lot of scammers online looking to take advantage of people."

"I'm not listing my social security number," Dale retorted. "I just need a place to explain what happened. Maybe there's someone else out there looking for answers like me."

"Dad," Carmen said carefully.

"Something's not right," Dale said. "You search for anything else and there is so much information. There is nothing about this."

"Maybe because it's exactly what the doctors say it is: rare, aggressive and without a cure."

Dale shook his head vehemently. "No, something doesn't make sense. I know it. And I won't stop, won't rest until I figure it out."

EMMA AND RUSSELL

In the two weeks since the diagnosis, life had become a slow-motion blur. Emma cried every day. Russell put on a brave face, only crying in private. The first day they sobbed together, after which, Russell wouldn't allow Emma to see him anything other than strong, determined. Together they would fight. Together they would prevail.

Emma's first question was about the prognosis. How bad did it look? How much time did she have? She couldn't bear the thought of leaving her children behind. She fought like hell to keep the image out of her head, but it constantly managed to seep back in. She'd be on the floor with Jocelyn and the innocence of her daughter that once made her smile instead made her weep. She'd hold on to Hope a little longer, a little tighter every time she ran to Emma.

"Why is Mom crying all the time?" Kaitlin had asked Russell one night as he tucked her in. It had been an especially emotional day for Emma and she was too upset to put the kids to bed.

Russell sighed and sat next to Kaitlin on her bed. He thought for a minute of how to put it in a context his daughter would understand.

"Do you remember the story of Snow White?" he asked. Kaitlin nodded. "Well, Mommy was given a poisoned apple and it made her sick."

"Sick?" The fear flashed across Kaitlin's face. "Who gave her a poisoned apple?"

"The hospital."

The confusion showed as his daughter's eyes grew wide.

"Do you remember when Mommy had to have surgery on her belly?" Again, Kaitlin nodded. "There was a doctor at the hospital who told

Mommy all the great things the surgery would do. It was like the witch who offered Snow White the poisoned apple. Mommy was nervous about the surgery just like Snow White was nervous about accepting the shiny, red apple from the stranger. Just as the witch persisted and took a bite of the apple to show Snow White it wasn't poisonous, Mommy's doctor told us we had nothing to worry about. She said the surgery was the safest. Mommy believed her and so did I."

"It wasn't safest," Kaitlin inferred. "Was it?"

"No," Russell replied, hanging his head. How could he have been so foolish as to have fallen victim to the Snow White effect?

"Is she going to be okay?" Kaitlin asked.

"That's what we're trying to figure out," Russell answered.

The cloud that loomed over the Speck household poured over Russell. A trained surgeon, and a good one at that, he knew the implications of a poorly performed operation where cancer was concerned.

Emma's hysterectomy was done laparoscopically, two small incisions instead of one large cut. Better for the healing process, bad for cancer removal. Any reputable surgeon stressed the importance of en bloc removal with clear margins. But the laparoscopic procedure performed on Emma didn't allow for either because the procedure, by nature, was used to minimize incision and scar size. She'd been talked into minimally invasive surgery because of her low risk of experiencing complications.

"It was morcellated," Dr. Stein replied when she'd met with Russell and Emma after the diagnosis.

"Morcellated?" Emma asked. While she and Russell were both doctors, they hadn't heard of morcellators and more specifically, hadn't known one would be used in her hysterectomy.

"It's a tool we use to cut up the tissue so we can remove it through the incision sites," Dr. Stein replied.

"Cut up?" Russell asked, his face going white.

"Yes."

"You cut up malignant tissue in my wife's abdomen?" he asked.

"I did a thorough wash after everything was removed."

"Everything?" Russell said. "How do you know you got everything if you cut it up inside her?"

Dr. Stein thought for a moment, opened her mouth and then stopped. Russell realized his worst fears were correct.

"Have you ever broken a glass?" he asked when Dr. Stein offered nothing else. "Try as you might, you can't pick up every broken piece, every shard. The fragments go everywhere. You just admitted to shattering a glass inside my wife."

That night, Russell researched morcellators and their history. He wanted to know everything about the tool that, by all means, sentenced his wife to death. The poor prognosis forced Russell into damage control mode. Based on what little had been published regarding morcellation, fibroids and leiomyosarcoma, Emma's only chance for survival was to remove any disseminated uterine fragments left behind by the morcellator.

Since so little was known about her disease, there was no clear direction to take. One doctor proposed she wait a couple of months to see what, if anything, would happen. The odds of cancer recurrence after morcellation were eighty percent. If the cancer was to recur, it would likely take her life within five years. Emma didn't like those odds. Being a mother, she certainly wasn't going to sit back and wait around to see which percentage she fell into.

Chemotherapy was an option, but Russell insisted more had to be done. He wasn't going to rely on Nicole Stein's promise of a thorough abdominal wash. Using his broken-glass analogy, he wasn't going to be satisfied with a good sweeping to gather all the shards. He was going to find a way to remove the floor completely.

RICHARD

Richard had just tucked Eli back into bed after a terrible nightmare when his phone lit up. *I wish I slept enough to dream,* he thought as he walked the long hallway back to his bedroom. Elaine refused to get up with either one of the boys when Richard was home. "I deal with enough on my own," she'd said. "It's your turn now." It didn't matter how exhausted he was, she wouldn't budge.

Through slit eyes, Richard unlocked his phone and read the new email. The subject read "Sentinel Event - Urgent," and was from one of Kendal Slate's doctors. Richard's sleepy eyes opened wide to make sure he'd read correctly. Sentinel events were not something any doctor took lightly, especially the department chair.

Dear Dr. Richard Oakley,

A tragedy has occurred in the operating room at Kendal Slate to one of our own, my wife and mother to our four children, Dr. Emma Speck. She had a routine laparoscopic hysterectomy to remove what was thought to be a benign uterine fibroid. However, pathology came back indicating the eight-centimeter fibroid was in fact a malignant tumor. A morcellator was used to cut up the tumor for extraction, causing disseminated cells to be spread in her abdomen.

I don't have to tell you the implications of removing a malignancy this way. Both my wife and I were unaware a morcellator would be used in her surgery and frankly, I'm appalled any type of mass would be removed in such a way. As we struggle to make sense of her diagnosis and come up with a plan moving forward, I implore you to halt the use of morcellators at Kendal Slate Memorial. The numbers are vague at this point, but it appears that the use of the morcellator upstaged Emma's cancer and dramatically reduced her chance of long-term survival. Allow Kendal Slate to pave the way in stopping this technique and save women's lives.

Sincerely,

Russell Speck

Richard sighed, turned off the screen on his phone and closed his eyes. He went over the email in his head, trying to put a face to Russell Speck or his wife Emma.

It was bad enough dealing with the grieving families of strangers. But to have an employee grieving the negative outcome of surgery at the hospital was something different altogether. Just because Kendal Slate had some of the best doctors in the country didn't make the surgeries performed there infallible. People got sick. People died. End of story. Sometimes patients were injured or even died in the name of medicine. "You have to crack a few eggs to make an omelet," he'd heard early on in his residency. At first, he was taken aback by such a brazen comment, but over time he'd come to agree. Medicine wasn't perfect. Sometimes setbacks were necessary in order to advance. Everyone at the hospital knew it. Until someone close to them got sick.

Richard had gained an understanding of sickness and disease from an early age. It wasn't anyone's fault. No one caused his mother to die. It just happened. His father blamed anyone or anything he could. Something like that couldn't happen to his Margaret. He'd never understood why his father couldn't grasp the reality of cancer. It had caused a rift between them and eventually, he believed, his father's death.

From the tone of Russell Speck's email, Richard could tell he was dealing with a grieving spouse and not a like-minded colleague. For Russell to be blaming the surgery and calling it a sentinel event was concerning. The term sentinel event was reserved for urgent matters in which patients suffered a negative outcome as the result of care which didn't relate directly to their illness. He couldn't have doctors from the hospital spreading rumors about procedures harming patients. Regardless of what had happened to his wife, Russell Speck needed to be reined in.

ADDISON

"I've made up my mind, Mom. I'm going to have the surgery."

"Oh Addy—"

"We've already done this, Mom. You say you don't know. I tell you I'll think about it even though I know what I want. We leave it alone until I bring it up again. I'm just so tired of it. I want to be done with wondering, hoping, fearing. It's too much. I just want to enjoy my life."

Addison's mom let out a sigh, which was as close as she could come to silent protest.

"It'll be good for me. I promise."

"It's surgery," her mom said.

"Barely," Addison said. "It's not the same surgery it was when Aunt Betty had it done. Nowadays it's done through tiny incisions. I won't have to be cut open. The risk of infection is reduced. Pregnancy for me has become riskier than this procedure."

"Don't let them brainwash you," her mom stated sternly. "They can call it a procedure but it's still surgery. Tiny incisions still mean they're cutting."

Addison smiled and took a long sip of the wine she had opened and poured before calling her mother. "I know," she said, gently placing her glass back on the coffee table in front of her. Keith, sitting next to her, patted her knee in encouragement. "But it's what I've decided to do. What Keith and I think is best."

"Well then, best of luck to you."

"Mom," Addison said. "Don't be like that. Trust me, we didn't come to this decision lightly."

"I'm sure," her mom replied.

"I'm sorry if you're upset, Mom. This is what's best for me."

"If you say so."

Addison decided to get off the phone and let her mom digest the news.

"You did it," Keith said, offering a toast when Addison put the phone down.

"I did it," she tapped her glass against his bottle of beer.

"Want to change your mind?"

She shook her head. "Not a chance. I know it's the right thing to do. My mom will come around."

"But…" Keith prodded, knowing there was more. If anyone would make Addison reconsider, it would be her mom.

"But nothing," she replied before taking a long and steady drink from her glass.

"What is it, Addy?"

Addison sighed, nodding her head. "Nothing new," she said. "I hate that it's come to this. I hate hearing the disappointment in my mom's voice. I need to fast-forward time and be done with this all."

Keith pulled her against his chest. "Don't wish time away, Addy. Everything is going to be okay."

DALE

"It's perfect," Carmen said.

The task of choosing a picture of Cindy for the website they were creating proved hard. To save Dale the heartache of going through their pictures, Carmen had offered to do it. But Dale insisted on finding the perfect representation of his Cindy.

For over four decades, they'd posed for hundreds of pictures—Polaroid's, developed and digital. Cindy had them well organized, negatives and all. It was one thing to page through the albums with the girls or grandkids when Cindy was alive and poke fun at the hair styles and clothing choices of their past. But without her he felt emptier than ever. Each smile and silly face tore at his already bleeding heart. And those were the pictures of the good times. The pictures taken at the end, the ones thrown haphazardly into a shoe box without her there to arrange into albums, he didn't consider those. He didn't even know why they'd been taken. He didn't want to remember his love as anything other than the radiant light she was.

His absolute favorite was a picture he'd snapped when she'd fallen asleep after they'd spent the day painting the walls in their first apartment. They'd spent all morning deciding on the perfect color for their living room before settling on Honeysuckle Happiness, a light shade of yellow she believed would brighten the tight living space. They painted two coats and when it was done, she fell into the bean bag chair that was in the center of the room along with the rest of their furniture and passed out, brush still in hand. She had specks of yellow on her face and in her humidity-curled hair. She'd never looked more beautiful. But that picture was too personal, so he opted for his second favorite.

"I took this one after we finished a hike in the Smoky Mountains." Dale paused to clear his throat. "Your mom is flexing because it had been so hot that day, we didn't know if we'd make it all the way. But you know your mom, she wasn't going to give up."

Carmen's eyes filled with tears. Dale's eyes glistened as he stared at the image of his wife on the computer screen. "We watched the sunset that night. We were exhausted and sweaty, but your mom turned and looked at me and said, 'Life doesn't get much better than this.' At the time she was right. But life just kept getting better with her every day."

Dale swatted the tears from his eyes.

"Dad," Carmen reached out to Dale. "It's okay. I miss her too."

"She didn't deserve it, Car," he said. "She was such a light, my light."

"I know," Carmen replied. "She'd be so proud of what you've done here. The page looks great."

Dale coughed away his hoarseness. "I'm not done. I'm just getting started."

Emma and Russell

"It's risky, I know," Russell explained. "But you have to do it, Em. We can't assume Stein got everything. We have to make sure."

"Ten hours? That's a long time to be under."

"I know," he said. "But it's the only way to make sure there aren't any microscopic pieces floating around in your abdomen."

Emma sat beside Russell at the kitchen table, where he'd brought up a controversial cancer treatment on the computer. The procedure he was suggesting was the complete and utter opposite of the minimally invasive hysterectomy she'd just had, and she'd been nervous about that. Ten hours under, organ removal, and a hot chemotherapy bath that would essentially scald her abdominal cavity. She didn't know which was worse, leiomyosarcoma or the shot-in-the-dark procedure Russell was proposing.*

She'd gone to Nicole Stein. She'd talked about her concerns of the behavior of the fibroid. Something, a tiny voice in her head, had been sounding a quiet alarm as Nicole reassured her of the benign nature of fibroids.

Emma didn't care about the scars a traditional hysterectomy would've left behind. Hell, if she went through with the treatment Russell was showing her, she'd be cut sternum to belly. Talk about a scar. *Why?* Why was this happening to her? Why didn't Stein receive her concerns? How could morcellation be an accepted method if it had the chance of disseminating and upstaging an occult cancer?

"Because the risk is so low," Nicole had told them. "It's one in ten thousand. All of Emma's testing came back normal. There was no way to know."

* The Sugarbaker Procedure, also known as HIPEC (hyperthermic intraperitoneal chemotherapy) was created in 1995 by Dr. Paul Sugarbaker.

"Which is exactly my point," Russell had said. "How can you morcellate

if you can't be sure?"

Nicole went back to the numbers—in all her years of performing hysterectomies, both traditional and laparoscopic, she'd never seen a case of leiomyosarcoma.

They were going around in circles and while Russell would have been more than content to sit across from Nicole Stein and argue the point, Emma wanted to leave. She wanted to be home.

"What are the success rates?" Emma asked Russell, debating the pros and cons of such a severe procedure.

"Impressive," Russell said. "No surgery is without risk."

"Thanks," she said and rolled her eyes. "I'm aware of that."

"You were assaulted," he said. "This is different. I'm going to make sure I know everything about this surgery."

"The damage has already been done."

"That's why we're going to fix it," Russell said.

Emma kissed Russell on the cheek and went up to bed. But who was she kidding? There was no sleep in her future. Only tears.

RICHARD

"Nancy," Richard beckoned from his desk.

Nancy walked in his office with a notebook in hand. "Yes?"

"Get me everything you can on Russell Speck. He keeps emailing me and won't quit."

"Yes," she said. "I've seen. Would you like me to filter his emails as they come in?"

Yes, Richard thought. "No, I'll deal with him."

Since the first email had come in from Russell, Richard received an email just about every day for two weeks straight, if not more. As if the constant barrage wasn't enough for Richard to deal with, Russell appeared to copy everyone he could think of on the emails: doctors, journalists, people who Richard had never heard of. While he would have liked to delete the messages as quickly as they appeared, he had to stay on top of what was being said about him and his surgical department. At first, he'd given Russell a pass because he was obviously grieving the bad news of a grim prognosis. However, as time passed and Russell showed no signs of letting up, Richard's understanding was quickly turning into annoyance.

"From what I've heard, he's a great surgeon," Nancy said. "A lot of potential."

"Potential won't get him anywhere if he keeps this nonsense up."

"Have you talked with anyone from legal?" Nancy asked.

"I didn't think he would be this unrelenting," Richard said and exhaled.

"Is there any truth in what he's saying? Is Dr. Stein at fault?"

Richard knew better. Even though he trusted Nancy completely, anything he said relating to Emma's surgery or outcome was a violation of HIPPA. "Call Henry Lewis and set up an appointment," he replied.

Medical malpractice and negligence were necessary evils to learn when Richard started practicing medicine. In his current position, they were even more vital to understand. People were always looking for somewhere to place the blame when they or someone they loved suffered a negative medical outcome. And yes, occasionally a doctor was at fault. But more often than not, the doctors were not culpable.

In part, Richard blamed television. He scoffed at the TV shows Elaine found herself wrapped up in. Every show presented the most difficult of cases and, if they were even feasible, they were solved in the end by a young, attractive hot shot doctor. He swore patients came to the hospital expecting George Clooney. When they were introduced to a white-haired doctor in his forties who wasn't able to perform the miracles so perfectly executed in sixty minutes onscreen, patients got testy. Lawsuits were often threatened but rarely filed. And the ones that did retain legal counsel brought nothing but headaches regardless of their merit.

Richard shook his head as Nancy walked out. Russell and Emma Speck were doctors. They, more than anyone, should've understood the imperfect nature of medicine.

ADDISON

Nine days had passed since Addison told her mother she was having the hysterectomy—nine days of her mom digging up everything she could in an effort to sway Addison against it.

Rachel, much like Addison's mom, wasn't keen on the idea of surgery. But she supported Addison. She always did. When Addison and Keith had first started dating, Addison had been a little insecure. In a half-drunken fit of jealousy, Addison convinced Rachel to do a drive-by. The only problem was that Keith was renting a house on a cul-de-sac. As Rachel's car crept by the front of the house, Keith came out with the trash. Panicked, Rachel slammed her foot on the gas, the tires screeching as she spun around right in front of Keith, who had dropped the bag in his hand and was staring directly at Rachel.

Rachel laughed as they drove off, Addison hysterical on the floor of the front seat. "Why wouldn't you tell me he lived on a cul-de-sac?"

When Keith asked Addison why Rachel was driving by his house, she'd confessed that Rachel didn't trust him completely and was just looking out for her best friend. It was a little white lie. How was she to know they'd end up married?

"I'm only going to ask you once," Rachel had said when Addison told her about the surgery. "Are you sure?"

"Yes," Addison replied.

"Then that's all that matters," she said. "Your body, your decision."

"You make it seem so easy," Addison said with a sigh.

"Because it is," Rachel replied.

"Can you tell my mom that?"

Rachel laughed. "Yeah, because your mom would love advice from me about you."

It wasn't that Addison's mom disliked Rachel. She more so disapproved of her lifestyle. Rachel was a floater according to Addison's mom. "She floats through life on her youth and looks," her mom had said once. "You better warn her that they'll both run out and she'll be left with nothing if she doesn't settle down."

"I thought you said we shouldn't rely on men," Addison said with a smirk, just to egg her mom on.

"You shouldn't," her mom replied quickly. "But men make children."

"That's all they're good for, then?" Addison asked. "Their sperm?"

"Most of them," her mom quipped.

Something about talking about sperm with her mom made Addison laugh. They were very close, but some topics would always be off limits no matter how old Addison was.

Rachel practically choked on her Diet Coke when Addison recounted the sperm conversation she'd had with her mother.

"I can't imagine your mom saying sperm," Rachel said, wiping her nose.

"She didn't," Addison laughed. "I did."

"It's a surprise she ever got laid in the first place."

"I think she was different then."

DALE

Dear Mr. Reichter,

My daughter passed along an email she received from you regarding my wife, Pauline. Thank you for your kind words. I am sorry to hear about your wife. It's never easy to lose someone you care so much for. My Pauline left us five years ago and I still miss her terribly. From your description, Cindy passed very similar to Pauline and I, too, find it hard to believe how quickly her health deteriorated. Please call me any time if you would like to talk.

Jason Harris

Dale's heart quickened as he read and re-read the email. He never thought he'd receive a reply to the emails he sent out to the families that had posted things online about their loved ones and LMS. But there it was, an email from Jason Harris who'd endured the same pain. The first piece in the puzzle, he thought as he printed the email.

"Are you going to call him?" Sophia asked. Dale could tell she had become emotionally invested in Cindy's story. "What are you going to say?"

Dale shrugged. "I don't know."

"You don't know whether you're going to call him or what you're going to say?"

"What I'm going to say," Dale said. "I'm not sure I'm ready to talk about Cindy with someone else."

It was easy to imagine the conversation when it was hypothetical. But now he had someone, a companion in the misery of what life had brought him.

"Just tell him what you told me," Sophia offered. "He wouldn't have replied if he didn't have anything to say."

"I'm not looking for someone to swap sad stories with. I want answers. If Jason Harris is looking for a friend, I'm not interested."

Dale re-read the email one last time before navigating to Cindy's web page. He looked at her beautiful smile, her perfect face. He then went to the page Pauline Harris's children had made, apparently when she first fell ill. They were looking for what could save her. They didn't appear to have found anything.

EMMA AND RUSSELL

How could this be happening? The question plagued Emma a million times a day. This was not supposed to be her life. Other people got sick and she took care of them. The sickness she saw every day in the hospital wasn't supposed to touch her. Things were finally getting easier for her and Russell. She wasn't supposed to be considering a ten-hour surgery that couldn't make any promises about her prognosis. *How could this be happening to me?*

Primum non nocere. First, do no harm. That was the main principal they, as doctors, were supposed to practice. How could Nicole Stein, or any gynecologist possibly believe that cutting tissue, malignant or not, to have it disseminated throughout the abdomen was a good idea? It was painfully clear to Emma that the benefit of minimally invasive surgery, including morcellation, was not worth the risk of spreading cancer or disseminating tissue.

She and Russell had read the findings that reported uterine tissue being known to implant itself to other parts of the peritoneal cavity after morcellation, causing bowel obstruction along with other complications. How could a procedure that undoubtedly had the potential to do more harm than good be practiced in a hospital as prestigious as Kendal Slate Memorial? Questions were all Emma had when she wasn't crying or distracted by the beauty of her children.

"It's assault," Russell sometimes yelled to himself when no one was around. "My wife has been assaulted."

After learning of her diagnosis, Emma's family wrapped themselves around her like a warm blanket. First came the phone calls, which she didn't, couldn't answer right away. It's not that she didn't appreciate the outreach, she just couldn't bear to hear the same condolences over and over. Just about everyone started off with "I'm so sorry." And if it wasn't an apology it was, "How are you?" That stupid question was definitely worse. How was she? She was horrible.

Their house was never empty. Someone was always dropping by, in town for this or that and wanting to check in. Flowers were sent, her mom was there cooking at least every other day. The constant commotion was a welcomed distraction. Eventually, however, the dishes would be clean and the kids bathed and in bed and it would be time for everyone to leave, to go back to their normal lives.

Those moments stung Emma. Sure, her family had their worlds rocked, but it was her news, her disease. They could return to their families and while they could be sad for her, for themselves, they could also hug and kiss their children knowing they had better odds of seeing them grow old. She appreciated the support but found it hard not to resent that this was all happening to her.

Thankfully, Russell refused to wallow in pity and turned his anger into action. He researched everything he could about the intruder in her body and how to fight it. When he presented Emma with what he deemed to be a lifesaving surgery, it was hard to refute it as her only option.

"Who knows if Stein left anything behind," he'd said in an effort to cajole Emma into agreeing to have the surgery a week and a half out. "The longer we allow these cells to circulate throughout your body, the longer we're giving this disease a chance to take root, to come back."

It was a grim reality that Emma didn't want to accept. To fight LMS, she'd have to be as aggressive and ugly as the disease itself. If it meant ten hours in an operating room and a long recovery, so be it. She'd read and re-read the statistics. They weren't in her favor. The surgery had the potential to sway the odds, which was better than doing nothing.

"I'll do it," she said, walking into the den where Russell sat in front of his laptop. He'd been spending just about every waking moment at the desk reading, emailing, researching. He was there when she went to bed, when she woke up in the middle of the night, and still in his wooden chair with bloodshot eyes when she came down in the morning. He slept just as little, if not less, than her.

Russell turned to her with a look of relief. "Great. I'll call first thing in the morning."

Overcome with anxiety and sadness, Emma turned to leave the room.

"Em," Russell called, his voice shaky.

"Yeah?" When she turned, tears streamed down her cheeks.

"This is the right call."

She nodded. "I know," she said walking through the archway to the stairs, unable to shake the voice in her head telling her she had thought the same thing about the hysterectomy.

"Schedule a meeting with Russell Speck and his wife," Richard ordered Nancy. "If she's available."

"With Henry Lewis as well?" Nancy asked.

"No," Richard replied. "Just Dr. and Dr. Speck."

Nancy looked at Richard skeptically. "Is that all?"

"Yes," he replied. "And make it as soon as possible."

The meeting he'd had with Henry Lewis from legal hadn't gone as badly as Richard had thought it would. In the end, Henry informed Richard that the hospital was not at fault. How were they to know Emma had cancer? According to her records, they'd done everything preoperatively to check for malignancy. She'd signed off on the surgery. Dr. Stein performed the hysterectomy successfully. Had Emma not had an occult cancer, they would have been more than satisfied with the procedure.

"So how do I proceed with Russell?" Richard had asked Henry during their two-hour discussion.

"Give him some time off," Henry offered. "Let him be with his wife and family. Give him time to accept the prognosis."

"I doubt that's going to get him off my back," Richard said. "He's clearly not stable."

"There's nothing you or anyone here could have done for them," Henry said. "Surgery didn't give his wife cancer."

"No, but he's claiming it made her prognosis worse," Richard said.

"That can't be proven," Henry answered.

"Although the outcome for any patient with LMS is not positive, statistics show a correlation between morcellated LMS and its increase in recurrence as compared to open, en bloc removal."

"What are the stats about the chance of a uterine fibroid being LMS?" Henry questioned.

"One in ten thousand," Richard said. He'd researched the numbers as soon as Russell started on his rant about morcellation and the negligence of the hospital.

Henry didn't appear concerned. "No one can be blamed for not detecting something that occurs in one out of every ten thousand patients."

Henry conducted himself similar to how Richard did around his patients. If Richard showed any concern or apprehension when discussing medical information, his patients tended to overreact. It became vital to control and hide his emotions. State only the facts, leaving nothing to interpretation. He didn't mind if it made him appear as an emotionless doctor. He'd rather have his patients angry than alarmed.

"What about his allegations of lack of informed consent?" Richard asked, feeling like a nervous patient.

"Let's give him some time to get over the shock," Henry said. "Bring him in, give him some time off, let him settle down. You know how these things go. His focus will shift from the hospital to his wife's care."

Richard nodded but couldn't agree less. Russell Speck was a successful surgeon because of his dedication and hard work. Surgeons were taught to be technical, precise, committed. That kind of training didn't shift easily. Richard didn't see Russell fading into chemotherapy treatments. Nonetheless, he would do as Henry instructed, meet with the Specks and offer Russell some time off. What was the worst that could happen?

ADDISON

Smile, Rachel sent Addison a text first thing Monday morning. *Only six Mondays until Christmas.*

Addison read the text and smiled. Christmas meant two completely different things for her and Rachel. For Addison, Christmas was quality time off with Keith. Addison's first miscarriage had come a couple of days before Christmas, sending her holiday cheer right out the window. As a surprise, Keith booked a last-minute getaway in the Pocono Mountains. Hesitant at first, Addison went along. It turned into one of their best vacations.

The fresh air on the top of the slopes and the thrill of skiing down the mountains was exactly what she needed to remind herself of how good her life was. Every year following, they returned to the same lodge and spent the days leading up to the new year skiing.

For Rachel there was no Christmas break. The holiday season was one of her busiest times of the year. She was always steadily booked with office parties, private parties, engagement parties.

"Why, Addy?" she'd ranted to Addison one particularly stressful holiday season. "Why must everyone want to make New Year's about themselves? Just because it's the start of a new year doesn't mean their life is going to change at the stroke of midnight."

"Aren't we just filled with optimism?" Addison replied. "You would think throwing parties would make you happy."

"Not when you see the stupid things people want to do," Rachel complained. "I'm actually in the process of planning a surprise engagement party for a guy who's going to propose to his girlfriend at midnight."

"Why is that so bad?" Addison asked. "It sounds kind of romantic."

"I'm not sure they've been dating that long, if they're dating at all."

"What?"

"Exactly. The guy sounds a little off, but he's offered to pay me very well."

"Still," Addison argued. "That doesn't sound so bad."

"It's pathetic," Rachel said. "The hope, the expectation. It's just another day!"

"You end things with Joey?" Addison asked, knowing there was something more to Rachel's hostility.

"He's another hopeless one, talking about love and our future. Where have all the real men gone?"

Addison laughed. As much as her mom disapproved of Rachel's freeness, they actually shared a similar view of men.

Let's get through Thanksgiving first, Addison texted back just as the bell rang. She was excited at the thought of Christmas and her and Keith gliding down the mountains, not a care in the world. But that was six long weeks away. First, she had to deal with Thanksgiving, and facing her mother.

DALE

"What can I do for you?" Jason Harris had a surprisingly animated voice, considering the loss he'd endured.

"I appreciate you taking the time to talk to me," Dale began. "I'm really sorry for your loss."

"You too."

"I guess I'm just looking for answers. None of this makes any sense."

"I stopped looking for answers," Jason said. "But if you find any, I'd sure like to hear them."

"Would you mind telling me what happened to your wife?"

Jason exhaled loudly over the phone. "If you think it'll help."

Dale tightened his grip on the phone in his left hand and with his right, picked up the pen sitting on the table in front of him.

"Pauline had fibroids as long as she could remember."

Dale wrote FIBROIDS as the first bullet point under Pauline's name on his notepad.

"They never really bothered her much. But over the last couple of years, she'd started having pelvic pressure. At fifty-six she'd already gone through menopause, so she went to the doctor. She waited until the end of summer because our granddaughter loves the beach and she didn't want to take any time away from her. The doctor said she had two rather large fibroids, but they weren't life-threatening."

Dale scribbled NON-LIFE THREATENING.

"He said she could get them removed laparoscopically, which would make recovery easier."

EASY RECOVERY.

"He explained the procedure, the incisions, the standard risks with surgery and she scheduled her date."

"Did he say anything about cancer?" Dale asked.

"No. He said fibroids were common and surgery was a standard treatment."

"When was her surgery?"

"The end of September. The doctor was happy with how things went, said it was routine and that she would be back to herself in a couple of days."

Dale tensed at the familiarity of Jason's story.

"A week later we got a call saying she had cancer. Within weeks she could feel the tumors growing inside her." Dale could hear the anger growing in Jason's voice as he recounted what happened to his wife. "By Thanksgiving…they were everywhere. She spent Christmas in bed, barely able to eat. The tumors were entangled in everything, obstructing her bowel. The doctors couldn't get ahead of them." Jason's voice cracked and he paused. Dale could feel the pain radiating through the phone. His soul ached for Cindy.

"Anyway," Jason said after a moment. "She passed away in March."

"I'm sorry," Dale said, fighting back tears of his own.

"She was such a fighter through it all. She was the picture of health and then in six months she was dead. After the doctor told her she had a bad cancer, you know what she said? She told me she wasn't scared to die. She was just scared of what she had to go through to get there." Jason's anger broke and he began to cry.

"Sounds like she was a strong woman," Dale offered.

"She was," Jason replied. "And you know the kicker of it all?"

Dale waited in silence.

"That son of a bitch doctor who was so confident Pauline didn't have anything to worry about actually had the nerve to show up in her hospital room the week she died asking for forgiveness."

It was more than what Cindy's doctor had offered. At least Pauline's doctor sounded as though he had some remorse.

"He said he had no idea she had cancer. In ten years of practicing medicine, he'd never seen it."

"What did you say to him?" Dale asked, imagining what he would've said had Dr. Clayton offered an apology instead of the robotic condolences he was undoubtedly taught to deliver.

"I told him to get out," Jason said. "It was too late. Pauline could barely breathe and this guy wanted her forgiveness? I wasn't going to let her waste one precious breath on him."

"Good for you," Dale said.

"Yeah," Jason chuckled. "It was the only thing I could do for her."

"I would've done the same thing," Dale said.

Jason sighed. "I don't know if what happened to Pauline helps any…"

"It did," Dale confirmed. "I know it's not easy."

"No, it's not," Jason replied.

Dale thanked Jason for his time and immediately went to the refrigerator for a beer. He knew the pain Jason suffered, felt the anger boiling over in Jason's voice. It could have easily been Dale telling his story and it seemed as though time hadn't helped Jason much. With a cold beer in one hand and his notepad in the other, Dale fell into his favorite recliner and went over his notes. With the exception of some specifics, Pauline and Cindy's stories were the same.

EMMA AND RUSSELL

"It's insane!" Emma's mom exclaimed after Emma told her the details of the surgery she had scheduled for the following week. Emma had invited her parents over for lunch to discuss the surgery and what she would need from them in terms of child care. Sara was a great option during the day, but the surgery would require an extensive hospital stay and Emma didn't feel comfortable with anyone besides her parents staying with the kids. "This can't be the only option."

"Sure," Emma said. "We could wait and see what happens, wait for the cancer to seed itself inside my abdomen and tumors to pop up."

"Em," her mom reached across the kitchen table, covering Emma's hand with her own. "I'm just saying that ten hours is a long time when we aren't even sure what we're dealing with yet."

"*I'm* dealing with an aggressive cancer," Emma barked. "I have to be proactive. None of the doctors we've talked to know what to do. I'm not just going to sit back and wait. I can't. I have to do something."

Emma's father cleared his throat. "What do you need from us?"

"If all goes well I'll be in the hospital about a week which means we're going to need someone to stay with the kids," she answered, calming her voice.

"Of course," he replied. "Whatever you need."

Emma looked over to her mom, who sniffled and wiped her eyes. "Whatever you need."

"I don't really have options here, Mom," Emma said. "Russell's done the research. He's reached out to everyone we know. This is the only approach that gives me any chance." As she spoke, Emma began crying.

"I know," her mom said, trying her best to sound reassuring. "I just wish there was another way. I wish we weren't in this mess."

The conversation hadn't gone as badly as Emma worried and she was so glad to have her parents on board. If it weren't for them caring for the children, she didn't know what she would have done. While Russell's parents would have been more than happy to step in and help, there was something comforting knowing her kids would be home with her mom and dad through the entire ordeal.

"Are you going to die?" Kaitlin had asked when Russell and Emma sat her down and explained that Emma had to go back to the hospital for a while. It would have been easier to explain that Emma had to work, but Emma wanted her to understand she was having surgery in case something happened, a thought which pestered her night and day. Because, really, how do you prepare yourself for a severely invasive surgery that could just as easily end your life as save it?

For years Emma had spoken with patients and their families about surgery, trying her best to calm any anxieties. For years, she had the utmost respect for and trust in the medical community. But since her hysterectomy and diagnosis, she'd viewed the medical community in a different light. Doctors weren't all out to make a positive difference. Some, she was beginning to see, lost their way along the road of patient care, detouring at corporate greed and arrogance. One in particular—Dr. Richard Oakley of Kendal Slate Memorial.

RICHARD

Dear Dr. Oakley,

I thank you for your response to my request to speak with you about the use of power morcellators at Kendal Slate Memorial. Being one of the country's premier hospitals specializing in women's care, I believe that taking action now to halt the use of morcellators will create awareness and pave the way for other hospitals to follow. I regret that my wife and I will be unable to meet with you until she is recovered from the surgery she will be undergoing next week in the hopes of eradicating any residual cancer cells she may have in her peritoneum. I will be in touch as she recovers and hope to see how you and Kendal Slate right this terrible wrong for the many unsuspecting women devastated by this procedure.

Sincerely,
Russell Speck

Great, Richard thought reading Russell's email. As with the many emails Russell had fired out since his wife's diagnosis, the latest was received at two forty-seven in the morning.

"Can you blame the poor man?" Elaine had asked. "I wouldn't be able to sleep either if I learned you were dealing with a terminal illness."

"At least this email was only to me," Richard said. The first email Russell had sent was only to Richard. As time passed and Russell became more demanding that the hospital stop using the morcellator, he'd started cc-ing everyone remotely interested.

"He obviously loves his wife very much," Elaine replied, paying no mind to what Richard had said.

Elaine, making the situation about her, immediately took Emma's side.

"It's not that cut-and-dried," Richard argued, regretting sharing with his wife. Elaine had an opinion for everything. And everything, every disease, somehow found a way back to being about her.

"Would you let them do that procedure on me?" she'd asked.

"Of course," he replied. The color in Elaine's face changed. She was angry. He didn't care. It was the truth. "The odds of you or anyone having an occult cancer masquerading as a benign fibroid are one in ten thousand. I'd tell you to have the surgery and play the lottery because your odds of winning would be better than having cancer."

Elaine shook her head. "I don't know. Remember how I had that pain in my side and had that ultrasound?"

"Yes." Richard rolled his eyes, having no idea where her story was going.

"Well I was all freaked out and you weren't bothered at all."

"Again, because the chances of it being anything were so small."

"But you didn't know that. That's how Dolly's sister passed. She had a pain, she had an ultrasound and they found a tumor. I bet her doctors didn't think it was anything, but it was."

They'd gotten so off topic and Richard was irritated. To be talking about Dolly, Elaine's new best friend who, like her, suffered every ailment one could think of, was more than he had the mental space for.

"I've got work to do," he said and walked out of the room.

ADDISON

"Don't be mad," Addison's mom began as soon as Addison answered the phone.

Addison sighed.

"I was talking with Megan about the surgery you want to have, and she said you need to see her holistic healer."

"Mom—"

"Just hear me out. I know you don't believe in essential oils and all that other stuff, but I'm telling you this lady has a really good reputation."

"Why, Mom? Because Megan told you?"

"Because she came very highly recommended to Megan's daughter when she was having conception problems and now she's pregnant with her third child."

"Well great for Megan's daughter," Addison said.

"Don't be fresh," her mom warned. "I'm just saying it can't hurt to talk to her."

Other than seeing everyone around her get pregnant, Addison was also faced with the unwanted advice everyone gave her to help get pregnant. Calendars, positions, juices to drink, juices to avoid. Everyone had something that was guaranteed to work. And when it didn't, they'd ask if she and Keith were doing it correctly. She was done with it all. No more experimenting.

"I'm having the surgery, Mom," she replied. "I don't want to talk to anyone else about it. It's a private matter and I'd really appreciate it if you didn't discuss it with Megan."

"Megan is my best friend, Addison Jean. We discuss everything."

"Well pretty soon there won't be much to say about me. I'll be as boring as they come." The thought made Addison smile. Nothing to think about, no more talk of pregnancy. No more options to be weighed.

"Let me give you her number in case you change your mind," her mom said, refusing to take no for an answer. "Or better yet, I'll give her yours. That way she can call you."

"No, Mom," Addison said. "Give me her number."

"Great, are you going to call her?" she said, victory in her voice.

"I'll think about it," Addison said, writing the number as her mom read it off.

"Don't lie to your mother."

"Good night, Mom," Addison said and hung up the phone.

"What's this?" Keith asked that night, picking up the notepad where Addison wrote Miranda's number.

"Yet another suggestion from my mother," Addison replied.

"Do I want to know?" he asked.

"Nope," she said, tearing the top sheet from the rest of the pad and throwing it away.

Technically she hadn't lied to her mother. She did think about calling Miranda. She thought about the load of bullshit she'd have to endure during the phone call and the time she'd waste. There was nothing left to think about. Addison was going to have surgery the good ole'-fashion way. Well, not good ole'-fashion because her doctor said it could be done less-invasively through tiny incisions.

"Barely even noticeable," the doctor had said.

Perfect, Addison had thought.

DALE

"Where is he from?" Carmen asked when Dale told her about his conversation with Jason Harris.

"East Meadow, New York."

"That's not too far, Dad," she said. "Did you guys talk about meeting up for coffee or something?"

"There's really no point. I got everything I needed from the phone call."

"It probably couldn't hurt to get to know him a little better." Her concern for his social life or lack thereof was apparent. There was no doubt that she or any of her sisters hadn't noticed his deteriorating support group once Cindy passed.

In the beginning their friends were amazing, checking in, bringing meals, whatever they could do. As Cindy became sicker, they doubled and tripled their efforts to support her and Dale. But once she died, they became more distant. Dale believed they didn't know how to relate to him once Cindy was gone. He didn't want to make anyone uncomfortable, so he gave them a pass, allowing them to slide guiltlessly back into their lives and out of his.

"I don't need a friend," he said. "I need answers."

When Jason sent Dale a follow-up email, his initial fear was that Jason was looking to start a friendship. He was relieved to read that Jason only wanted to pass along another contact who'd lost his wife in a similar fashion.

Dale didn't want to get too excited as he wrote Phil Santerberry's number down, but his grumpy old man bones were telling him he'd been right. There was more to this disease than what the doctors had said, or more than what they knew. He didn't know which scenario was worse.

EMMA AND RUSSELL

Dear Russell,

I understand your focus is on your wife right now and I wish her the best in her recovery, as all of us here at Kendal Slate Memorial do. Please take the next couple of weeks to be with your wife and family during this difficult time. In addition, I have contacted Dr. Vislat and he will be reaching out to you to offer his assistance anyway he can.

Richard Oakley

Russell read the email and laughed out loud.

"What?" Emma asked.

"Oakley wants me to talk to Vislat," he replied, staring at his computer screen in disbelief.

"The psych guy?" Emma echoed his disbelief.

"The one and only," Russell said.

"Why?"

"They probably think I'm cracking up."

"I told you sending those mass emails wouldn't help."

"It got their attention, didn't it?"

"Probably not in the way you wanted."

"Positive or negative, I still got their attention and now they're listening."

"Are they listening?" Emma asked. "Or are they discrediting you as crazy?"

"It's how they operate. What do you do when you give a patient horrible news? You ask if they have anyone to talk to. And if they don't, who do you recommend?"

Emma thought and smirked. "Vislat."

"Vislat," Russell repeated.

"Have you ever met him?" Emma asked.

"I think a while back, but I can't be sure. You?"

"I had a consult with him last year."

"And?"

"And what?"

"What's he like?" Russell asked.

"You're not going to like him. He's one of those doctors that tries to be your friend, listens attentively, really cares for his patients."

"Well it doesn't matter because I'm not going to meet with him."

"You're not?" Emma asked.

"They can't make me," he said. "Can they?"

"I don't think so," Emma said. "But do you really want to give them a reason to discount you? Not to take what we're saying seriously?"

"Maybe you should talk to him," Russell offered. "You're the one who was recently diagnosed."

"You're the one sending mass emails to the entire world," she rebutted.

"Fine," Russell huffed. "But talking to him isn't going to make me back off of the hospital and what they did to you."

"No one is asking you to," Emma replied.

"I'm not buying their caring act one bit," he said. "I know what they're doing and frankly, I'm insulted they think I wouldn't see it. Guy causing a stir? Label him crazy to discredit him. Yes, I sent mass emails. But how else am I going to get the word out about the dangers of morcellation?"

RICHARD

The emails poured in. Each one more frantic than the previous, more desperate, with words like "assault" and "criminal" thrown about. Richard only hoped that everyone receiving the blasts saw Russell for what he was, grieving and disturbed. How could anyone take him seriously? The first email Richard received concerned him. The second and third even, but by the seventieth email in a mere three weeks, Russell was becoming obsessive and reflecting poorly on the hospital.

Russell's public outcry made him appear unstable, and Kendal Slate could not afford to have a staff surgeon going off the deep end in the public eye. While Russell was certainly in no condition to step foot in an operating room, the hospital couldn't let him go without paying him because technically, he hadn't done anything wrong. Besides, letting Russell go would only fuel his campaign against the hospital.

Russell was just one of the many fires Richard had to extinguish as department chair. He was also in the midst of a debate about plastic surgery procedures for teens with Hailey Mason, who wasn't a fan of elective surgeries in anyone under twenty-five.

"They're still figuring out who they are," she'd argued. "Let them get out into the real world, experience life a little before altering their appearance."

Richard thought about Elaine and her appearance. She'd had implants when they first met and, after having the twins, had them and other areas of her body touched up.

"If their parents are on board, who are we to question the decision?" he countered.

"The parents who are on board are stupid. If I hear one more sob story about a girl with a poor body image needing surgery to get her out of depression—"

"Why'd you go into plastics?" Richard cut her off.

"To help people who feel hopeless feel better about themselves," she answered. "People who have no other choice. Some girl wanting to go to a size D because her best friend is more developed isn't why I chose this field. And now you want to market this hospital, *me*, as a nose repair wizard?"

"I'm suggesting something that will help people needing rhinoplasties see the benefit of coming here for a total reconstructive experience."

"Is this a theme park now?" she asked. "We're selling an experience? I don't mean any disrespect, Richard, but marketing plastic surgery to kids is where I draw the line. I understand you want the hospital to make money, but at what cost? I fix what is broken, not what is human."

Richard was taken aback by Hailey's stance and had no logical rebuttal. In one aspect, he was upset with her for questioning his vision for the plastic surgery department, but on the other, he respected her defending what she believed in. He'd had beliefs when he first started. However, career aspirations and the administrative side of medicine slowly killed his dreams, replacing them with less noble ones.

Ultimately, it was his call. He just didn't want to go through the hassle of finding a plastics replacement so quickly after enduring the pain of hiring her if she threatened to leave. He had Hailey who he couldn't have leave and Russell who he'd wished would just quit.

ADDISON

Addison stood in front of the mirror staring at her reflection. She was having a good hair day, her curly auburn locks just tight enough to rest on her shoulders. The sweater she'd chosen to wear accented her hazel eyes, making them appear emerald. She ran her hand over her stomach, sucking in the unwanted softness to imagine what she'd look like if she lost a little more weight.

For the past couple of years, she'd maintained a healthy diet and weight, never obsessing about her body because she knew it would go when she got pregnant. She had no disillusions of being one of those women who only gain twenty pounds and leave the hospital in their pre-pregnancy clothing. Addison was honest enough with herself to know she'd pack on the weight under the glow of pregnancy and be happy to do it. Keith would love her no matter what. But now that she wasn't ever going to get pregnant, she had no excuse not to focus on her body and its round edges.

"You couldn't look any more beautiful." Keith interrupted her self-critique.

Addison dropped her hand from her stomach and turned to smile at her husband as he admired her from the doorway. "I think I'm going to train for a marathon."

"A marathon?" he asked, clearly thinking she was kidding.

"Yep," she said. "I've heard the Philadelphia one is fun."

"You're serious?" he asked. "What brought this on?"

"I've always wanted to run one," she answered, which was true, even if it had never come up in conversation.

"Do you know how far a marathon is?"

"Yep. You want to do it with me?"

Keith, like Addison, kept himself in good enough shape. However, unlike Addison, he could get away with eating and drinking a lot more without taking on a different shape. If Addison wasn't careful, a couple extra pounds could easily find a home on her.

"It's already getting cold out," he said. "How are you going to train?"

"On the treadmill."

"Train for a marathon on a treadmill?"

"Just until the weather gets nice. Besides, I'm sure we'll have a few good days here and there to run outside."

It was hard to describe the way Addison felt while talking about running a marathon. It was a goal. It gave her direction, allowing her to focus on something besides her inability to have children.

"What about the surgery?" Keith asked.

"What about it? The doctor said the recovery was minimal. I can train up until the surgery, take some time to recover and then start back up again."

"Sounds like you've thought this through," he said.

"Not at all," she admitted. "You with me?"

Keith crossed the room and hugged her from behind, staring at their reflection in the full-length mirror that hung on their closet door. "Heck yeah. For all twenty-six miles."

"Twenty-six point two," she corrected.

"Point two? Forget it then," he said.

Addison laughed.

"Maybe we should start with training for a ten-K or half-marathon?" he offered. "Work our way up?"

"It depends." Addison turned and eyed him suspiciously. "Are you going to stick with me? I don't want to do a half and have you say you're good with that."

Keith wrapped his arms around her. "I've never left you hanging before. Why would I start now?"

Addison's recent experiences had sucked her into an unhappy place. If running more than he thought was sane would keep her happy, he'd do it. All twenty-six point two miles.

"Hello, Phil?" Dale asked when a deep voice came on the line.

"Who's this?" the voice asked.

"Dale Reichter." Silence. "Jason Harris gave me your number. I'm calling to talk about your wife Leslie."

"Hold on."

Dale waited, his heart pounding in his chest, until a softer voice came on the line.

"This is Phil."

"Hi Phil. My name is Dale Reichter."

"Yes, Dale," Phil said. "Jay told me you might be calling. Not sure what I can do to help but Jay said you recently lost your wife."

"Yes. Cindy. In September."

"I'm sorry for your loss," Phil said. "I'm sure you haven't gotten sick of hearing that one yet."

"It beats people asking how I am."

"That's true," Phil said. "So, what can I do for you?"

"I lost my wife so quickly. I'm still trying to figure out what happened. The doctors say it's just one of those things, that nothing could be done. But it just doesn't feel right and I've lived by my gut my whole life."

Phil chuckled softly. "The doctors don't know anything. At least Leslie's didn't."

"Can you tell me what happened?"

Phil exhaled loud and long. "Nothing and then everything."

Dale began taking notes. *NOTHING AND THEN EVERYTHING.*

"Leslie went in healthy as can be. With the exception of her fibroids, she was great. The doctors weren't concerned, so we weren't.

Laparoscopic surgery seemed like a no-brainer with no downside."

NO DOWNSIDE.

"She had surgery on a Thursday morning, was home Friday for dinner. Sure, she had a little discomfort, but appeared no worse for the wear. The doctor gave her a clean bill of health so we went on with our life. Our youngest daughter Suzanne was getting married, so she and Leslie were always out and about.

"About a month after the surgery, Leslie started having some abdominal pain. Talk about gut feelings," Phil said. "The first time she mentioned it, I knew something was wrong. She decided to give it a couple of days but the pain didn't get better. It got worse and when her belly started to bloat, she made an appointment. By the time she saw the doctor, she looked four months pregnant.

"Scans showed a ten-centimeter mass in her abdomen, one in her bowel and another on her spleen. We didn't understand. The doctors had just given her a clean bill of health the month before. Hell, they were in her stomach and said everything looked fine.

"She had surgery to remove the tumors and started on chemo shortly after. The chemo made her so sick." Phil paused. "I'm sorry, it still feels like it was just yesterday."

"Nothing to be sorry about," Dale said.

"Leslie didn't let the chemo stop her. She had Suzie's wedding and refused to allow how she felt get in the way of any of the plans. There were mornings she'd be vomiting right until the time Suzie came over. She'd put on a brave face and tell Suzie she felt great. But as soon as Suzie would leave, she'd be back in the bathroom and in bed for the rest of the night. I joked with her that if the cancer didn't kill her, the wedding would."

Dale laughed sympathetically. "And the doctors didn't know what happened?"

"No," Phil said. "Like I said, they were just as surprised as we were. They ran tests on the tumor and said it was LMS, stage four."

Dale shook his head. *STAGE FOUR LMS. NO IDEA.*

"Did the chemo help?" Dale asked, though he already knew the answer. LMS didn't respond to chemotherapy the way other cancers did. There was little research available and little in terms of a cure, especially when it was stage four.

Dale made Cindy's doctor explain the stages of cancer very clearly, so he understood what they were facing. Stage one meant it was small, that it hadn't spread or grown too deeply in the surrounding tissues. Stage two and three meant the cancer was larger than stage one and had grown or spread into the surrounding tissues, possibly the lymph nodes, but not to other parts of the body. Stage four, the explanation Dale was waiting for, meant the cancer had spread, and not just locally. It was advanced. Metastatic. That was the word of the day for him. He would learn the abbreviation, METS, when Cindy was scanned to see if the cancer had spread. It was like *Where's Waldo*, except in her condition, the tumors weren't a small, thin object blending into the background. Cindy's tumors were huge, everywhere and anything but discreet.

"How many stages are there?" Dale had asked. The oncologist had looked at him with so much pity, Dale wanted to punch him square in the jaw. Dale wasn't a violent person, but his lack of understanding frustrated him, especially when dealing with the doctors who needed translators to get their points across.

"Four," Dr. Chemo—as Dale and Cindy referred to him—said with a look of hopelessness.

"We were hopeful even though the doctors told us we needed to be realistic," Phil answered.

"Did you go back to the doctor who did the hysterectomy?" Dale asked. "To see what he had to say about the operation."

"We tried," Phil said. "But he left the practice shortly after Leslie's diagnosis."

"What about the practice? Did they have any information?"

"They were pretty closed off to any discussion," Phil said, frustration evident in his voice. "Said they couldn't comment on behalf of Dr. Falzgrove."

"Were you able to track him down?" Dale asked.

"No," Phil said. "And it wasn't for a lack of trying. I'm pretty sure he stopped practicing medicine."

Alarm bells sounded in Dale's head. Why would a doctor up and leave a practice, the medical field altogether unless he'd done something wrong? *DOCTOR STOPPED PRACTICING.*

"So that was it?"

"Pretty much. The cancer consumed her belly and the doctors said she wasn't a candidate for surgery because of the chemo. They gave her three months. She lived three, pushed herself to five for Suzie's wedding and held on for another two just to prove the doctors wrong."

"Sounds like an incredible woman," Dale said, admiring her strength. He couldn't help but be reminded of Cindy and her tenacity in the face of the insurmountable odds the disease gave her.

"She was," Phil said. "I miss her every day."

Another conversation and the similarities continued. Healthy, beautiful women one day. Sick, overcome with tumors shortly after surgery. How was it that a cancer could attack and grow so quickly, moving throughout the body undetected until it was too late? Dale now knew of three women who'd suffered horrific deaths after they'd all had a simple, non-invasive surgery. Surgeries didn't cause cancer. Smoking, lifestyle, shit luck caused cancer. Still, there was something here. He was sure of it, and he was getting closer. He was sure of that, too.

EMMA AND RUSSELL

"Come in," Nicolai Vislat welcomed Emma and Russell into his soft-hued office, directing them to take a seat on one of the plump couches.

Emma smiled and entered, followed by Russell who was making a point to show no emotion. Although by exuding no emotion, he was exhibiting plenty.

"If he asks me how I'm feeling, I'm going to leave," Russell had said on the drive to the hospital.

Emma laughed. She appreciated Russell for his antics. While he was dead serious about leaving, she found him amusing. "I think they learn that in psych 101," she said.

"Sixty minutes," Russell said. "This man gets sixty minutes as a professional courtesy and not one second more."

Once everyone was seated, Nicolai spoke. "I'm sorry about what you're going through. Cancer is not an easy diagnosis to deal with, even to seasoned doctors such as yourselves."

Russell stared out of the window. Emma felt a surge of sadness.

"I've been asked to make myself available to you," Nicolai continued. "To help in any way I can."

"I'm not crazy," Russell blurted out.

Nicolai furrowed his brow. "Have I given you the impression I think that?"

"I know what the hospital is saying about me. They don't appreciate the emails, the truth."

"I'm not here as the hospital. I'm here to offer my assistance during this difficult time."

"We appreciate that," Emma said. "But we're dealing with this the best we can given the circumstances."

"How have you found yourself accepting the diagnosis?" Nicolai asked.

"We accept that Emma was assaulted in this hospital by the doctors we trusted," Russell replied.

"It's absolutely normal to try to find somewhere to place the blame when something of this magnitude occurs. Do you blame the hospital for Emma's cancer?"

"And you say you're not representing the hospital," Russell scoffed.

"I'm merely inquiring about your feelings about Emma's cancer."

"It's pretty simple, Nicolai. Kendal Slate took what could have been a manageable disease and turned it fatal. To be clear, we're not blaming Emma's LMS on the hospital. We're blaming the upstaging of her cancer on the hospital."

"I see," Nicolai replied.

"Do you?" Russell asked. "Because no one else in the hospital appears to. Cancer should never be cut up, let alone shredded inside of a patient. If Richard led you to believe I'm blaming Emma's cancer on the hospital, he clearly doesn't get it."

"My impression is that the concern lies with your approach of handling what has happened."

"That should be the least of their concerns," Russell said. "They're assaulting women. It needs to stop."

"What about you, Emma?" Nicolai asked. "You haven't said very much."

"There's not much else to say," Emma replied.

"I tried going directly to Oakley," Russell said. "He didn't care to listen. He wrote me off. I know the emails seem a bit much, but they're getting attention. There needs to be a moratorium placed on uterine morcellation. I'll do whatever it takes to make that happen."

Sixty minutes later, Russell thanked Nicolai for his time and stood to leave.

"I've found that having a person who isn't emotionally tied to you to talk with can really help," Nicolai said to Emma. "Sometimes people who are sick get stuck forcing themselves to look brave or feel better than they really do in an attempt to be strong for their loved ones. I can provide a safe place for decompression if you ever need it."

Russell laughed. "Emma's fine."

Nicolai looked to Emma. "One other thing to consider is keeping a journal. It's a private way to vent your emotions. Writing your fears and frustrations can help."

Emma smiled, rose from her seat and extended her hand. "Thank you for talking with us. I appreciate your willingness to hear us out."

Emma didn't need a place for decompression. She was capable of taking care of her own mental needs. But she understood what Nicolai meant. Some of the people who'd reached out since her diagnosis appeared more devastated by the news than she was. Emma's youngest sister had broken down the first time she came to visit, and Russell's parents were practically in tears every time they spoke. It wasn't hard to see how cancer patients needed a safe place to vent. But she didn't have time to vent. She needed to prepare for a ten-hour surgery.

"What if I don't make it through?" Emma asked Russell at four thirteen in the morning.

"You're going to make it through," Russell said firmly. He wasn't open to the thought of any other outcome.

"It's risky," she said. "Just in case—"

"You're going to make it through and we're going to go back to our life," he said with a finality to his voice.

Russell had been so tired, but the thought of life continuing without Emma kept his eyes wide open. He couldn't let her see or hear his fear. His job was to guide her through the surgery. He had to exude confidence, much like when he was in the operating room. Whatever the cases of the day brought in, Russell had to be in charge. His patients' lives depended on it. Emma was now his most important, precious patient. Her life was his to save.

RICHARD

"Good start to the day," Nancy said as Richard passed her desk. "No emails from Russell."

Richard shook his head and continued to his office. While it was good he hadn't heard from Russell, it also unnerved him. People like Russell didn't go quiet so quickly. Especially with the degree to which Russell was depicting Kendal Slate Memorial as a treacherous castle with Richard as its head villain.

Admittedly, bedside manner was not Richard's best asset. He excelled because of his steady hands and great technique. Patients, however, presented a challenge. Thankfully, he'd been born with a nice smile, though it was sometimes mistaken for arrogance. Some people were just going to hate doctors, he believed. No matter what he said or did, they were going to hate him, accuse him of getting paid too much and caring too little.

Empathy was preached at every lecture he attended regarding doctor-patient relationships. "Make contact," he'd heard repeatedly. "Patients want to feel like they are being heard, that their health matters."

"What's the biggest complaint you have with your doctor?" Richard had asked Nancy after the latest published study on patient satisfaction had crossed his desk.

"The wait time in his office," she answered quickly. "His staff is so quick to reschedule me if I'm a second over ten minutes late. Never mind that they are always at least twenty minutes behind and give me an attitude if I ask when I'm going to be seen."

Richard laughed. "Okay, but once you are seen. What's your biggest complaint?"

Nancy took a minute before responding. "He doesn't always listen, especially if I'm the last appointment of the day."

"How can you tell he's not listening?" Richard asked.

"Because I'm usually in and out in less than ten minutes. And he'll make his diagnosis, cutting me off before I even finish talking."

"Is he usually right?"

"I don't go to the doctor often," she said. "So, I like to be heard out when I do. I don't care if he knows what's wrong with me after one or two symptoms. Would it really pain him to hear what I have to say?" Nancy paused and chuckled to herself. "You know, sometimes, if I really feel like he's rushing my appointment, especially if I've waited a ridiculous amount of time, I talk longer on purpose. I refuse to allow him to cut me off. I ask extra questions just to make sure I really get my money's worth."

Richard leaned back in his chair and laughed. "I'm sure you do."

Aside from giving insight as to why Nancy was on her third marriage, Richard's conversation with her helped him think of a better way to deal with Russell. If a major key to patient satisfaction was allowing the patient to be heard, maybe all Richard had to do was allow Russell to be heard, or at least give him the impression he was being heard.

ADDISON

So maybe training for a marathon wasn't as easy as all the blogs and articles online made it seem. Four miles here, six miles there, ten-mile-long runs and rest days. Four miles didn't seem that hard on her first day of training. Four miles didn't seem to hurt that first night after she stretched and showered. Even the second run of the week, another four miles, didn't really bother her. But on the third day of consecutive running, Addison was tired.

"Come on," Keith had jogged back to her when she'd slowed her pace. "Don't give up, it's only day three."

Addison didn't, wouldn't give up despite her heavy legs. But it was cold and the November air burned her lungs with each breath. The tip of her nose was practically frozen. She should have agreed when Keith suggested they run at the gym. With every stride she took, the fresh, cool air that she thought she'd wanted assaulted her lungs. The only thing that kept her motivated was knowing that every step brought her closer to the warmth of home and the ever important, and much-needed, rest day.

Being a beginner training for a marathon, the training calendar she downloaded allowed her two rest days per week. Addison thought that day four, rest day one, was going to be her favorite day. But then she had her long run on day six, which was supposed to be ten miles but turned into seven run and three walked (totally acceptable according to her beginner's schedule) and the next day she hurt all over. Her body was officially on strike. Keith showed some signs of soreness and equally welcomed lounging on the couch to allow his muscles to "repair."

"You know I'm in this with you, Addy," he said, still in his pajamas at noon. "But is torturing your body and mine really making you feel better?"

"It is," she nodded. "I can't explain it, but it is. It's something to focus on."

"How about you focus on giving me a kiss?" he asked.

"Oww, oww, oww" Addison sat up and leaned into Keith, planting a large kiss on his lips before lying back down repeating, "oww, oww, oww."

DALE

"Dad, I think this plant is done," Carmen said, taking a giant bite of a burger from the local diner. She and her sisters had surprised Dale with lunch, bringing him one of his favorites, a Reuben.

"It's fine," Dale replied. "Been there so long I've gotten used to it."

"It's dead," Rebecca said. The room went silent. Everyone stopped chewing. "What?" she asked. "It is."

"I'll get to it," Dale said.

"Why don't you let us straighten up a bit?" Rebecca suggested. "You know mom taught us well."

"I know she did," Dale said. "But I'm okay with the house the way it is."

"We don't mind," Rebecca continued. "In fact, we could do a little bit after lunch."

"Is that why you're here?"

His girls looked back and forth at each other, just as they did when they were kids, no one brave enough to answer.

"We just thought it might be a good time to start going through Mom's stuff," Gail finally took the lead. "We can do it if it's too hard for you."

Dale shook his head and pushed the Styrofoam container with half a sandwich still in it to the center of the table. "I like the way the house is," he repeated.

"Dad, it's never going to be an easy thing to do," Rebecca said softly. "But it needs to be done."

"Why?" Dale barked. "Give me one good reason why."

"We just thought," Carmen said with a shaky voice.

"You just thought you knew what's best for me," Dale yelled. "How insensitive can you be? She was my wife! If I want to keep her belongings, I will. If I want a dead plant on my table, then so be it. It's my house!"

Carmen burst out into tears.

"Who's the insensitive one now, Dad?" Rebecca snapped back. "Do whatever you want. Silly us for caring about you."

"We're just trying to help," Gail, always the mediator, said. "It doesn't have to be today. It doesn't have to be ever. Just know that we're here."

Dale knew he was eventually going to have to clean up, dust the shelves, put Cindy's clothes away. He just wasn't ready. Leaving the house how she left it gave him a piece of her. He liked seeing her robe hanging on the back of the bedroom door and her water glass next to the book she'd been reading on the nightstand, though the water had long since evaporated. She'd have had a fit if she saw how he'd allowed the house to get and in a weird way, that also gave him a sense of peace. He was taunting her memory, her spirit because he knew if there was a way for her to hang around after her death, she would. Just as he'd never leave her.

He knew the dead plant was an eyesore but didn't care. It was part of his and Cindy's story. When Cindy had gone in for the surgery that was supposed to be the answer to her troubles, she'd made him promise to water the plants. It didn't matter it was only a one-night stay, she wanted her green babies cared for. Being the good husband, he did as he was instructed and watered her plants. As a get-well-soon jest, he bought her a peace lily because the woman in the plant store had told him peace lilies did better under-watered than overwatered. Cindy laughed and made room for the plant on her dresser, saying it would make her smile every morning and every night.

After Cindy got sick and went in to the hospital, Dale cared for the peace lily as though it was directly related to Cindy's health. He had to make sure it stayed alive, that it thrived. He checked it every day and at the first sign of dryness or any drooping, he watered it right away. When Cindy's health deteriorated, Dale brought the lily to her room in an attempt to brighten her spirit. She smiled the best she could through the pain. The lily blossomed in the hospital and Dale so badly wanted to believe its white flowers were a sign of hope.

He'd brought it home from the hospital after Cindy passed, unable to throw it out. He tried to take care of it, along with the rest of her plants, but in his ups and downs he didn't always remember or care to water the plants. Some days he did everything the way Cindy did or would have wanted him to, fighting to keep her present in the house. But on his low days, his darkest days, he didn't want to do anything.

The peace lily held on the longest, bouncing back from Dale's intentional dehydration a number of times before having had enough. Yet, despite it being dead, Dale couldn't throw it out. So now the pink ceramic pot sat on the kitchen table, where he put it the day Cindy died, still housing the lily and what used to be its beautiful blooms but were now a collection of dried, lifeless sticks.

After the girls left, he returned to the kitchen table and stared at the decrepit plant. *How could it spread so quickly? How do the doctors not know?* Working as a general contractor as long as he had, Dale had become extremely proficient in his trade. He had to because people trusted him with their homes. Many of his clients didn't know which beams throughout the house were structural and which were not. If he knocked down the wrong wall, it could be catastrophic. One of his uncle's favorite quotes was, "Don't take anything for granted." If something wasn't working the way it was planned, Dale always took a step back and reevaluated. If he was Dr. Clayton, he would be taking a huge step back and reevaluating everything about Cindy's surgery to see what went wrong.

Had the doctors in Cindy, Pauline and Leslie's surgeries taken their patients' health for granted? Had they assumed nothing else was going on and so proceeded with the surgery without hesitation? One in ten thousand was what Dr. Clayton had told Cindy and Dale the odds of her having undiagnosed leiomyosarcoma were. One in ten thousand. At the time Dale and Cindy both couldn't believe her bad luck. But after speaking with Jason Harris and Phil Santerberry, bad luck no longer seemed like a plausible explanation. He wondered how statistics like those were developed, who controlled the numbers.

"Do the numbers even matter?" Sophia had asked the next day at the library. "I mean what do the numbers matter when you're the one it happens to? If you tell me my odds are one in a million of getting hit by a truck when I cross the street, I'm going to do so confidently. But if I'm that one that gets hit, will I really care there were another nine hundred ninety-nine thousand nine hundred and ninety-nine people who didn't? It's still going to be bad for me."

"Of course it is," he said, grateful she'd explained her remark. "But if the odds are one in a million and let's say five people get hit in one day, wouldn't you be suspicious?"

"Sure," Sophia agreed.

"That's all I'm saying. These two other guys lost their wives the same way. Three women in two years with the same story. I don't buy it."

"What are you saying?"

"I'm saying I think the doctors have it wrong."

"What wrong?"

"The numbers. How can they know numbers on something they have no clue about?"

"That's a pretty big accusation."

"I know." Dale nodded. "But I don't think I'm wrong."

He was on the verge of something. What, Dale wasn't quite sure of, but the pieces were starting to come together in his head. With just a little more research and investigation, he might be lucky enough to see the bigger picture.

EMMA AND RUSSELL

The table was set, a beautiful spread laid before them. A golden turkey weighing at least twenty pounds served as the centerpiece, surrounded by bountiful bowls of salad, green beans and potatoes. Water glasses sparkled under the chandelier illuminating the room filled with family. Conversations were being spoken with smiles and speckled with laughter. Emma observed it all.

Would this be her last Thanksgiving? The last holiday she shared with her loved ones? It was hard to be thankful when she knew what she was up against. But at the same time, watching her children squeal in delight as they ran through her parents' house with their cousins, she'd never been more thankful. She loved her life, her family, her job. She'd been so elated to get the position at Kendal Slate, considered herself one of the lucky ones. What a cruel twist of fate that the same institution she'd been so grateful to work for would in turn, upstage her cancer and sentence her to death.

The moment wasn't lost on Russell either. The last thing he wanted to do was celebrate, be around anyone, be thankful for anything. He watched Emma interact with her family, watched the kids run and play. He watched it all with an empty, forced smile. The conversations he had were short and superficial. Everyone made a point to show their concern, offer support any way they could. And while he appreciated the outpouring of love, he didn't want any of it. He didn't want to celebrate Thanksgiving, especially with other people. But Emma insisted. She wasn't going to take the holiday away from her children and family.

"It's not about them," Russell had protested when Emma insisted they go.

"This is what *I* want," she said. "*I* want to be around everyone. *I* want the kids to have fun family memories."

How could he argue with that? With her? He would do anything for Emma. Whatever she wanted, whatever she needed.

Getting ready for dinner was no small feat for either of them. They both had to prepare themselves for the sympathy, the questions, the awkwardness intruding on almost every conversation. Cancer made people forget how to be normal. Try as they might, if their unease wasn't conveyed in words, it came through their eyes. After crying it out in the shower, Emma got dressed and chased her children down to dress them up for the evening. In the midst of changing diapers, socks, shirts and pants, she also had to pry Russell from his position in front of the computer and urge him to put some effort into his appearance.

Once he had taken leave from the hospital, Russell let go of everything that "didn't matter anymore." What he had meant was anything that didn't include fighting against morcellation or researching a cure for Emma. Never one to wear sweatpants, Russell barely changed out of the only gray pair he owned, a souvenir from his med school days. The stubble on his face came in quickly and was soon replaced by a beard, something he'd never sported before. But he didn't care. Those things didn't matter. He didn't have time to waste on his appearance when there were much more pressing issues requiring his attention. While it wasn't her favorite look for Russell, Emma was growing used to the extra facial hair. The kids thought it was funny. Hope laughed every time he kissed her, saying it tickled her chinny chin chin.

Emma hadn't let herself go one bit, despite her worst days. Because they were all bad days and if she gave in to how she felt, she wouldn't get out of bed. She had four blessings who relied on her to endure the sadness, despite the crippling fear of the unknown. It surprised Emma how shocked people appeared to see her put together, dressed well, hair done. Had they'd expected her to melt into a puddle? It would take more than a diagnosis to keep her down. She and her children would visit with friends, celebrate birthdays and holidays as long as they could, including Thanksgiving. And they would be thankful they had each other today because really, that was all anyone really had anyway.

RICHARD

"Happy Thanksgiving," Elaine toasted from the opposite end of the table as Richard.

"Happy Thanksgiving," everyone responded in unison.

Thanksgiving was Elaine's holiday to host and yet another way to one-up her sister Madeline. They had a strange competition between them which Richard didn't understand and didn't care enough to learn about. Every time Elaine complained about Madeline and what she'd done, Richard tuned her out, thankful he was an only child. Yet despite whatever issue Elaine and Madeline were in the midst of, they always showed up for family get-togethers with a smile. Elaine could be bitching about Madeline right up until she knocked on the front door. Then it was all hugs and kisses and compliments.

"I am thankful for my precious family," Elaine continued in the tradition of going around the table announcing what everyone was thankful for, "and our health."

The twins rolled their eyes and muttered something about family.

"I'm thankful for our family, wonderful friends, and Stan's new promotion." Madeline beamed with pride. "Oh, and that our kitchen addition is finally finished so Christmas dinner will not be interrupted."

Elaine rolled her eyes when Madeline brought up Christmas. "Richard, your turn."

I'd be happy if we could eat in silence, he thought. "I'm thankful for all of this," he said, forcing a smile.

It was a redundant question and one Richard dreaded every time the holiday approached. While he had a lot in his life, it was his hard work and sacrifice that allotted him the luxuries and successes he enjoyed.

Being thankful meant he had gratitude toward someone or something when it was his efforts that got him to where he was. Apart from a surprise baby early on, Richard pretty much handpicked his life. The twins were obviously out of his control but he and Elaine were trying to conceive. In fact, they'd planned on having two children. Having them both at once just made it easier, at least for him. One pregnancy, one delivery. As an added bonus, the chaos two babies brought into their life and the damage it wreaked on Elaine's size four frame pretty much guaranteed she wouldn't want to get pregnant again.

"How's that doctor?" Madeline started up conversation while everyone loaded their plates with the food Elaine had prepared. And by prepared, she meant giving their cook a menu.

Richard's head snapped up at the mention of a doctor, staring directly at Elaine. Elaine's cheeks flushed as red as the cranberries under the heat of Richard's glare.

"Doctor?" Madeline's husband asked.

"You know, the one I was telling you about," she forced through a mouth full of candied yams. "The one from Richard's hospital who had the surgery and now has cancer."

Richard felt the heat rise from his cheeks to his forehead.

Elaine, in panic mode, tried to correct the situation. "The surgery didn't give her cancer."

"Obviously," Madeline laughed, oblivious to Richard's mounting fury. "Just because we're not doctors doesn't mean we don't have common sense."

Stan nodded as the recollection clicked. "Right."

"It's just so sad," Madeline said. "I can't begin to imagine. Especially now, around the holidays. It can't be easy. How is she doing?"

Richard was pretty sure smoke was billowing from his nostrils. He knew better than to discuss the Speck case with Elaine, but at the same time, trusted his wife would know not to discuss it with anyone. Especially her loud-mouth sister.

"It's a violation to discuss that matter," Richard said as calmly as his irritation would permit.

"Madeline wouldn't say anything to anyone," Elaine offered.

"Except Stan," Richard replied, slightly above what would be considered a growl.

"Come on Richie," Madeline said in an attempt to make the mood light. "We're all family here."

"It's Richard," he replied. "And family doesn't matter when I could lose my job."

Elaine picked the napkin off her lap, threw it on her plate and excused herself from the table. Richard knew she was going to pout, somehow make her indiscretion out to be his fault and yes, she should be able to tell her sister things and no, she hadn't told anyone else, and why did everything have to be such a big deal? It's not like she'd told Madeline Emma's name. And of course, the big issue Elaine would have was that Richard had made dinner awkward, which Madeline was absolutely going to rub in her face at Christmas.

If nothing else, Richard was able to finish his Thanksgiving dinner in silence.

ADDISON

"You're losing weight," Addison's mother greeted her at the door with a disapproving glance and peck on the cheek hello before turning her accusatory look to Keith.

Keith threw his hands up in surrender. "Don't look at me. This is all Addy."

"Happy Thanksgiving to you too, Mom," Addison said.

Addison and Keith had just arrived at her mom's for Thanksgiving dessert after celebrating dinner with Keith's family. There couldn't have been more of a contrast between the happiness at Keith's parents' and Addison's mother's place, where the years of anger and bitterness clung to the walls like dusty old drapes.

"I take it you're still training for the marathon," her mom said as she cut and plated three pieces of pumpkin pie.

Addison placed each plate at the kitchen table. "Every day."

"That's too much. I can practically see your bones."

"Mom," Addison said with a sigh.

"Tell her, Keith," her mom said, turning her attention to Keith.

Keith had learned it was better to side with Addison's mother over not saying anything at all. "I told her she was perfect just the way she was when she said she wanted to train for the marathon. But it has been fun training together."

"You're going to run it too?" her mother scoffed.

"I told you that, Mom," Addison said, taking a seat next to Keith.

"It seems a bit excessive if you ask me," her mom replied.

"That's why I didn't ask you," Addison joked.

"You don't ask me about a lot of things," her mom retorted.

"This pie is delicious as always," Keith cut in, stopping the conversation from the argument it was only seconds away from becoming.

Addison's mom smiled weakly and pushed the pie dish toward his plate. "Good. Have some more. You both look like you could use it."

When dessert was finished they took their coffee into the living room in awkward silence. Addison's mother, usually ready with a list of grievances, sat on her maroon couch, coffee cup in her hands, staring out the window.

"I heard we might be getting snow," Keith offered.

"If the weathermen are right, it should only be a dusting," Addison's mother replied. "We probably won't even see a drop of rain."

Addison started the countdown in her head. *Three...two...one.*

"Weather forecasting is probably one of the only professions where it's acceptable to be wrong more often than right...and no one seems to care! They say it's going to rain, people load up on umbrellas and boots. Snow, everyone rushes out to stock up on bread and milk. I think they're all in on it together."

"The weathermen and the stores?" Addison held back her amusement. "Seriously, Mom?"

"Makes perfect sense to me," Keith chimed in.

Addison shot him a dirty look. He winked at her.

"Everyone has an agenda, Addison," her mom said. "You might not see it, but that's how the world works. Angles are being worked all around you."

"So what's your angle, Mom?"

"What?"

"You just said angles are being worked all around me. What's your angle?"

"Mothers don't work angles," she replied.

Addison just about choked on her coffee. "Moms probably work the most angles out of anyone."

"That's different. If we have a concern for our children, it is only right to find a way to address it. If you consider that an angle, well then."

"Guess I'll never know," Addison said, a hint of sadness in her voice.

Keith reached over and took her hand.

Addison's mother exhaled. "That's your decision."

"Yes, Mom. I decided to have endometriosis."

"You know what I mean, Addison."

Addison looked across the room, directly at her mother. "It's Thanksgiving, Mom. Can you please let it go just for today?"

Her mother let out a loud sigh, contorting her face in what appeared to be pain. For a second, Addison thought her mother was about to cry. But just as quickly as the pain surfaced on her mother's face, she replaced it with indifference. With one final sigh, she looked across the room back at her daughter and said, "Whatever you want Addison."

DALE

"I've got something for you," Sophia exclaimed when she saw Dale walk into the library. The expression on her face gave Dale a feeling of excitement and hope, both of which he needed after enduring his first Thanksgiving without Cindy.

The girls had put together a wonderful dinner, but no one was hungry. The desserts could've easily been plucked out of any culinary magazine, yet with the exception of the cookies ravaged by the kids, the pies and sweets remained untouched for the most part. His sons-in-law ate, not that they weren't saddened, they just didn't feel the loss the same way as the girls. He didn't fault them. They hadn't lost their mother.

"I'm all ears," Dale said, forcing a smile to his face.

"Do you read *The Times*?" Sophia asked.

"Just *The Tribune*," he replied. The girls had been on him for years to get a tablet, so he could read things electronically, but Dale liked walking out front in the morning and getting the paper from the end of the driveway. There was something about reading the paper with his breakfast that he knew he'd never be able to feel with a piece of metal, or whatever they were made of, in his hand. With the paper he didn't have to worry about internet connection and battery life.

"Kendal Slate Memorial is in the paper this morning," Sophia boasted, producing a copy of the newspaper for Dale. "And it has something to do with the hysterectomies they've been performing there."

Dale snatched the paper from her hands and read the article as quickly as possible. His skin raised with goose bumps as the words processed. *Drs. Emma and Russell Speck. Hysterectomy. Leiomyosarcoma.*

The reporter, Alyson Baker, claimed that Emma Speck, a doctor at

Kendal Slate, had undergone a routine laparoscopic hysterectomy to treat what she believed to be benign uterine fibroids. However, the operating doctor discovered after she'd performed the procedure that Emma had leiomyosarcoma and her prognosis was not good. According to Emma's husband Russell, also a doctor at Kendal Slate, the procedure the hospital used had in fact upstaged her cancer by mincing up the malignant tumor and disseminating it throughout her abdominal cavity and introducing it into her bloodstream.

Dale looked at Sophia with wide eyes.

"I know," she said. "This is it. You were right."

Dale didn't want to get ahead of himself. He knew Cindy's sudden sickness and untimely death were not a coincidence after surgery; something had happened. His lack of medical knowledge stifled his ability to get answers. But now he had not one, but two doctors not only asking questions, but making allegations. He had to get in touch with Russell Speck.

The first question that came to Dale's mind was whether or not Cindy's doctor had used a power morcellator. Dale was pretty sure he'd never heard the term before, but the article in *The Times* made it appear to be a commonly used tool in laparoscopic hysterectomies.

When he searched power morcellator and fibroids on the internet, the videos that came up made his stomach turn. At first glance, the morcellator appeared harmless, a small tool with a claw that reached out and pulled the fibroid to its base, sucking the mass inside. However, masses larger than the opening at the end of the morcellator had to be cut by a small blade and hacked up so that they could be removed. He couldn't believe the destructive nature of such a small innocuous instrument.

Sophia couldn't tolerate the graphic images on the screen and patted Dale on the shoulder as she left him watching video after video of uterine morcellations. He read up on the morcellator, its design, the companies that made and distributed them. The Specks were right. Morcellators were commonly used and widely accepted.

He found little information about any downsides. In fact, he found himself reading a lot of the things that had been sold to him and Cindy before her surgery. *Precise, safe, quicker recovery times.* If the machine did all of the work, what exactly had Dr. Clayton done? Did Dr. Clayton perform the surgery or a robot? Dale felt ill. He pushed back from the computer and stood up, his mind filled with questions.

Had Cindy been morcellated? After what happened to her, why was the hospital still performing the same operation? How could he get in touch with the Specks? The article had said something about an upcoming long and invasive procedure Emma Speck would have, in the hopes of stopping her disseminated cancer from recurring. But it didn't say when. Dale wanted to respect the Specks' privacy, but at the same time he needed to talk with Russell. If the Specks were serious about bringing their fight to Kendal Slate, Dale wanted them to know they had at least one other family in their corner.

EMMA AND RUSSELL

How do you say good-bye? The question beat Emma down most days every time she looked at her children, her husband, her life. She wasn't ready to say good-bye to any of it. And while the surgery she was about to undergo gave her the best chance at leveling the unfair advantage Nicole Stein had handed leiomyosarcoma by morcellating Emma's tumor, it also had a good chance of complete failure, death.

The human body is only capable of handling so much. Being in the operating room day in and day out, Emma witnessed the miracles of bodily strength, but also its limitations. Her mental strength was ready for the fight. She prayed her body would be as well. Double-digit hours under anesthesia, open on a table. Organ removal. Being scalded internally with chemotherapy. It was a lot for even the healthiest of bodies.

Her parents were hovering—she knew they had to be plagued with the same question. How could they say good-bye to their daughter? Their firstborn? Sure, they put on brave, positive faces and talked a favorable outcome, but she could see the fear, the pain. They, too, were trying to figure out how to say good-bye. They just weren't admitting it.

Russell was more on edge than she'd ever seen him. For starters, he was staring at her, a lot. Coming from hectic schedules where they barely co-existed in the same space, she wasn't used to having him around all the time, especially looking at her.

"Stop it," she'd said after catching him for easily the third time in half an hour.

Russell quickly looked away. "What?"

"Staring at me like it's the last time you're going to see me."

"Emma," he said sharply.

"What?" she replied just as pointedly. "I know what you're doing and I need you to stop."

"I'm not doing anything," he offered. It was a weak attempt and they both knew it. "Why can't I look at my wife, admire her beauty?"

His remark made her chuckle. "Because in ten years, you've never stopped to admire my beauty."

"Maybe you just haven't paid attention for the past ten years."

For brief interludes in the nightmare that had become their life, Emma and Russell escaped by way of flirting and foreplay. But as things progressed to what normal couples would enjoy as intimacy, Emma and Russell snapped right back into their sad reality in which one or both of them would end up crying.

The truth was, Russell did stop to admire Emma's beauty. He admired her for all that she was and all she had planned on becoming. In all his life, he'd never met a woman as driven as her.

Emma could tell every time Russell looked at her how much he loved her. He wasn't one to get sappy or spout off a romantic poem, but his eyes often beamed brighter than hers with each of her professional milestones. He boasted about her research more than he did their kids. He was smitten with her, not that she ever let on that she knew.

Russell must have told her he loved her a million times in the days leading up to the procedure. Everyone Emma knew checked in via text, phone calls, emails or random drop-ins. It was clear to see the reassurances family and friends were giving her were more for themselves than Emma. They wanted her to know everything was going to be okay, but on the off chance something happened, they needed to get in one last hug, one last good-bye. Though no one actually said good-bye. "See you when you wake up" or "I'm not going to say good-bye..." It all became noise.

"How do I prepare the kids for this?" she'd asked Russell in a moment of utter despair. "How can I tuck them in the night before, kiss them in the morning and not know whether they'll ever see me again?" The thought was too much to bear and Emma broke down sobbing uncontrollably.

"You don't prepare them for anything because you're going to be fine," Russell insisted.

"Stop!" she yelled through the tears. "Just stop it. You know what this surgery is. You know how risky it is. I'm not going in for a routine procedure. There is nothing routine about what is about to happen to me. Can you just for one second admit that I could die?"

Russell shot Emma a look of utter hurt, possibly verging on betrayal. He took a second to gather his thoughts before responding calmly. "No."

"No?" she scoffed.

"No," he said. "I won't. I believe you are going to be okay and I need you to believe it too."

"But what—"

"But nothing," he said. "You know better than anyone how fragile life is. Think of some of the worst cases you've seen come through the doors at the hospital. People going about their days, normal as can be until something completely unexpected and horrific happens. You've had the unexpected and horrific happen. You had a malignancy minced up and introduced into your bloodstream. This surgery is going to fix that atrocity. I believe it and you need to as well."

Emma sunk into the couch as Russell paced and ranted. When he finished, he sat beside her, wrapping his arms tightly around her forlorn frame. She desperately wanted to believe like he did. She wanted to be positive—attitude was huge when it came to physical rehabilitation. She just wasn't there yet. She was a mother petrified at the thought of leaving her children.

If something happened to her, her pain would be over, her anxiety gone. But her babies, they wouldn't understand. They'd be so lost, as would Russell. The thought made her want to cancel the surgery. But she had to attack the cancer strong. Russell was right. There was no outcome allowed other than success. Her children deserved it and she would fight with everything she had to not leave them.

The night before the surgery, she spent extra time getting each child ready for bed. She brushed the girls' hair longer than was necessary after baths and showers. She allowed them extra dessert and to cuddle in bed with her and Russell until they fell asleep. She tried her best not to cry, not to give in to the sadness and fear gripping her heart, her breath. But it was unnatural not to. Seeing Hope's tiny fingers resting on her leg or feeling Jocelyn's tiny feet dig into her ribs as she snuggled into Emma and fell asleep. Even Jacob and his usual too cool attitude made Emma's heart ache. Kaitlin didn't have any qualms cozying up with her parents and siblings. She always had been a cuddler. Lying there surrounded by love, Emma was overwhelmed with a mélange of happiness, pain and regret.

Before dawn, she kissed each one of her angels on the head, taking in the smell of their skin and crept downstairs where Russell waited with her parents. Her mom was in tears, her dad a statue. Emma hugged them both quickly, not wanting to break. Her mom didn't let go until Russell mentioned the time.

"I love you," her parents said in unison, her dad holding her mom up.

"I love you," Emma replied.

"Thank you," Russell said. "I'll be in touch."

With that, they were out the door, no one having said a single good-bye.

RICHARD

"You see the paper?" Nancy asked, dropping it on Richard's desk as soon as he sat down.

"Yes," he replied, annoyed Nancy would think he hadn't been informed his hospital was being spat on in the news. Richard had called Henry Lewis before sunrise.

"Yes," Henry replied when Richard asked if he'd read the article. "Yes," he repeated when Richard asked if he'd known the article was going to be printed.

"How could you not tell me?" Richard demanded.

"They reached out to the hospital for a comment," Henry said. "We didn't have one. We're not at liberty to discuss a patient's medical care."

Richard laughed. "Right, but a patient can talk about the hospital care all they want. What about libel? Can we get them on defamation?"

"No," Henry said. "Technically, they didn't say anything defamatory about the hospital."

"They're blaming us for her cancer," Richard protested.

"They're blaming morcellation for upstaging her cancer," Henry corrected.

Richard re-read the article, hoping to find something defamatory.

"It's *The Times*, Richard," Henry said. "They know what to print and how to print it without getting into trouble."

"I still don't understand why you didn't feel it necessary to tell me they were going to publish an article about the Specks."

Henry sighed. "Do you know how often the hospital is asked to provide a comment? Enough to make it a full-time job. Someone always has an axe to grind. They rarely make it to the papers."

"So how did the Specks get this in *The Times*? Do they know"—Richard skimmed the article—"Alyson Baker?"

"I have no idea," Henry replied.

"Is the hospital going to comment now?" Richard asked. "I have a few things I'd like to say."

"No, we're not," Henry said. "And no, you don't. You have no comment. Like the rest of us here at Kendal Slate, you are very sorry to hear of Dr. Speck's unfortunate diagnosis. You understand how difficult news like that is to receive and wish her the best in her recovery."

"Seriously?" Richard asked. "That's what we're going with?"

"People love scandal. They thrive on it. If we engage the Specks in a verbal war over what happened and why in the newspaper, the story is going to gain traction, an audience. If we present the hospital as empathetic to what the Specks are going through and show no ill-will, there is no story."

"I don't know," Richard disagreed. "Russell Speck has been all over this since the beginning and hasn't let up. He's not going to go away because we acknowledge how he and his wife are feeling. He wants more than that."

"And it's your job to find out what he wants and give it to him. Stop this fire from igniting. Right now it's a sad story. Let's leave it at that. The worst thing you want is patients asking questions."

"He wants to stop morcellation," Richard said.

"Is that a feasible option?" Henry asked.

"Not unless we want to lose considerable revenue. Morcellation has allowed us to perform hysterectomies quicker with less complications and reduce hospital admissions."

"Sounds like you need to find another way to pacify him."

"His persistence tells me he's not the pacifying type."

"You'll find a way," Henry said. "You always do."

"So, what's the plan?" Nancy asked as Richard stared blankly at the newspaper on his desk.

"Were you ever able to schedule a meeting with the Specks?"

Nancy shook her head. "No. Russell hasn't returned my phone calls."

"Call again," Richard said.

"I will but he might be a little busy with his wife's surgery."

"Do you know where she's having that done?"

"The article didn't say," Nancy replied.

"Well find out," he all but barked. "Find out where and when her surgery is. I want you to send them flowers. A nice, big arrangement wishing her our best and a quick recovery."

"I'll see what I can do."

Richard nodded. Nancy, recognizing his dismissal, turned and walked out of the office, closing the door behind her. As soon as she was gone he picked up the phone and dialed his wife. Elaine answered on the second ring.

"Is everything okay?" she asked.

"Has anyone called the house looking for me? Any reporters?" he asked.

"No, why?" Richard could hear the excitement perk up in Elaine's voice and it made him angry. "Is this about that article?"

"How do you know about the article?" he snapped. Elaine had still been asleep when he left in the morning, so he hadn't had a chance to discuss the importance of keeping her mouth shut.

"I read the news," she said with a hint of annoyance.

Richard didn't have time to debate what Elaine considered news.

"If any reporters call, tell them nothing," he instructed. "No comment."

"How would they reach us at home?" she asked. "Don't you think you're being a bit paranoid?"

"Tell them no comment."

"Richard, no one has called for you. The only person who's called was Madeline and she—"

"Tell her to keep her mouth shut," he interrupted.

"Richard," Elaine snapped. "I don't know what has gotten into you, but do not talk to me that way."

Richard grabbed a pencil from his desk and snapped it in half. He hadn't meant to, but his agitation had boiled over and it was either the pencil or Elaine's neck. How could she not get the severity of the situation? All he needed was for a reporter to show interest in how Elaine felt or what she thought and it would be all over. He'd have the Specks teaming up with his own wife against him and the hospital. And Madeline, he wouldn't put it past her at all to contact the papers or reporters on her own.

"Look," he said through gritted teeth. "This story cannot gain traction. If it does, it won't be good for the hospital which won't be good for me. If anything gets out that even hints at a HIPPA violation or wrongdoing on the hospital's part, I could lose my job. We could lose everything."

"I see."

"So please call your sister and explain to her the importance of having no comment or opinion on the article."

"Fine," Elaine huffed. "I will. But only because you asked nicely."

Richard hung up the phone, Elaine's words taunting him. *Only because you asked nicely.* Was she really that childish and immature? She was the most difficult, stubborn person he'd ever dealt with. That was, before Russell Speck. Russell Speck was relentless and now Henry Lewis had put it on Richard to appease him. What if nothing would? Unlike with Elaine, Richard severely doubted that talking nicely to Russell would get the job done.

ADDISON

The cold weather had finally forced Addison indoors. While she didn't miss the burning lungs or chapped skin that accompanied running in thirty-degree weather, she did miss the fresh air. The gym felt stuffier in the winter with its foggy windows and circulating hot breath. Running on the treadmills next to smelly, sweaty people was not her idea of a good time. When a particularly sweaty man bumped into her as she made her way to the treadmill, she questioned her resolve to train the whole winter indoors.

For her first indoor workout, Addison packed her phone full of upbeat music and tried to block out her surroundings. She imagined the weight falling off, crossing the finish line with Keith by her side after twenty-six-point-two excruciating miles. She was picturing the happiness of it all when a tiny woman got on the next treadmill with an equally tiny-yet-protruding belly.

Addison didn't realize she was staring until she found herself stumbling to catch her step and flying off the treadmill. Of course everyone stopped and stared and one of the workers from Fitness 4 U came to investigate, making the ordeal even more embarrassing.

"I'm fine," Addison stammered. "Just lost my step."

After assuring the desk clerk at the gym she was fine and didn't feel the equipment was faulty, she made a quick escape to the locker room where she showered and promptly left.

"You did what?" Rachel laughed into the phone.

"Yep, got so caught up staring at the pregnant woman next to me, I busted my butt."

"Oh Addy," Rachel exclaimed.

"It's fine. You told me training for a marathon would be bad for my health."

"I didn't mean like that," Rachel laughed. "What are you doing now?"

"Going to find a rock to crawl under," Addison groaned.

"Why don't you come over?"

Addison looked at the clock on her dashboard. It was only four thirty in the afternoon. "Are you home?"

"I can be," Rachel said. "And I could definitely go for a drink. It's been that kind of day. I mean, not falling off the treadmill kind of bad, but stressful enough."

Addison laughed. "Ha. Ha. Kick me while I'm down. I'll see you soon."

"You know you don't need to have the surgery," Rachel offered fifteen minutes later, pouring Addison a generous glass of wine once they were seated at her kitchen table. "Who knows, maybe they'll have some crazy medical breakthrough in the next couple of years."

"Short of paying for a surrogate, which we can't afford, there are no more options. Unless..." Addison gave Rachel a look.

"Don't make me laugh," Rachel said, pouring herself an equally generous serving. "Can you imagine me, pregnant?"

"I can," Addison said with a sigh. "Because apparently everyone can get pregnant except for me."

"Addy, don't do this to yourself."

"It's kind of hard not to when it's constantly being thrown in my face. I mean come on. If I were pregnant, I'd be at home with my feet up getting fat and loving every second of it. Yet there I am, trying to better myself, training for a marathon and little miss perfectly pregnant has to come and run next to me. There were easily ten other open treadmills.

Why did she have to run next to me?!?"

"You don't know what she's going through," Rachel offered. "Maybe she has no idea who her baby's father is."

"Nope, she had an impressive diamond on her finger," Addison said, defeated.

"Wow, you got a good look, didn't you?" Rachel asked.

"I told you I fell because I was being nosy," Addison said. "Is it bad I was hoping she wasn't married?" Addison asked. "As if that would somehow make it better."

"I can't imagine how you feel," Rachel said. "So I'm not going to pretend to. But I can tell you pregnancy isn't all it's cracked up to be."

"How do you know?"

"Well, I know Tracy has just about had it with Tina."

Addison perked at the mention of Tina not being perfect. "I'm listening."

Rachel smiled. "Apparently she is really sick and making everyone around her miserable. Tracy has even considered calling off the shower."

"Really?"

"Yeah. Tina is so unhappy, she said she understood why some women choose to terminate their pregnancies."

"No, she didn't," Addison said, taking Tina's comment personally. "How can someone be so arrogant, so self-centered?"

Rachel nodded. "Keith dodged a bullet with that one for sure."

Addison gulped down her glass and held it up for Rachel to refill. "I'm not so sure. Who knows whether he'd rather be with her and have a baby or be with me with no chance of a family?"

"You can't be serious, Addison," Rachel said. "It's you every day."

Addison didn't reply.

"You need to stop looking at yourself as damaged," Rachel said, setting her glass on the table. "So you can't have children. That doesn't make you a bad person, or even faulted. I've told you how I don't want to have kids. Does that make me a bad person?"

Addison looked at the table. "It's just hard to want something so bad and know I'm never going to have it."

"So why have the surgery?"

"Because it's better to know there's no chance than to have a glimmer of hope and constant disappointment or worse, kill myself trying."

"Are you sure?" Rachel asked.

"I'm sure I'm done hoping."

"Well that's a sad stance to take, don't you think?"

"It's realistic," Addison said.

"You're one of the most optimistic people I know, Addy. If there's hope for anyone, it's definitely for you."

"And yet Tina is the one who has no problem getting pregnant."

"You know what?" Rachel said. "Let's stop talking about pregnancy, Tina and everything else that sucks. Let's finish this bottle and maybe another two and forget about it all."

"Sounds perfect," Addison said. "Let me call Keith and tell him I won't be coming home tonight."

Dear Alyson Baker,

I read your article in The Times about Kendal Slate Memorial and laparoscopic hysterectomies. My wife, Cindy, had her hysterectomy done there and died three months later from leiomyosarcoma. I believe Kendal Slate had something to do with my wife's death. In fact, I've spoken with other men who lost their wives the same way. Because I'm not a doctor, my concerns have been discounted by the hospital. If you could put me in touch with Dr. Speck, I'd really appreciate it. I understand he and his wife are going through a lot right now. But after I read your article, I'm sure there is something the hospital isn't saying and I have made it my mission to figure out what it is.

Sincerely,
Dale Reichter

Figuring a writer for The Times had to be busy, Dale composed the email in his head over and over before actually typing it and sending it to Alyson Baker. His wording, as well as his spelling, had to be perfect. He'd become quite proficient at writing and saying laparoscopic, hysterectomy and the dreaded leiomyosarcoma. Not one for words, he tried to ensure he came across as direct and professional. He didn't want his email to be discarded, not when he was so close to finding real answers.

He knew he wasn't going to get an immediate response, but that didn't stop Dale from checking his email hourly. If Alyson Baker wrote him back, he wanted to know. He was giddy, the anticipation of a response almost the same as waiting for a call back from Cindy after their first date. What he wouldn't have given for a call from Cindy. If only he could just talk to her again. To hold her, touch her. That would be heaven.

Dale closed his eyes and thought of her voice, the sweet melody her words carried. He'd been on dates with women whose voices made him cringe, wish he was deaf. Not Cindy. Her voice carried a tune he believed was meant only for him. Even leading up to her final words, before the pain of the masses growing inside her was too much to bear without medication, her voice was music to Dale's ears. He chuckled, thinking of how someone with such a sweet voice couldn't carry a tune for anything.

The first time he'd heard Cindy sing, she'd had no idea anyone was listening. Sure, she'd sung along to songs here and there on the radio, but it was never loud, never unrestricted the way she sang when she thought she was alone.

Shortly after they'd gotten married, Dale and his crew had finished up a job early and he headed home, deciding to surprise her with a bouquet of flowers. The radio was on upstairs when he walked through the front door, its music traveling easily throughout their quaint house. At first Dale couldn't tell whether Cindy was singing or in pain. Her tone didn't improve as he walked up the stairs and the volume of her voice increased. He found her in the bathroom, washing the floor, belting out Bohemian Rhapsody. He tried to keep quiet, wanted to watch and listen to the remainder of the song. But when she started making up words because she didn't know the actual lyrics, he lost it.

Cindy jumped, startled by the sound of his laughter and turned to him, half embarrassed, half amused. "What?"

"You know what," he replied.

"You think you can do better?"

"I don't think I could do worse," he jested.

"Is that so?" She threw the sponge at him.

"It's a good thing we're married," he said. "That's all I'm saying."

"Really?" Cindy asked, rising to her feet. "Are these for me?"

Dale held the bouquet out with a smile. "Of course."

"Thank you, they're beautiful," Cindy said, taking the flowers and giving Dale a peck on the cheek.

"Just don't sing to them," he said. "I'd like them to last a little while."

Cindy hit him with the bouquet but smiled. "I didn't realize I married a comedian."

"Well looks like we're learning a lot about each other today," Dale said and pulled her in for a hug.

Dale couldn't hear Bohemian Rhapsody play without grinning ear to ear after that day. Cindy was glad when its popularity waned and was no longer played in regular rotation on the radio. When the movie Wayne's World brought it back in the nineties, they both had a good laugh. He'd heard the song only once since Cindy's death and while the melody brought a smile to his face, Dale shut it off immediately. The memory stung the open wound of her absence too much.

Dale checked his email one more time before heading out to have lunch with Carmen. He was excited to share the article with her. He couldn't believe how anxious he was to log in and how disappointed he was when he didn't have a response. However, he wasn't losing hope.

EMMA AND RUSSELL

Russell sat in the waiting room, paced the waiting room, stood in the waiting room and when he'd had enough of the waiting room, he went to the cafeteria. Not that he was hungry. He was restless. Russell couldn't sit silent and wait like Emma's sisters Casey and Jordan. He needed to be doing something more.

When the nurse came out three hours into the surgery, Russell all but jumped directly on the woman, hanging on to every word she spoke.

"The doctor has found some evidence of the disease," the nurse reported. "But your wife is doing well."

"Evidence of the disease?" Russell repeated. "Where? How much?"

"I'm not quite sure," the nurse replied. "Dr. Sauer will be able to tell you more after the surgery."

"You don't know where?" Russell asked.

"Dr. Sauer will give you the details after the surgery," she said. "I'll be back with another update."

Russell looked to Casey and Jordan in disbelief as the nurse walked out. "Well she was useless," he said.

"At least we know she's doing well," Casey offered.

Her remark only served to irritate Russell. She wasn't a doctor. She couldn't understand the complexities of the surgery Emma was undergoing. Doing well meant nothing if there was evidence of disease. Doing well meant nothing three hours in. The risky part of the surgery had yet to start and then there was always the recovery. Hell, just getting Emma out from anesthesia with no complications after being under for ten hours would be doing well. But rather than vocalize all that, Russell let his sister-in-law continue believing Emma was "doing well."

"Let's get some coffee," Jordan offered.

"I'll stay here," Casey said. "In case the nurse comes back."

"I doubt we'll see her again," Russell grumbled.

"She's going to be okay," Jordan said, following Russell to a table by one of the large windows lining the cafeteria. She sat down across from him, her heart aching for both Emma and Russell. "Emma is as strong as they get."

Russell shook his head. "She shouldn't be here. We shouldn't be here. This isn't right."

Jordan, knowing her brother-in-law for more than a decade, remained silent and let him vent.

"Your sister is a great doctor, a great person. She doesn't deserve this. What they did to her is reprehensible. I'm not going to let them get away with this."

"Let's just focus on getting her through this procedure," Jordan suggested. "There will be plenty of time for all that later."

"No," Russell said. "Morcellation needs to be stopped. With every day that goes by, more women are subjected to its senseless practice. More women are going to end up like your sister."

"But it's really rare, right?" Jordan asked.

"Leiomyosarcoma is rare," Russell agreed. "But I don't think it's as rare as the doctors claim. Even if it is, it's unjustifiable to disseminate malignant cells throughout a person's abdominal cavity, especially when they asked for a traditional hysterectomy in the first place. It's not right to sentence one person to death for the sake of a quicker procedure."

"No, it's—"

"Regardless of malignancy, morcellation is not a safe practice. Women have reported nicked bowels, morcellated tissue adhering elsewhere in the peritoneum, all causing a wide array of obstructions and serious complications. It has to be stopped."

Jordan waited until she knew Russell was finished talking. "How do you stop something like this?"

"Tell the world," Russell replied, staring out the window. The gunmetal November sky over the hospital complemented his aura perfectly.

"I read the article about you guys," Jordan said with a smile. "It seems like a good start."

Russell chuckled. "This is only the beginning. Kendal Slate has no idea what's about to hit them."

"Aren't you worried about your job?"

Russell smiled patronizingly. "That's not how things work at a place like Kendal Slate."

But the truth was, Russell wasn't so sure what Kendal Slate stood for anymore. For all his adult life, until the day of Emma's diagnosis, Russell was certain he was destined to be one of Kendal Slate's finest. For all intents and purposes, he'd made "it" when he accepted his position there, donning the white lab coat with the prestigious KS logo above his name, Russell Speck, M.D. That white coat was the culmination of his hard work, his dedication. However, in the wake of Richard Oakley's response to morcellation, Russell was questioning everything he'd once believed about the prestigious community of Kendal Slate Memorial.

"Has she been back?" Russell asked Casey upon returning to the waiting room.

Casey shook her head, Russell fell into the open seat next to her. He'd been in many hospital waiting rooms, but never really stopped to notice the drab colors, bland décor and overall lack of visual stimulation. Out of all the thought and money he'd witnessed going into hospital design, Russell was shocked more effort hadn't gone into the ambiance of the waiting room. If the goal was to make people hopeless as they waited for news on their loved ones, the hospital had succeeded.

It bothered Russell that he was even considering the decoration of the waiting room. He was a specially trained, board certified surgeon whose hands were insured for more than most people's houses. He should've been in the operating room, saving someone's life. Instead, he was restless, anxiously analyzing the colors of the room he was trapped in.

Dinner came and went without any word from Dr. Sauer or his useless nurse. Russell could see Casey and Jordan's anxiety. He, too, was nervous at the lack of information. Silence meant complications. Silence meant things were changing too fast to get ahead of, to update the family. Ten hours and twenty-three minutes after Russell kissed Emma on the forehead and promised her things would be okay, Dr. Sauer walked into the waiting room. Russell's heart jumped into his throat. Casey and Jordan sprang up like their seats were on fire.

"The procedure went well. Emma's recovering in the SICU. It's going to take her some time to come out from the anesthesia."

Russell wasted no time in getting to the point. "The nurse said there was evidence of disease."

Dr. Sauer nodded. "Yes, we found a piece of likely tumor attached to her bladder."

"Attached?" Russell asked.

"Adhered," Dr. Sauer replied. "We were able to remove it with no complications."

Russell's stomach turned. It was just as he'd feared. There was no way Nicole Stein could have cleared Emma's entire abdomen. How could she when she wasn't aware she needed to? "Did you find any other remnants?"

"No. Everything else looked clear. She did great."

Russell shook Dr. Sauer's hand. "Thank you very much."

"If you follow me, I'll take you to see her," Dr. Sauer replied.

Russell, Jordan and Casey followed Dr. Sauer like obedient schoolchildren out of the surgical waiting room to the critical care waiting area. Emma's sisters took a seat while Russell went in to see Emma first.

Although Russell knew what to expect, the sight of Emma fresh out of surgery took his breath away. Her body was swollen from head to toe and she could barely keep her eyes open long enough to acknowledge he was in the room. He'd never loved her more. As much as he knew the technical aspects of what Emma had just undergone, Russell couldn't fathom what it felt like.

"You did fantastic." Russell bent over his wife's still body and kissed her gently on the forehead. "I'm so proud of you."

Emma opened her eyes, smiled weakly and was immediately out again. After ten hours of surgery, it would take her a while to wake up. He sat with her, reassuring her each of the brief times her eyes popped open. The alarmed look in her eyes quickly dissipated when she saw Russell sitting next to her, and she'd nod back to sleep. Russell hoped she was drifting to a good place, a place far from the hospital, far from cancer where she could be happy.

He hoped, rather than prayed, because lately his faith had been put to the test. There was a time he'd believed in God. But what God would do this? Both of Emma's parents made it a point to remind him that faith was most important when tested. Russell didn't buy it. He didn't buy anything anymore. Everything he'd believed in had crumbled down around him. The establishment he held in the highest regard, felt proud to be a part of, had assaulted his wife and showed no remorse. His religion hadn't protected his family the way he'd prayed for. Russell had lost belief in everything except for himself.

RICHARD

"I found the hospital. The flowers have been ordered," Nancy said, quite happy with what she considered a job well done.

"Thank you," Richard replied, not even lifting his head from what he was reading on his desk.

Unhappy with his lack of appreciation, Nancy remained in the door, waiting for his attention. Sensing her hovering frame, Richard looked up, annoyed. "I said thank you."

"I heard you," she said, acting more like a wronged spouse than a secretary.

"Is there anything else you need?" Richard asked.

Nancy put her hands on her hips and exhaled loudly before responding. "I didn't know if you wanted to know how I found out where the Specks were."

"To be honest, I don't," Richard replied. "I don't want this hospital accused of doing anything else illegal."

"Who says we've done anything illegal?"

"Russell is all but saying it in the paper, claiming he and his wife were in the dark about morcellation and its practice."

"Surely they can't sue the hospital. Especially since they work here," Nancy said in disbelief.

"They can sue whoever they want," Richard said.

"But they won't win."

"I don't know," Richard said with a sigh. "I didn't think his claims would gain traction, but you read the paper, as did the rest of the city. Obviously, the journalist bought their story and allegations of wrongdoing."

"So, what is the hospital going to do?" Nancy asked.

Richard shook his head. "We need to get Russell in here, listen to what he has to say. Get him to drop this nonsense."

"Do you think it'll work?"

"I think we had a shot before the article was published, when he was just ranting at the hospital. But now I'm not so sure. People are empathetic to the underdog, especially when the bad guy is a big bad institution of doctors."

"This hospital has done great things for this community, especially women," Nancy shot back. "Do you think the hospital is at fault? That Dr. Stein is to blame?"

Richard knew better than to answer. "What did you have the message on the card read?"

"From your family at Kendal Slate, wishing you the best in your recovery."

"Family," Richard said. "I like it."

"Thought it might evoke a sense of loyalty and love," Nancy replied, proud of herself.

"Yeah, well, let's hope it works, or this family is about to see an ugly divorce."

ADDISON

The sun was bright, more bright than normal when Addison opened her eyes. She didn't think she'd had that much to drink, but the pounding in her head told her differently.

"Coffee," she moaned. "I need coffee."

"Already brewing," Rachel answered.

Addison pushed herself off of the couch and squinted her eyes to deflect the intrusive rays of light. This time of year it was pitch black when Addison got up for work. The sun practically blinding her made her realize she was late, very late. "What time is it? I have to get to work."

"No, you don't," Rachel said. "I called Keith, told him you needed a day and asked if he could call the school."

"No." Addison shook her head which proved to be a mistake. "I have to go in. I didn't leave any plans."

"Addison, you never call out sick. You can take a day. You *need* a day."

The idea of a day off did feel rather fantastic. Her head and stomach, not so much. It had been so long since Addison had had an actual hangover, this felt like the worst one of all time.

Drinking excessively wasn't conducive to fertility, so she'd limited herself to only a couple of glasses at a time, which, sadly, was more than enough to take the edge off. When she thought about it, Addison's entire life had become restricted to what gave her the best odds of conceiving. She couldn't be too heavy, she couldn't be too thin. Tobacco, though a non-issue, was a no-no. Alcohol was frowned upon, but she wasn't going to give that up. STD's were another thing she was routinely screened for, despite being in a committed relationship. And those were the things she had control of.

Stress, her doctor had told her, was another big factor that could contribute to her inability to conceive. How could she not be stressed? And any medication she could take for anxiety or depression was bad for fertility. As common as her doctors said endometriosis and infertility were, Addison had a hard time believing them.

If it was so common, how come no one talked about it? How come the only time she heard or read anything relating to her predicament was when she was at the doctor's office? To be honest, she didn't care if it was common. She cared that it affected her. In fact, she cared very much. And that's when it hit her.

The surgery wasn't going to change anything. Running a marathon wasn't going to change anything. She would be unable to bear children, no matter what she did or didn't do. The only thing the surgery guaranteed was that she wasn't going to go through the heartbreak or risks of failed pregnancies. Sadly, this hangover was the closest she was ever going to get to morning sickness.

"Do you want to meet for lunch?" Keith asked when Addison called him on her way home from Rachel's. "We can do Italian or Chinese. There's also that Indian restaurant you've been wanting to try."

"Stop talking about food," Addison begged, feeling her stomach turn at the mere mention of eating.

Keith chuckled. "That bad?"

"When did I become such a lightweight?"

"Rachel said you were hitting it kind of hard last night. She told me about the treadmill. How are you feeling from that?"

Addison had completely forgotten about her intimate encounter with the belt of the treadmill. "I'm okay. Just want to take a hot shower and get into bed."

"This lunch date keeps getting better," Keith said. "Who needs food?"

Addison laughed. If the thought of food made her nauseous, sex was definitely out of the question.

"Is that a yes?" he asked.

"It's an I love you," she said.

"Get some rest," he replied. "Don't worry about dinner, I'll bring something in tonight. Just sleep."

"This is why I married you," she said.

Addison hit her bed harder than she'd had in a long time. The soft sheets welcomed her in, the warm blanket draped over her body, still chilled from getting out of the shower. Normally she would put the TV on, click through the channels until something caught her eye. Not today. Today the only thing she wanted to do was close her eyes and drift off.

She was sleeping soundly when her phone rang, wrapped up in a dream that Keith was calling to tell her he was bringing in three-foot-long hoagies stacked with every Italian deli meat possible. The image of salami and pepperoni piled high with cheese and onions, lettuce and tomato onto long loaves of bread made Addison sick. Her sweet state of slumber was quickly morphing into a nightmare she couldn't escape quickly enough.

"I thought I told you I couldn't stomach any food right now," she barked into the phone.

"Addy?" he replied, though it sounded a lot like her mother.

"I told you I wasn't hungry," she said. "Why are you bringing me hoagies?"

"Addison? Addison, what's wrong? Are you sick?"

The change in voice gave Addison pause and she realized she was no longer asleep and that she'd answered her phone.

"Sorry, Mom," she said. "I was taking a nap."

"A nap? Is everything okay?"

"Everything's fine," she replied. "I had dinner with Rachel last night and stayed up a little later than I'm used to."

Her mother's disapproval came through the phone just as clear as her voice. "Well, I'm calling because I want to talk to you about your decision."

"Mom, we've been through this."

"Don't *Mom* me," she said. "My job is to protect you. I need to make sure you're completely informed about what you're choosing to undergo. What you are voluntarily going to put your body through."

Addison thought for a minute. "No more painful periods? No more GI issues? I'd say my body has been through quite enough already that I haven't voluntarily chosen. I'd say what I'm doing is giving it a break."

"It's major surgery, Addison," her mother said. "Regardless of what your doctor says. You're going to have organs removed. You're going to alter your anatomy."

"I'm aware of what the surgery entails, Mom," Addison replied, tired of the same old conversation.

"Are you?" her mother shot back. "Has your doctor gone over everything with you?"

"She's been pretty thorough. I'm sure we'll go over more during my pre-op appointment."

"Did you read *The Times* this morning?"

Addison laughed.

"Fair enough," her mom answered, realizing Addison had never read the paper in her life. Why would she start on the morning an article was published about laparoscopic procedures done at Kendal Slate?

"You should go online and take a look. Read it on your phone. There's a great article about the dangers of minimally invasive surgery."

"Of course there is," Addison said.

"I get it, Addison. You've been through a lot. I've been by your side the entire way. I always will. If you think I'm paranoid or biased, then so be it. But I didn't write the article. I just happened upon it. I find the timing rather coincidental. It's an interesting article and at the very least, it might lead you to ask some more questions, be better informed. That's all I want for you, to make the best decision you can with all the information available."

While she'd started out annoyed by her mother's insistence that she was making the wrong decision, Addison appreciated her mother's devotion. She always went to bat for Addison, even when Addison didn't want to go to bat for herself. Why wouldn't an article come out accusing Kendal Slate of wrongdoing? That was all Addison's mother needed to ignite her rage against doctors, hospitals, anything related to medicine.

"I'll read it, Mom," Addison conceded. "But my doctor is really good. She cares about women."

"Don't be fooled, Addison. They all appear to care. It's their job."

DALE

Dale hated waiting. He liked to be in control, taking action, making things happen. Sitting, waiting for a return email was driving him nuts. It was all Cindy's fault too. Before her, his life had been boring and time passing wasn't a concern. But once they'd gotten together, he grew impatient wasting minutes. He'd been consumed by her.

"It was cute in the beginning," Mickey had complained once he realized Cindy wasn't going anywhere. "I mean, she's cool and all but you've got it bad."

"Yes, I do," Dale agreed all-too-happily.

"That's not a good thing, man."

"Why not?" Dale protested. "I love her. I'm going to ask her to marry me."

"No," Mickey groaned. "You can't. You're too young. You haven't dated enough girls yet."

"I don't need to. She's the one."

"How do you know for sure?"

Dale thought for a minute, knowing he had to come up with the perfect analogy to get his feelings about Cindy through to Mickey, the man who'd never been in love.

"You know how you love bacon cheddar cheeseburgers?" Dale asked.

Mickey nodded, a smile spreading across his face.

"It's just like that. Sure, you could have cheeseburgers with American cheese or a hamburger with bacon. You could mix up the variety until you try every combination possible. But I bet at the end of the day, you'd still choose a bacon cheddar cheeseburger. That's how I feel about Cindy. She's the one for me. Do you get it now?"

"I get that I want a burger," Mickey said.

Telling Mickey he wanted to marry Cindy was easy compared to saving for a ring and asking Cindy's father. While Dale knew Cindy's father liked him, he couldn't be sure that would translate into him wanting her to marry him. And Cindy loved her father. There was no doubt about that. If her father said no, things would be over. Dale couldn't bear the thought.

In order to buy the only ring perfect enough to grace Cindy's delicate finger, a quarter of a carat set on a thin, gold band, costing a steep one thousand dollars, Dale had hit his uncle up for any extra work he had to offer. He was working so much that Cindy felt neglected. In the end, however, Dale's rigorous work schedule impressed Cindy's father so much that when he learned why Dale had been working so hard, he gladly gave Dale permission to marry his daughter.

"I'm not going to lie, son," Cindy's father had said after Dale showed him the ring. "The way Cindy was moping about, I thought you might have been running around on her."

"I would never, Sir," Dale replied.

And he would never, could never have imagined being anything but faithful to Cindy. The time he spent away from her working was agonizing. He didn't want to wait. He wanted to propose every time he was with her. In fact, there were so many times he almost popped the question just because he couldn't wait another minute. On one of his Friday nights off, they'd gone to the movies where he'd tied a Twizzler into the shape of a ring but lost his nerve at the last minute. A week later, they were grabbing a late bite at a diner and he'd tied a straw wrapper into a ring. Dale was about to get on one knee when a friend of Cindy's slid in the booth. He took that as a sign to wait. Cindy deserved a real proposal. Even if the anticipation killed Dale.

He'd give anything to go back, propose all over again, to see the smile on Cindy's face as she realized what he was asking. And of course, once she agreed, he couldn't wait to get married, to start their life together. Life with Cindy was an adventure. Without her, it was like running on a track. He could move fast or slow, but he'd always end up at the same point, exactly back where he started, without her.

EMMA AND RUSSELL

Time was one of the most interesting facets of medicine according to Russell. In the operating room, he was always up against the clock. The body could only be subjected to so much for so long, even with the great advances in surgical technique and equipment. However, when it came to recovery, time was often the only cure. The more invasive the procedure, the more time required to heal. For everything surgeons can do, they are limited when it comes to recovery. Yes, antibiotics help prevent infection, narcotics help with pain, and anticoagulants help protect against blood clots. But those don't touch the surface of what the human body accomplishes when it heals.

Emma was very groggy after her surgery; the anesthesia would take some time to process though her system. Anesthesia wasn't over when the patient woke up. It wasn't a simple night-cap to a sound sleep, but rather a mixture of drugs that rendered the mind unconscious and unable to remember.

Emma tried her best to talk, ask Russell about the surgery, but her throat was on fire and her words incoherent.

"Dr. Sauer did a fantastic job," Russell offered, knowing she didn't need the exact details right away.

Emma slipped in and out, sometimes even mid-conversation. Between the exhaustion and medication, it was a wonder she was able to stay awake at all.

The nursing staff was great, though Russell didn't trust the nurses with Emma's care. He checked and rechecked every order they made. The only person he listened to was Dr. Sauer, who had his utmost respect. Russell owed Dr. Sauer so much for getting Emma through the surgery.

Russell waited while Emma dozed, speaking disjointedly halfway between consciousness. He waited, as he would every second of every day until Emma was back on her feet. He would wait, making sure Emma had the care she needed to ensure they had more time together, the time they'd planned for. He wasn't ready to say good-bye anytime soon.

Just after two thirty in the morning, Emma started to struggle. Russell jumped from his bedside chair, pressed the call-button for the nurse and turned on the light in the room. Emma's complexion had gone from the usual post-op paleness to ashen. She gasped, unable to catch her breath. Russell waited for the nurses to come, for a doctor, anyone to answer his repeated calls.

Emma's breathing was loud, labored and irregular. The panicked look in her eyes made him panic.

"I'll be right back," he said, kissing the top of her head. Emma grabbed his hand, as if to beg him not to leave. "I'm just going to get some help," he answered her unspoken plea, trying his best to remain calm, for her. He pushed the privacy curtain back so Emma was in plain view to anyone in the hall. When Russell got to the door, he lost his bearing completely.

"I NEED A DOCTOR!" he screamed. "NOW!"

RICHARD

Richard didn't want to go home, didn't want to deal with what was undoubtedly waiting for him as soon as he walked through the door. But he was tired. So tired. All he wanted was to change and collapse into bed. He'd missed dinner and bedtime with the boys on purpose, knowing he was at the end of a very, very short rope. In fact, he'd waited in his office, hoping Elaine would also be in bed by the time he arrived home.

Waiting wasn't Richard's best quality. In fact, most of the major mistakes he'd made in his life were due to rash decisions and impatience. His ex-wife ended up pregnant because he was horny and wanted to have sex. The baby wasn't conceived in love, she was conceived in lust, an immature and hasty coital act. He probably would have never married Janine if she hadn't been pregnant. That, too, was another hasty decision. He wasn't ready for a child, but also didn't want the stigma of having a pregnant girlfriend either. What would his fellow medical students think of him? He had plans for his career and at the time he believed he loved Janine.

But love, he'd learned, was both easily fleeting and replaced, as evidenced by what happened when Elaine walked in the emergency room. Out went Janine, in came Elaine. He'd lost a daughter and gained twin sons. He didn't look back, didn't regret. Richard did what he needed to do to get where he wanted to go. Some said he was heartless, detached even. He preferred "driven."

The house was dark when he arrived home, putting a smile on his face. It was the first time he'd smiled all day. Starting at six a.m., his email and phone had been flooded by people curious if he had a comment, if the story was true. Had he seen other cases like Emma Speck's? That's when he remembered that man, the one he'd mistaken as homeless. His wife had leiomyosarcoma. The only reason he'd known that was because he'd, what was his name, begged him to look into her file. And rather than be faced with some kind of malpractice lawsuit, he did.

Her fibroids were assumed benign. She'd opted for the total laparoscopic hysterectomy and oophorectomy. The surgery presented no complications and she was discharged the day after surgery. It appeared standard—until he read the follow-up notes and emergency room admittance notes. Things spiraled rapidly after her initial recovery period. There was already tumor growth and metastases present during her four-week post-op appointment. Eight weeks after that, she was dead.

"She had a name," he remembered the man, Dave, no, Dale, saying. *Cindy*, Richard thought. He knew why Dale was asking questions. But there wasn't anything to indicate the hospital had done anything wrong. Although Dale was clearly dissatisfied, Richard believed he had conveyed what had happened to Cindy in a way that would remove any accusation or suspicion of wrongdoing. He was confident he'd succeeded until *The Times'* article stated the possible cause and effect of morcellating leiomyosarcoma.

Richard crept through the house. He didn't even peek inside the boys' rooms like he normally did. He wanted to sleep. He was going to sleep. Then he saw the light glowing from under the master bedroom door. *Shit, she's still awake.*

ADDISON

She'd be lying if she said the conversation with her mother hadn't made her second-guess the decision to have the surgery. Her mother was a professional when it came to instilling doubt and fear. "The world is going to give and it's going to take," she'd told Addison. "And it's not an even exchange. So, save for the good, prepare for the bad, and never get too comfortable where you stand."

Addison disagreed. She believed the world was good with only sprinkles of bad. She had faith in people, which her mother obviously lacked. She had faith in her doctor, Dr. Elizabeth Yorker. As much as Addison's mom thought she didn't follow her advice, Addison rarely strayed too far from it. For example, her mother only saw female physicians. She'd wait a month if it meant getting in to see a female provider. Addison had grown up with only female doctors and as an adult, that's who she wanted to see—especially when it came to gynecology.

Dr. Yorker was receptive and empathetic to Addison's struggles from the first time they'd met. She was optimistic Addison would be able to conceive, carry and deliver a child. But as time passed and the miscarriages added up, Dr. Yorker agreed that pregnancy might not be the best option for Addison. While she was more than willing to continue treatment, she had also told Addison it was okay if she wanted to take a break from trying so hard.

"If I take a break," Addison had told her, "it's going to be for good."

"Don't feel like you have to put restrictions on yourself," Dr. Yorker replied. "Sometimes a little break here and there is all the body needs."

When Addison got pregnant, Dr. Yorker was almost as ecstatic to hear the news as Addison was to deliver it.

"It's early, I know," Addison had said. "But I feel pregnant this time. My breasts are sore. I'm super nauseous all the time. I can feel it."

As the pregnancy progressed, the pain got worse and her spotting turned into bleeding. She didn't even make it to the first prenatal appointment, the one where she and Keith would get to "ohh" and "ahh" over the tiny bean on the ultrasound.

She'd known something was wrong the first time she saw a drop of blood in her underwear but pushed the fear out of her head. Some women spotted during pregnancy, it was normal. She wanted so desperately to be normal. According to the internet, some women even felt dizzy from time to time. So, when Addison's head got so fuzzy she couldn't see straight, she'd told herself it was fine, to be expected. She would wait it out.

But in a perfect storm, her idea of a normal pregnancy, a normal life was ripped from her. First came the increased pain, pressure on her left side that made it almost impossible to breathe. Then the blood. There was so much blood. Then she fainted.

"It's okay, Addy. You're going to be okay, Addy." Addison came to in the front seat of Keith's car. He was repeating his reassurances, unaware she was coherent.

"It hurts," she said, putting both of her hands to her left side. "What happened?"

Keith exhaled in relief. "Oh, Addy. You passed out. You're bleeding. We're going to the hospital."

"Something's wrong."

"It's okay, honey," he said, his tone heightened by panic. "We're almost there."

Addison awoke in a recovery room with a vague memory of what happened. Keith and her mother were by her side, smiling, but unable to mask the sadness of yet another failed pregnancy.

"It was ectopic," Keith said. "In your fallopian tube. That's why you had so much pain."

Addison nodded.

"It ruptured," Keith continued. "They had to remove the ovary."

Addison was numb. The implications of what she'd just been through was too much to process.

"You still have your right fallopian tube," he offered, optimistically. "And Dr. Yorker said it looked just fine. That we can keep trying."

Addison chuckled. As if it were that easy.

"Don't think about that right now," her mother stepped in. "You need to rest so we can get you home."

"How long do I have to stay here?" Addison asked.

"Just another day or so," Keith answered. "Dr. Yorker wants to observe you, make sure your blood levels even out."

Addison tried to adjust her position in the bed but could barely move.

"What do you need, honey?" Keith moved in to help her move. "Your belly is going to be tender. Dr. Yorker said not to engage your core too much right now."

Addison gave up trying to move. She gave up on everything.

"I get it," she confessed to God. "You want me to stop. I'm not supposed to have children of my own. I don't know what I've done to deserve this. Surely there are more unfit women than me who have kids. But I hear you loud and clear."

Addison reflected guiltily on the thoughts she'd had about having a C-section. When she and Keith discussed delivery, she was adamantly against a cesarean because she didn't want the scar. She wanted a vaginal delivery, no cuts, no extra recovery. She couldn't help but feel as though her vanity led to a scar across her abdomen but no baby. *You can scar my entire belly*, she'd pleaded, one last effort. *I don't care about the scar. I just want a baby.*

Dr. Yorker repeated the encouraging words Keith had said about her having a fully functioning ovary and fallopian tube on the right which was all she needed to conceive. She told Addison not to lose heart. It was too late; her heart was already broken.

When she was discharged, Addison looked on the internet for stories of women like her, who saw their fertility dwindling by the day. The heartache Addison came across in just a few searches would've scared anyone from wanting to have a baby. If every woman read the stories she did, she was certain human procreation would cease. Woman after woman vented about their near-death experiences, the pain, the sadness, some in vivid detail beyond Addison's comfort level. Then came the women who ranted about how their husbands left them for younger, fertile women. At the time, Addison hadn't even considered that an option. She was grateful for Keith and knew his love for her was real. However, a tiny seed of doubt was planted after she'd read the woes of unknown women on the internet. How could she be sure Keith wouldn't be tempted by a fruitful, younger woman?

Discouraged after reading the article her mom had called about, Addison decided to search for personal accounts of hysterectomies. She was looking for stories of relief, of success. What she got was more tales of sadness. She couldn't win. Failed pregnancies, ectopic pregnancies, endometriosis. But it was comforting to read how many women turned to a permanent surgical solution. For the first time, she didn't feel so alone. However, it was not comforting to learn of the complications afterward.

When Addison happened upon ShellyBee42's story, her stomach turned. ShellyBee42 was married to a wonderful man named John. It was her first marriage, his second. He had two children with his ex but wanted to have more with her. They tried and tried but were unsuccessful. After two rounds of failed in vitro fertilization and thirty thousand dollars down the drain, they decided to stop trying. She opted for a hysterectomy because of a condition she called adenomyosis. Addison made a mental note to research that. At first ShellyBee's husband supported her decision. But she wasn't even recovered when he told her he was getting back with his ex, who was pregnant with their third child.

Addison poured herself a large glass of wine after that story, unable to separate herself and her situation from ShellyBee's. The only thing giving her solace was knowing Keith hadn't been married before, and his ex was currently pregnant with another man's child... or was it? She'd been sucked into the world wide web of crazy and needed to escape. It was all her mother's fault, too. If she hadn't placed a speck of doubt, Addison would've never researched hysterectomy outcomes. Instead of feeling better, Addison now felt more pitiful than ever, convinced Keith was going to leave her for someone with a hospitable womb.

DALE

"She got back to me, Car," Dale practically burst through Carmen's front door.

"Hi to you too, Dad," Carmen replied, happy to see so much energy coming from her father.

"Hi, hi," he said. "Where's my Lois?"

"Napping," Carmen said. "She just went down so if you could keep it down."

Dale lowered his voice. "Yes, sorry. I'm just. I'm so excited."

"Wow," Carmen said, leading Dale into the family room. "Do you want something to drink? Should we be celebrating? What are we celebrating?"

"She got back to me," Dale repeated, sitting in one of the two recliners.

"Who?" Carmen asked.

"The reporter. Alyson Baker. She got my email and wrote back."

"That's great, Dad," Carmen said, taking a seat across from Dale. "What did she say?"

"She offered her condolences for your mom, said how grateful she was for me to get in touch and that she passed my information on to the Specks."

For the first time since her mother had passed, Carmen saw a hint of animation from her father. She knew he was depressed, they all were. But Carmen was still able to enjoy the little pleasantries of life. Her dad had completely withdrawn. Until today.

"So that's it?" Carmen asked, feeling she'd missed something.

"That's it?" Dale huffed. "No. This is just the beginning. She said she wanted me to talk with Russell Speck and if your mother's story and his wife's are the same, she'd like to write a follow-up piece on me."

"Oh wow," Carmen replied.

Dale could see the hesitation in his daughter's eyes. "What? This is great news."

"Is it, Dad?"

"Of course it is. I told you something wasn't right with what happened to your mother."

"I know that," Carmen replied. "But the thing is. I guess I'm trying to figure out what you want from all this? An apology? A lawsuit?"

Dale exhaled. "You know I'm not interested in money. I've only wanted the truth. I knew your mother's doctor wasn't honest about what happened. Your mother didn't understand what was happening to her. I promised her I'd find out."

"If the Specks are right and the hospital is upstaging women's cancers by how they're performing the surgeries, would you consider suing?"

"I haven't thought about it," Dale replied. "I'd hope the hospital wouldn't knowingly make their patients sicker."

"Me too," Carmen agreed. "But what if they did know? They couldn't have, right? I mean, how could they…" Carmen trailed off, thinking about her mother and the last month of her life. Tears burst from her eyes. The thought of her mother withering away, writhing in pain was too much to contain. "I hope not, Dad," she managed. "Because if they had any idea what they were doing and Mom ended up like that because of them…"

"I'm going to give them a chance to explain," Dale said. "After that we'll see what happens."

Dale didn't know anything when it came to the law. Cindy had cancer. She died from cancer. He'd known that and never had any intention of pursuing legal action. He just didn't understand how quickly the cancer had spread. While Dale had his suspicions that the doctors had missed something, he'd never once considered that they'd made her sicker. He thought Cindy's condition was an unfortunate oversight, not a negligent act. The article in the paper told a different story.

"What if there are other women?" Carmen asked. "Like the ones whose husbands you spoke to. Didn't you say their stories were all the same? What if this is happening all over the country? Dad, if this is as bad as the Specks are saying, it needs to be stopped."

The resolve building in Carmen was palpable. He saw the fire ignite but knew she had to be managed carefully. Carmen was explosive and passionate. To have her behind a cause was a wonderful thing. But he couldn't bear to see her mount a fight in a senseless battle.

"One step at a time, Car," he said. "I'll make the same promise to you that I made to your mom. If there is anything behind what happened to her, I will find out. If she was wronged, I will right it. Make no mistake about that."

Dale was a general contractor, not a crusader. And up until a month prior, he'd had very limited technological knowledge. But what he'd endured with Cindy, what she suffered through, if someone was at fault they would be held accountable. And if it was something that could be stopped, he would do his best to do so. He wouldn't be able to sleep knowing more women were at risk for such a tragedy.

"Do Becca and Gail know?" Carmen asked.

Dale shook his head. "Not yet. They haven't exactly been happy with what I've been doing."

"This is different," she said. "I was a little unsure at first, too. But things are coming together in what appears to be an undeniable way."

"Let's take it one step at a time. For all we know, I'll talk with Russell Speck and he'll tell me the same thing Dr. Oakley did, that your mother had cancer and while it's unfortunate, there's really nothing different they could've done."

Carmen was about to answer when the baby started crying.

Dale stood quickly. "Let me get my Lo-Lo."

Carmen was all-too-happy to have a glimmer of her father back. Selfishly, she said a quick, silent prayer that the path he was on was correct. She'd missed him. In many ways, she'd lost both parents the day her mother died. If Russell Speck held the key to keeping her father upbeat and positive, she was all in. While she knew he had a lot going on in his own life, she hoped Russell Speck would get back to her dad. He had to. Too much depended on it.

EMMA AND RUSSELL

Russell sat alone in Emma's room and sobbed. The hard part was supposed to have been over. She was out of surgery. She had made it through double-digit hours of surgery. She was awake. Why did she have to have any complications?

It was a pulmonary embolism. A small blood clot had traveled to her lung. The nursing staff in the SICU responded quickly, summoning a doctor and supplying Emma with oxygen and the blood thinners she needed. It was a tricky equation, a delicate balance of how much to thin Emma's blood to prevent more clots from forming while keeping it thick enough to prevent bleeding. Russell knew too much to be a silent observer yet had no authority to do anything for Emma other than watch.

As he waited for Emma to return from imaging, he sat in the dark room and let the stress of the day crash on him like a wave at the beach and the sorrow of it all pull him down like an undertow. He didn't like the quiet of the room, the separation from Emma. He wanted to be with her, reassure her everything was fine. But everything was far from fine. She couldn't catch a break. Was it not enough that she'd been assaulted by the colleagues she trusted most? Was it not enough she'd been subjected to a consequent surgery that further battered her barely healed body? And now a pulmonary embolism to boot? How much more would she be subjected to? Russell threw his faith out the window. No just God could allow such a wonderful woman, a mother to four beautiful children and devoted doctor to suffer such an unfair fate.

Why me? Emma thought as the table slid her into the CT machine. It was a stupid question, one she'd asked many times. She was still waiting for an answer. Emma considered herself a religious person, but her diagnosis had shaken her foundation. She needed an answer, something to make sense of how her life had gone from being exactly what she wanted to its complete antithesis.

Emma was scared going into the surgery. Scared of never seeing her family again, leaving her babies behind. When she awoke in recovery, the first thing she did was thank God. Even with the intense pain, of which the medication did little to quell, and unrelenting nausea, she reminded herself things could be worse. But when her breath became short and her head light, all positivity went out the window. There was no good to focus on. No silver lining.

Working day in and day out at the hospital brought no shortage of examples of the cruelty of life. Maybe it was naïve and a bit pretentious of Emma to think she was somehow excluded from the unfair twists of fate she witnessed, but she had. She was thankful for what God had blessed her with and never once considered that misfortune would land on her doorstep. She was a good person, a good doctor and a great Mom. Didn't that amount to some type of casualty avoidance points? Other people got bad news. Hell, she was often the bearer of such news. She wasn't supposed to be on the receiving end. She wasn't supposed to have cancer.

The machine rattled to life and she was told to hold her breath and remain still. *Is this the rest of my life?* She thought, staring up at the eggshell colored popcorn ceiling. Scans, surgeries, pain, complications. Maybe it would have been better if she hadn't made it through the surgery. It wasn't like her to wallow, to even entertain the idea of death, of her children existing without her, but today she was lost. She hated to admit she felt part of herself giving up.

Russell perked up when he heard Emma's bed being rolled down the hall. The frown that had taken residence on his face was quickly replaced with a smile. "All done?" he said, looking at her admiringly.

"For now."

Emma appreciated that Russell didn't show his despair around her, but did he really have to smile like that? It was so forced, even he had to know it.

"How are you feeling?" Russell asked. "Do you think you can get some sleep?"

Emma shrugged.

"Why don't you try?"

Closing her eyes wasn't difficult. It was opening them that pained her. When she closed her eyes, she drifted into unconsciousness, even if it was short-lived because of the million and one checks the nurses performed in the SICU. But when she was asleep, she wasn't thinking. It was only when her eyes opened and she saw the machines, the tubes running from her body, that the harsh reality came crashing back.

Russell watched as Emma's chocolate eyes closed and she was still. He hoped the pain meds were enough to keep her comfortably numb while she slept. He leaned his head back in his chair, wishing it offered any option of recline. It didn't budge. The SICU wasn't set up for companion sleeping. He had to fight with the staff at the hospital just to be allowed to stay the night with Emma. It was a good thing he had. There was no way the nurses would have caught her embolism before it turned into something much worse. Though he didn't need a reason not to leave Emma's side prior to the pulmonary embolism, he sure as hell wasn't going to leave her for one second, no matter how tired he was or uncomfortable the chair.

Since Emma had just had a workup done and was fast asleep, Russell closed his eyes, but only for a couple of minutes. All he needed was to knock the cobwebs off, nothing more. For once, he was grateful for the brutal schedule of surgical residency and the unrelenting fellowship hours that followed. Sleep was something both Russell and Emma had learned to function well without.

Five minutes turned out to be closer to twenty solid minutes of deep and refreshing sleep. When Russell opened his eyes, it only took the sight of his princess lying still on the bed across from him to remember where he was. She looked angelic, beautiful enough to be the heroine in any fairy tale. If only a simple kiss from him would save her. He wished it were that easy. He wished his love was enough to undo the damage of a poisoned apple.

Completely distraught and recharged from his nap, Russell took out his computer and opened his email. He'd seen the article Alyson Baker had written and was curious to see if there'd been any feedback. He was half-expecting to receive a phone call from Kendal Slate saying his services were no longer needed. But then the flowers arrived, a beautiful and slightly over-the-top arrangement from their "family" at Kendal Slate Memorial. The gesture infuriated him. Did they think he and Emma would forgive all because of a ridiculous floral arrangement? Did they think he would be fooled by their use of the word family? It was insulting.

Russell took the time while Emma slept to check his email. Just as he'd suspected, he had a couple related to the article. Most of them were from friends and family members congratulating him on having the courage to go up against the hospital, to speak out against what he perceived to be a wrongdoing. It was all fluff. He wanted to know the truth, what people really thought about what Alyson Baker had written. When he saw her email mixed in with the others, he read it immediately.

Russell,

I wanted to thank you again for sharing your story with me and allowing me to give you and Emma a voice. The feedback I've received has been overwhelmingly positive. I look forward to covering your journey as I believe it's a story that needs to be told. I also wanted to forward an email I received earlier today. I think you and Mr. Reichter may have a lot to talk about. I'll be in touch. ~ A

Russell scrolled down to the forwarded message, reading Dale Reichter's email three times before exclaiming, "Son of a bitch!" The fury in his voice was deeper than he'd intended.

"Is everything okay?" One of the nurses who happened to be walking by stopped in.

"Sorry," Russell whispered. "Everything's fine."

The nurse glanced over at Emma who was still thankfully asleep before smiling at Russell and leaving. Russell's hands started to shake and his head felt like it was going to explode. Kendal Slate knew women were dying and yet continued to perform the surgery. While he found it hard to believe, Russell really wanted to trust the hospital's claim of ignorance, have faith in his "family." But to know they'd lied to him and Emma—to have proof they were knowingly and willingly committing this atrocity. That was the ultimate betrayal.

RICHARD

At first she'd feigned to be sleeping, a skill she'd perfected over the years after countless arguments. Not that Elaine was scared to straight up ignore Richard. Her tactics went above and beyond the standard silent treatment. But at night, when she was too exhausted to deal with him, she pretended to sleep.

Richard, not wanting to open the door to any possible conversation, turned Elaine's bedside lamp off before walking into his closet to change. His closet, filled with cashmere sweaters and wool suits that cost more than the rent of his first apartment, made him feel better. Elaine wouldn't be mad for long, especially when she got changed in her equally large closet overflowing with designer brands. She could play the empathetic patient, make the morcellation issue about something that could happen to her all she wanted. But she needed to be careful, and Richard would quickly remind her if she got too overzealous in her defense of unsuspecting women. She was sleeping with the enemy. Except he wasn't the enemy and neither were minimally invasive surgeries.

The flak he'd heard from patients and surgeons alike after that damn article was already more than he wanted to deal with. And it was only day one. Patients, some of whom weren't even candidates for laparoscopic procedures, let alone power morcellation, were questioning their doctors and the safety of the hospital. Already, families of patients who'd passed from cancer had contacted the hospital, inquiring if their loved ones had been morcellated.

Richard understood what Russell was causing a stir about. He wouldn't go so far as to validate Russell's claims, but he at least understood the basis for why Russell was calling out the medical profession. What

Russell didn't understand was that most of the readers of the article couldn't differentiate between laparoscopic power morcellation and other laparoscopic procedures. Russell had created an environment for hysteria and the fallout came knocking on Richard's door. It had already invaded his bed.

The advances in laparoscopic surgery brought a breath of fresh air to the very stagnant world of open operations. The benefits surely outweighed any potential risk associated with the technique. And the technique was no small thing to learn.

"They need to write a piece on laparoscopic procedures," Richard had told Henry Lewis when they discussed the fallout from the article. "Explain how they are a good thing."

"We're not going to engage them in a battle of words," Henry replied calmly. "Let's just see how it plays out."

"I know patients," Richard said with a hint of annoyance. Henry understood the law and what was best for the hospital, but Richard knew how patients internalized any bad press about surgery. "They're going to get nervous. I wouldn't be surprised if we see a drop in elective procedures."

"Give it a couple of days," Henry said.

"Can't we at least release a statement explaining the rigorous training and practice our surgeons go through? Explain that minimally invasive surgeries are quicker with less bad side effects for the patient and require the same amount of technical expertise from our doctors. We need to reassure the community that Kendal Slate is still a premier facility with some of the best surgeons in the country."

"By continuing to practice medicine and perform surgeries without getting tangled up in a debate on power morcellation, you are doing just that."

"I think staying quiet makes us look culpable," Richard said.

"Arguing the point makes you look defensive. If the hospital has done nothing wrong, there is nothing to defend."

"And I suppose we don't need to stop using power morcellators either, if we're saying there's nothing wrong with its use."

"Precisely," Henry said. "This might gain a little traction, but the Specks aren't the first couple to blame medicine for bad health."

"I hope you're right," Richard replied and hung up the phone.

Maybe Henry had a point. Maybe it wasn't worth the debate. But then again, Henry also thought Russell would let it go once he got everything off his chest. Richard had never felt so helpless. His hands were tied on what he could say to anyone outside of the hospital regarding the Specks, morcellation, or the competency of Kendal Slate. And he couldn't tell Russell what he really wanted, which was to get over himself and stop blaming the hospital for his wife's condition. Russell Speck had sought out his position. Kendal Slate didn't beg him to work for them. If the hospital was such a bad place filled with deplorable surgeons, why did both he and his wife work there? Furthermore, why did they decide to have Emma's surgery done there? There were ten other hospitals within a thirty-five mile radius. Richard knew the answer and he knew that Russell knew it as well. They came to Kendal Slate because it was one of the best in the country. They came to Kendal Slate because they knew they would be in good hands.

Elaine was breathing deeply when Richard crawled into bed. He wanted to join her in sleep but couldn't stop coming back to the idea of posting an anonymous comment on the online article. He'd made the mistake of reading the few comments posted throughout the day. Each comment highlighted a story of medical malpractice and the bad doctors involved.

"You shouldn't read these things," Nancy said when Richard asked her to print out the comments. "People who comment online have no lives and live to put other people down."

"It sounds like you're speaking from experience," Richard said with a chuckle.

Nancy soured her face and huffed. "I hate the internet and everything that comes along with it. It does nothing positive for humanity."

"I'm not interested in what these people have to say," he said. "I'm interested in who these people are."

"You lost me," she replied.

"If—and that's a big if—if there is a lawsuit brought on by the Specks, people are going to come out of the woodwork to join in and try to make some money."

"So what does a list of internet trolls have to do with a lawsuit?"

"I'm not sure," Richard said. "But I want to keep a record."

It wasn't just about keeping a record of what people said. Richard planned to have a meeting with the surgeons to discuss protocols moving forward, especially relating to what they said and didn't say about power morcellation. He wanted a list because he wanted to keep track of names in case they popped up again. Henry Lewis may have thought it would pass, but Richard wanted to be prepared in case it didn't.

Disgusted, Richard closed the browser on his phone and set his alarm for five a.m. If he fell asleep in the next seven minutes, he would get three solid hours of sleep before facing the same problem tomorrow.

ADDISON

At two thirty-seven a.m. Addison rolled over and sighed. She'd been tossing and turning all night while Keith snored contently beside her. His loud, labored sounds normally didn't bother her to the point where she couldn't sleep. But since she woke up at midnight and almost hourly after that, his breathing, choking and gasping held her hostage from falling back asleep. Instead of focusing on what was really bothering her and keeping her awake, she instead focused her agitation on her better half. He was her better half, snoring and all, but it didn't prevent her from shoving and poking him. At two thirty-seven, she just about pushed him out of bed completely.

The words from the article circled her mind, even in sleep. The article addressed it as elective surgery. But Addison hadn't elected to have endometriosis, she was born with it. If she could have elected for anything, it would've been to have a baby. The article talked about fibroids. She wasn't quite sure what they were other than usually benign growths. Of all the things she'd been subjected to because of her condition, fibroids were not one. She wasn't necessarily concerned so much about the risk of cancer as she was the risk of tissue adhesion or organ damage. While she didn't remember everything she and Dr. Yorker talked about, she was pretty sure they hadn't discussed morcellation or organ damage.

Addison's mind raced back and forth. She and Keith had come to a decision on the surgery. It was her best option. But after talking to her mom and reading things online…having an open surgery didn't exactly sound ideal. However, neither did a nicked bowel or damaged ureter which, although rare, was still something to consider, especially since endometriosis was a predisposing factor for surgical complications.

She'd told her mother she knew what the surgery entailed. However, as Addison read about the procedure Emma Speck had undergone, she realized she had no clue about what went into a total laparoscopic hysterectomy. Addison knew what was going to be removed: uterus, fallopian tubes, cervix. But she didn't know how. It had never occurred to her to ask.

At five-thirty, Addison decided to give up on the idea of sleep and went to the gym. She couldn't stay at home because she'd be drawn to read more horror stories on the internet. Despite being extremely exhausted, she hoped the positive energy of people burning calories first thing in the morning might help lift her spirits. If not for anything else, she'd at least get in a good run.

Since she started training she'd lost six pounds. At five-foot-four, any extra weight made her look shorter than she was. The subtle lines forming on the sides of her abdomen elongated what she thought to be a short core, making her feel like a model. Addison wasn't delusional enough to think she actually looked like a supermodel. However, losing the weight gave her a greater appreciation of herself.

Addison struggled to get going on the treadmill, but once she did, the time flew by. Before she realized, she'd run six miles without feeling winded at all. The ups and downs of the past four years were an anchor tied to her waist. When she made the decision to have the surgery, the load lightened. But then doubts about the safety of the surgery crept in and she felt bogged down again.

It wasn't a decision anyone could make for her. It was a decision she had to make for herself. Surfing the internet with her symptoms, she'd learned that both grave and non-life-threatening conditions often mimicked each other. A headache could be a migraine, caused by dehydration, or a tumor. A tumor could be benign or malignant. Human illness and conditions, including endometriosis, ran a gamut which the internet could not properly interpret. Despite years of hearing her mom bad-mouth the medical industry, Addison believed doctors knew better. It was time to get advice from a trusted source. Surely, Dr. Yorker wouldn't steer her wrong.

DALE

The email came at two forty-three in the morning. Dale, who thought of himself as an early riser, didn't check his email until seven thirty. Maybe Russell Speck didn't sleep, much like Dale didn't in the early days of Cindy's diagnosis and illness. However, when the days dragged and Cindy's condition worsened, Dale found himself so drained that exhaustion often pulled him under. It was mentally taxing to see his love deteriorate the way she had and extremely frustrating to hear the doctors say there wasn't anything they could do. How could they not do anything? They were doctors.

Dale couldn't imagine the predicament Russell Speck was in as both a doctor and husband. Maybe where Dale fell short in caring for Cindy, Russell would come through for his wife. Maybe Russell's medical training would help him find his wife a way to beat the cancer. Although Dale became envious at the thought, he hoped it would happen.

Dear Mr. Reichter,

Thank you for reaching out. I am sorry to hear of your wife's passing. If you wouldn't mind giving me a little more detail about your wife, her procedure and diagnosis so I can better understand what happened, I would really appreciate it. If she was morcellated, I can guarantee you there is more to her illness than the hospital let on. My number is listed below. Please call me at any time to further discuss.

Russell Speck

The emotion Dale felt reading and re-reading Russell's email overwhelmed him more than he thought was possible. Every step along the process of finding out what happened to Cindy invigorated Dale's resolve to live. When Cindy died, he'd lost his will to go on. Sure, he loved his kids and the grands, but he loved Cindy more. If there was any chance he could be with her again, he would've gladly taken it. But now, knowing she might have been the victim of some kind of hospital cover up, to know she didn't have to suffer the way she had. Someone had to pay. While no one would probably have listened to a retired construction worker, they most certainly were going to listen to one of their own. Cindy no longer had a voice, so Dale would be hers. And now where Dale didn't have a voice, Dr. Russell Speck would be his.

With trembling hands, Dale picked up the phone and pressed each number on the keypad slowly and accurately.

EMMA AND RUSSELL

Thankfully his phone was on silent when it started vibrating in his pocket at eight a.m. Emma had had a rough night and she'd finally just dozed back off after a refresh of pain medication. Every time she winced, Russell felt it. Every time she moaned, he moaned internally. If only he could take her pain away. He knew it was bad when the tears fell from Emma's eyes. Yes, she missed the kids and wanted to be home, but Russell could see the agony she was trying so hard to suppress. He told her to let it go, to get it all out, but Emma refused to cave to the pain.

"Mind over matter, right?" she'd said through gritted teeth an hour before when the pain medication had begun to wear off.

The weight was falling off of her bones, evidence of her diminished appetite.

"Everything hurts," she'd confessed. "Everything."

"You've been through a lot," Russell offered. "It's going to take some time, even for you, to bounce back. But you will."

"I can't even stand up straight," Emma replied. The scar from the incision practically ran the length of her torso and was sewn up so tightly, she was unable to stand fully erect.

"But you will," Russell repeated.

"Before or after the cancer comes back?"

"Em," he said.

"What if this doesn't work? What if the cancer still comes back?"

Emma couldn't bear to look at Russell. Her head was bent, she was staring at the sheet draped across her belly. The tears ran down Emma's face, pooling in the lenses of her glasses.

It was hard not to go down that road with Emma, but Russell refused.

She was going to get through this, even if he had to carry her.

"It did. And it won't." Russell said with as clear of a voice as he could muster.

Emma was a different person when the meds were fresh and the pain was less. Russell knew he just had to walk with her along the dark path, reminding her of the sunlight, until the medication coursed through her body and offered some relief. As soon as the worst of the pain subsided, Emma usually stopped ranting and fell back asleep, her body taking advantage of the reprieve. It was cyclical and Russell was prepared to wait it out with her as long as it took.

Russell looked at the phone, then to Emma. Not recognizing the number, he was about to let it go to voicemail, but something told him to answer.

"This is Russell Speck," he said softly as he slowly left Emma's room.

"Dr. Speck," an unfamiliar, rough voice said.

"Yes," Russell confirmed.

"This is Dale Reichter."

Russell exhaled. "Dale, yes. Hello."

"Is this a good time?"

"As good as any," Russell said. "You said your wife was treated at Kendal Slate Memorial?"

"Yes," Dale replied. "She'd heard such great things about the hospital. Didn't look anywhere else."

Normally, a statement like that would have filled Russell with pride. But now, every compliment given to Kendal Slate was an insult to Russell and a slap across Emma's face.

"Was she morcellated?" Russell asked.

"I'm not sure," Dale replied. "How can I find out?"

"Did you go to her appointments with her?"

"Most of them."

"Did her doctor ever talk about morcellation?"

"No."

Russell took a moment to collect his thoughts. "Why did your wife have surgery?"

"She was bleeding," Dale replied. "Said she could feel something in her belly."

"Did she have a big scar, little scars or no scar at all after the surgery?"

"She had a total laparoscopic hysterectomy," Dale said, a hint of agitation in his voice.

Russell nearly dropped the phone. This man had gone from saying his late wife could feel something in her belly to stating she'd had a total laparoscopic hysterectomy.

"You're certain?"

"Listen, doctor. I might not be an overly educated man. But I knew something was wrong from the second Cindy got sick. Even I know you don't go from having no cancer to tumors all over your belly. I promised her I would find out what happened. I've done my research. I might not know whether she was morcellated, but I can tell you she was fine when she went into the hospital. Sure, she'd been bleeding, but it didn't slow her down much.

"After the surgery, things looked normal. Her doctor, Dr. Clayton, said everything went as planned and he wished us well. Then, when she started to look pregnant and started with real pain, he was quick to blame it on the cancer."

"Did he mention anything about the surgery?" Russell asked.

Dale thought for a second. "No. He called when the test results came back saying she had cancer, leiomyosarcoma. He referred her to an oncologist and that was the last time we heard from him. I tried to contact him to get more information, but his office either didn't give him my messages or he chose to ignore me."

"He never got back to you?" Russell asked, though not completely surprised. Especially since Dale and his wife had been passed off to an oncologist.

"Nope," Dale said. "So I went above him, to the department chair."

"You talked to Richard Oakley?"

"Yes."

Russell's anger swelled. Richard Oakley knew of a patient who'd more than likely had her cancer upstaged and didn't raise any flags? "What did he say?"

"That man is a piece of work," Dale said. "If I were any younger, I probably would've punched him in his mouth."

Russell laughed. He was starting to like this Dale Reichter.

"He talked to me like I was a bum. He had no time or patience."

Russell exhaled, letting his anger subside. Had Dale even gotten a chance to explain what happened to his wife?

"But I wouldn't take no for an answer. He tried to send me away, to talk to someone else if I had a complaint. But they did enough of that to Cindy. I told him I wanted answers and wasn't going to leave until I got them."

"How did that work out for you?" Russell asked.

"He took his time, but he did get back to me. Said he'd reviewed Cindy's case personally, that he didn't see anything wrong in her notes. He explained her disease the same way Dr. Clayton did and said it was unfortunate, but just one of those things."

"So, he knew?" Russell, feeling his anger reignite, wanted to make sure he understood Dale correctly. "He knew exactly what happened to your wife?"

"He read her file," Dale replied.

"I need to get back to my wife," Russell said, realizing he'd stepped out longer than he'd originally planned. "But I'd like to review your wife's medical file, if that's all right. Can you request a copy of her surgical notes and gather whatever medical paperwork you have for her?"

"Sure thing," Dale replied. "I have the notes she kept after her diagnosis. Not sure if they could help."

"They can't hurt," Russell replied. "Please let me know when you have everything together."

Russell hung up with Dale and quickened his pace back to Emma's room. He didn't like to stray unless someone was there to stay with her. She'd had such an outpouring of love and support, friends and colleagues were constantly stopping by to check in. But when Dale called, Russell had left her alone.

Emma was awake when Dale slid past the privacy curtain. He smiled weakly.

"What?" she asked, reading him easily. "What is it?" The digital display of her heart rate increased on the monitor beside her bed. "Did they find something else? How long was I out for?"

Russell shook his head and approached Emma's bed, taking her iv-free hand in his. "No, it's not that. You're doing great."

"Then what?" she persisted. "Something's wrong."

Russell nodded. How could he tell her? Knowing that the hospital had prior knowledge of a case similar to hers without doing anything about it would devastate Emma.

"Russell," she demanded.

"They knew, Em," he said, regretfully.

"What? Who?"

"Kendal Slate. Richard Oakley. They knew."

"What do you mean they knew?"

"There was a woman who died from LMS right before your surgery. She'd had an elective TLH three months prior."

The color drained from Emma's already pale face.

"They knew?" she whispered.

"They knew," he said.

RICHARD

"We need to revise our informed consent process," Richard said to Nancy. "Everyone needs to be up to date with what's going on."

"What about our informed consent?" Nancy asked.

"The Specks are claiming the informed consent process with regards to laparoscopic hysterectomies utilizing morcellators is not clearly defined. They're saying the doctors here never told them Emma could have had an undiagnosed cancer," Richard said. "They're saying they were never warned about the potential damaging effects of morcellation."

"Were they?" Nancy asked. Richard could see the empathy in her eyes.

"If doctors listed every possible surgical outcome or complication, well…they couldn't. There is no way to imagine everything that could go wrong. And forget the great majority of the time when things work out exceedingly well. No one has much to say about that. But God forbid something goes unexpectedly, we are demonized. Medicine is not perfect. Doctors are not perfect. Try as we might, we can't get it right all the time."

Nancy remained silent.

"Did you have an epidural when you had your daughter?" Richard asked.

"Of course I did."

"Do you remember signing a paper giving consent for the epidural?"

"Sure."

"Do you remember what the anesthesiologist said before you signed?"

Nancy closed her eyes as though visualizing the delivery of her daughter. Richard shuddered at the thought. She shook her head. "Not really. I was in a lot of pain. I didn't really care what he had to say. I'm pretty sure I would've signed anything for that needle."

"The paperwork you signed clearly states that, while rare, complications from epidurals include nerve damage, paralysis, and even death. You signed a paper saying you acknowledged you could die from having the epidural placed in your back. Did the anesthesiologist tell you there was a chance you would die? Probably not. But it was on the paper you signed."

"So were the risks of surgery on Emma's consent form?" Nancy asked.

Richard sighed. "Not specifically about cancer, no."

"And morcellation? Did she really not know she was being morcellated?"

"That's not clear," Richard said.

"I see," Nancy replied.

"I don't think you do." He couldn't have his own staff questioning Kendal Slate's practices. "There is always a risk of an undiagnosed condition. Do we really need to put that on everything? Do you know how many times people have gone into surgery for one thing only to have doctors discover something else in the process? You don't know what you don't know."

"So the hospital didn't know about morcellation and undiagnosed cancers in women?"

Richard opened his mouth but closed it quickly. He was in dangerous territory. He wasn't at liberty to discuss what the hospital did and didn't know.

"We need to revise our informed consent process," Richard refocused the conversation. "That is our number one priority."

"The Specks are calling for hospitals to stop the practice of morcellation altogether," Nancy said. "Is Kendal Slate going to stop?"

"We are evaluating the use of morcellators as it pertains to female laparoscopic procedures here at Kendal Slate. We are and always have been devoted to ensuring patient safety and see no need at this time to stop a procedure that has, up until now, proven to be very beneficial to women."

"Is that your official statement?" Nancy asked.

"It's my only statement," he replied.

"Got it," Nancy said. She took three steps toward the door before turning to Richard. "If I ended up paralyzed because of an epidural, I would've sued the hospital, regardless if I signed a consent acknowledging the risks or not. Hypotheticals don't matter until they become a reality. For the Specks it's very much a reality."

"But they're both doctors!" Richard exclaimed, allowing himself to get pulled back into the discussion with Nancy. "They know the risks of everything we do. Even if they weren't explicitly told the risks of her procedure, they were implied with the nature of the surgery. If you were paralyzed because of an epidural, you could sue, and probably win, because you weren't paralyzed prior to coming in to the hospital. Forget that you willingly allowed a doctor to put a needle in your back. You even said you begged for it. I'm pretty sure even if the doctor had said to you right before placing the epidural that paralysis was a risk, you would've bent over and shown him your spine. The procedure, morcellation, neither of them gave Emma cancer. She had cancer that was discovered because of her surgery, a surgery which by all intents and purposes, was a success. The stuff they are claiming now is pure hearsay. It's all hypotheticals. They should know better."

"That's what they're saying about Kendal Slate and our doctors," Nancy said.

"Yes," Richard said and sighed. "I'm aware."

"Addison, hi." Dr. Yorker walked in the room where Addison sat anxiously, crinkling the paper beneath her on the exam table.

"Hi," Addison said as Dr. Yorker gave her a hug. Never in Addison's life had a doctor offered any contact other than a handshake, and even that was becoming rare. But Dr. Yorker was different. She'd made a personal connection with Addison, treating her more like a friend than a patient.

"I don't trust it," Addison's mom had said when she'd made the mistake of telling her about Dr. Yorker's personal touch.

"Of course you don't, Mom."

"I've been seeing doctors longer than you've been alive and never once has one put their hands on me that way."

"You make it sound dirty," Addison replied.

"Her medicine should do the talking for her, not personal touches."

Addison sighed. "Her medicine is great. And so is she."

It didn't matter that Addison's mom wasn't impressed with Dr. Yorker because Addison was. Addison's condition made her more vulnerable than she liked to admit. Having an understanding and approachable doctor like Elizabeth Yorker was a necessity.

"I'm sorry you had to wait," Dr. Yorker said. "Things are a little crazy around here today."

Addison smiled. "No problem. I'm just really glad you could fit me in."

"Me too," Dr. Yorker replied, sitting on the stool across from the exam table. "Heather said you sounded upset when you called to be seen. Is everything okay? Has something happened?"

"No," Addison said and looked down at her hands. Suddenly she felt stupid for asking to be squeezed in. She could've, and probably should've, waited until her nerves settled.

"What is it?" Dr. Yorker asked, putting her hand on Addison's knee.

"I'm sorry," Addison said. "I don't mean to waste your time. I'm just really confused and scared about having the surgery."

Dr. Yorker smiled. "I see."

"It's just that I was set. I really was. And, well, you know my mom is against it. But I was okay with that because it felt right. And Keith, he just wants to make me happy. But then that article was published in the paper about Kendal Slate and minimally invasive surgery. My mom called as soon as she read it, telling me to reconsider, which left me more confused." Addison paused to breathe. "I'm sorry I'm rambling. I've never been so confused before."

"Well for starters, you don't need to have the surgery. I know it's very appealing for your condition. Given your medical history, it makes a lot of sense. But if you're having doubts, you can always wait until it feels right. And if you decide not to do it at all, surgery is not your only option."

"Did you read the article?" Addison asked, consumed with the downsides of the surgery she'd believed to be safe.

"Yes," Dr. Yorker replied.

"Is it true?" Addison asked. "I mean, does Kendal Slate not inform their patients about the true risks of the surgeries done here?"

"What is happening to Emma Speck is very unfortunate. But her case is also unique."

"Do you know about morcellation?" Addison asked.

"I do," Dr. Yorker said.

"Is that how you were going to do my hysterectomy?" Addison asked.

"Were you going to morecellate me?"

Dr. Yorker looked at Addison and smiled. "That article has some valid points which are being overwhelmingly overshadowed by grief. And trust me, you are not the first patient of mine who read it and has questions. Based on your overall health, yes, I was planning on using a power morecellator in your procedure. You are a prime candidate."

Addison felt her stomach drop.

Dr. Yorker continued. "Laparoscopic surgery has its advantages and disadvantages. But like we've discussed, the benefits of minimally invasive surgery outweigh the very serious complications that can arise with open surgery. There is no way around it."

"I guess I didn't realize how many bad things can happen during laparoscopic procedures. I mean, I really thought it was a no-brainer. But then I read about all the things that could happen. For example, I read that having a laparoscopic hysterectomy could cause endometrial symptoms. I already have those. In fact, that's a big reason I considered the surgery. Does that mean they could get worse? That after the surgery I'd be worse off?"

"I can't promise you there won't be any surgical complications, Addison," Dr. Yorker said. "But I can tell you the risks of serious complications in your case are extremely low."

"What about cancer?" Addison asked. "Could I have cancer?"

"Again, I can't give you a definitive answer on that until after the surgery, but I don't expect to find anything abnormal."

Addison felt her breath release. She didn't realize she'd been holding it since asking her question.

"All of your bloodwork and exams have shown nothing of concern. If I had any doubts about performing this surgery, I wouldn't do it. This is a routine procedure with very high success rates."

Addison sighed and looked at her hands in her lap. "There are so many stories on the internet. People put everything online."

"I liken medical stories online to product reviews," Dr. Yorker said. "People only take the time to write about the bad experiences. Sure, you have people willing to give praise where it's due. But the internet has become more of a hub of dissatisfaction than true information. I've always been honest with you, Addison. I'm not going to stop now. The article you read brought up valid points. But if Dr. Speck didn't have cancer, there wouldn't be an article. Her procedure was successful. Unfortunately, she had an occult tumor masquerading as a fibroid. In all my years here and hysterectomies performed, I've never come across a case of morcellated LMS."

Addison sat quietly, processing the information, trying her best to clear her confusion.

"You don't have to make a decision today," Dr. Yorker continued. "Do as much research as you need to make an informed decision. Ask me as many questions as you'd like. There is no right or wrong answer. It comes down to what you want to do."

"I don't want another ectopic pregnancy," Addison admitted, feeling tears forming behind her eyes. "But I don't want to elect to do something that could cause more harm than good."

Dr. Yorker smiled at Addison. "I understand completely. Why don't you talk with Keith about it and let me know if you have any questions? There is no rush to do anything."

Although Addison left Dr. Yorker's office feeling better, she was still undecided about what to do. When she thought about her own reaction to negative experiences versus good ones, she agreed with Dr. Yorker.

Admittedly, she would find the time to write five bad reviews before writing one good one. Was it that the internet was filled mainly with angry, unhappy people? Maybe she should've searched for hysterectomy success stories. Maybe she only read about the bad stuff because that's what she was looking for. It made perfect sense when she thought about it. Her mother was the world's best cynic, viewing life through a pair of very thick, pessimistic lenses. That was not who Addison was. Surely, if laparoscopic hysterectomies were so bad, they wouldn't be allowed. Right?

DALE

"It's going to be a day or two," the receptionist at Dr. Clayton's office said, sounding annoyed by Dale's request for Cindy's medical record.

Dale returned the attitude. "A day or two? I'm not asking for a lot, just a copy of her file. Does it really take twenty-four to forty-eight hours to print a couple of pieces of paper?"

"You're not the only one requesting records, Mr. Reichter."

"I'm sure I'm not," he said. "But this is important."

"I can put your request in," she replied. "That's all I can do. Someone from our staff will call you when they are ready to be picked up."

"Look," he said, losing his patience. "I can wait for the copy of her record. I just need to know if she was morcellated during her procedure."

"Mr. Reichter, I can't read your wife's medical record."

"Somebody there can. Hell, I'm sure Dr. Clayton can tell me. Is he available?"

"He's with patients."

"How about his nurse? She used to return calls to my wife."

"I can put you through to her voicemail if you'd like, please hold."

Dale didn't have a chance to respond before his call was redirected to Susan Washington's voicemail.

"Hi Susan," he said through gritted teeth. It was all he could do not to go to Dr. Clayton's office and demand to speak with him. "This is Dale Reichter. I have a question about my wife's operation that I would like answered today. Please call me back as soon as you can. Thank you."

The message was nicer than he wanted to leave, but Cindy had taught him better. "You get more bees with honey," she loved to say. She was so much better than him. She didn't deserve to die the way she did. She didn't deserve to die at all.

If the roles were reversed, Cindy would've known all of Dale's doctors' names, where they studied and exactly what they did or were planning on doing to him. She would've researched the procedures. She would've protected him. He'd failed her so severely, taking her thoroughness for granted and not asking any important questions himself. He would carry that guilt to his grave, if it didn't take him there itself.

After calling Dr. Clayton's office, Dale reached out to Jason Harris and Phil Santerberry.

"She was morcellated," Jason Harris confirmed. Dale's grip on the phone tightened. "I checked her records just to make sure."

"Did Pauline know she was going to be morcellated?" Dale asked.

"No," Jason said. "Her doctor talked to us about a lot of things, but he never once mentioned morcellation or cancer. He told Pauline it was a safe procedure for her benign condition."

SAFE. BENIGN. Dale's notes were mounting more and more evidence in favor of Russell Speck's claims. Were the doctors so oblivious that they really didn't think these women had cancer? Or were they so arrogant they didn't look deeply enough at each woman individually to assess her specific symptoms? Had these patients, these women, become nothing more than routine?

Dale was just as guilty at falling into routine as everyone else. As a contractor, he approached all repairs by the description of the home owners. More often than not, water in a basement was due to improper grading or a slight crack in the foundation that could easily be fixed. But he had come across houses where the water in the basement was a result of structural issues that required more than soil movement or epoxy injections. The number one solution for most waterproofing contractors was a water management system. Countless homeowners had been lured into the appeal of a "dry" basement through the installation of a drain around the perimeter that would collect water in a sump pump that expelled it from the basement. While this often did the job of keeping the basement "dry", using the term dry to describe a basement made him laugh, it didn't address any other potential issues, if there were any.

He saw the ninety-percent solution work wonders for homeowners. However, for the unlucky ten percent who had moisture in their basement because of a more serious issue, the drain was pointless. Dale felt the same way about Cindy's procedure. All Dr. Clayton had said after her diagnosis was how rare LMS was. One in ten thousand. He'd claimed to never have seen a case of LMS in any of his patients. At first, Dale took his words to heart and thought it was a freak occurrence. At first. But what Russell Speck brought up in the article that Dale hadn't really questioned, was whether the doctors had done their due diligence with regards to eliminating the concern for cancer prior to surgery.

"This is what fibroids do," Phil Santerberry said to Dale. "That's what Dr. Falzgrove said, anyway. He was so certain of it he had both Leslie and I convinced."

"Was she morcellated?" Dale asked.

"Yes," Phil said. "Her doctor recommended laparoscopic power morcellation. He said it would cut her recovery from six weeks to three."

"Did he mention any risks with the morcellator?" Dale asked.

"The only thing he talked about were the standard risks of surgery," Phil said. "Never once did he mention cancer."

"And when she was diagnosed, did he mention anything about the surgery?"

"No," Phil replied. "Like I said, he left the practice shortly after."

"What about her medical record? Did that say anything?" Dale pushed on.

"I looked through it once after Leslie passed," Phil admitted. "But it was too hard to read, so I packed it away."

Dale nodded. He understood what Phil had gone through and didn't want to push him further than he wanted to go. Quickly, he read through his notes from their first conversation.

"I know this is extremely difficult. I wouldn't be asking these questions unless I felt it was necessary, but you said her abdomen was invaded by tumors within a month of her surgery?"

"Yes," Phil said. Dale could hear Phil's energy draining.

"Could any of the doctors explain that?" Dale asked. "How, if her belly was clear during the surgery, could she develop such a quick growing cancer in the exact same area?"

"They said it was very characteristic of LMS. It grew fast and uncontrollably."

Dale shook his head. The doctors who were so certain of their patients not having cancer were then so quick to blame rapid patient deterioration on the disease. If Dale tore down a wall in a house one day and the next month the ceiling collapsed in that same area, he would be sued, and rightfully so. Yes, sometimes things just happen. But for tumors to appear exactly where the doctors had performed surgery, how had no flags been raised?

DECEMBER

EMMA AND RUSSELL

Nine days after having several organs removed, her peritoneum scalded, and suffering a pulmonary embolism, Emma returned home. It was Emma and Russell who pushed for her discharge. Dr. Sauer would have gladly kept her a couple of more days, but Emma refused to extend her hospital stay into the double digits. She was still considerably sore and the taut staples spanning the length of her torso made it impossible for her to walk completely upright. But none of that mattered. She was happy to be home, with her babies.

Hope and Jocelyn were beyond ecstatic when Emma walked through the door. However, their excitement paused when they saw the hunched way she walked.

"It's okay girls," Emma said softly, holding back the tears. She smiled at her littlest angels, overwhelmed with the raw emotion of finally being home.

Hope stepped toward her cautiously. "You have boo-boo, Mommy?"

"Yes." Russell stepped in. "Mommy has a big boo-boo so you have to be very careful around her, okay?"

"Tay," Hope replied.

It broke Emma's heart to see the guarded way in which her babies approached. She wanted so badly to receive them with wide, open arms, but her body was screaming in pain.

"Why don't you go up and take a nap," her mom offered. "You both could probably use some rest in your own bed."

"In a couple of minutes," Emma said as she shuffled over to the couch. "I want to hear all about what these little ones have been up to."

Russell stood guard as Emma sat gingerly on the couch, monitoring the girls as they bounded forward. Emma's parents watched from the doorway, all eyes on her.

"Can I get you something to drink?" her mom asked. "Are you hungry?"

"I'm actually due for my next round," she said to Russell, referring to her pain medication. Hunger wasn't something Emma had felt since the surgery. The weight she'd lost was evident in the way the sweatpants she'd worn into the hospital now fell below her hips.

Russell turned and looked at Emma's mom, obviously uncomfortable with leaving Emma unattended in the presence of the girls. "Hope, Joce, why don't I put on a video you can watch with Mommy?" The girls squealed and shouted out which movies they wanted to watch. "Okay, okay, why don't we make a picnic on the floor and you can watch from there?"

Emma smiled as the girls bounded off the couch and onto the blanket and pillows her mom arranged in the middle of the living room. When the girls were entranced by the television, Emma's mom walked over and kissed her on the top of the head.

"I'm so glad you're home," she said. "How are you feeling?"

"Like I've had my insides ripped out," Emma said.

Emma could see the words strike her mother. "But you made it," her mom managed.

"Barely," Emma said.

Russell walked in the room, stepping over the girls, and offered Emma three pills, a large glass of water, and a small container of red Jell-O. "You need to eat something."

"I made soup, too," Emma's mom said.

"Or I can run out and get anything you want," her dad added.

"Jell-O's fine," she said. "Thank you. I think I'm going to lay down."

"That's not a bad idea," her mom agreed.

Russell waited until Emma was finished taking her medicine to help her to her feet and then up the stairs. Step-by-step, he held Emma's right hand as she clutched the railing with her left. Step-by-step, they took their time, his grip tight on her. When Emma was settled in bed and fast asleep, Russell returned downstairs.

"So, what's the plan?" Emma's mom asked.

"We give her a couple of weeks to heal and then we start chemo."

Emma's mom gasped. "Chemo? I thought you said they got it all?"

"They did, but we don't know what was seeded, what is growing microscopically."

"Can't they test for that?" Emma's dad asked.

Russell nodded. "We'll only know if something is growing when we see it, or she feels it." Emma's mom reached for her husband's hand. "This is a nasty monster we're up against."

"Is it safe for her to start so soon? Doesn't she need time to heal?" her dad asked.

"We can't afford to leave anything to chance with this disease. She has a fast growing, highly aggressive cancer."

"But right now she's cancer free, right?" her mom asked.

Russell sighed. "Yes and no. We don't know what was introduced into her bloodstream during the morcellation. We know the tumor was cut up, which means it could very reasonably be in her blood, circulating through her body."

"What does that mean?" Emma's dad asked with wide eyes.

"It means it could be spreading throughout her body as we speak. They took a contained beast and let it loose inside her body. We need to fight

226 | A.K. MILLS

it with everything we've got before it starts breathing fire."

Emma's parents looked horrified.

"LMS is known to those affected by it as the purple dragon," Russell said. "It has a high propensity of rapidly taking the lives of innocent women. I intend on slaying this dragon."

RICHARD

"It's ten after," Richard said as he paced the room.

Henry Lewis glanced at his watched and shrugged from his seat in one of the two chairs opposite the beige couch in Richard's office. Richard was not a nervous man by nature, but the meeting scheduled to take place in his office had his anxiety at an all-time high.

"He'll be here," Henry said.

At twenty-five after, Nancy let Richard know that doctors Russell and Emma Speck were on their way in. Richard stood by the door.

"Russell," Richard said, extending his hand when the Specks walked in.

"Richard," Russell replied, returning the handshake.

"Emma," Richard turned his attention to Emma. "I'm glad you could make it. How are you feeling?"

"I've been better," she replied, walking past him to the couch.

Russell followed behind Emma and helped her ease into her seat. Richard had been surprised when Russell sent an email, requesting a meeting so soon after Emma's procedure. Her recovery would take months, if not an entire year. Yet there she was, seated in his office, ready to talk morcellation. Richard was impressed by Emma's resolve. However, her languid movements and pallor concerned him.

"This is Henry Lewis from risk management," Richard said. "He wanted to sit in on the meeting."

"Should we have our lawyer present?" Russell asked, half-joking.

Richard ignored the comment and sat down, followed by Henry and finally Russell.

"I think we should start with—" Richard began.

"You knew," Emma interrupted with a quiet, sharp voice that sliced through the air.

"I'm sorry?" Richard asked.

"You knew," she repeated. "You knew laparoscopic power morcellation upstaged another woman's cancer and yet, you did nothing to stop it or prevent it from happening to me."

"I'm sorry?" Richard repeated, stealing a glance at Henry.

"Cindy Reichter passed away the day I scheduled my surgery. Her husband, Dale, questioned what happened to his wife."

"You know I'm not at liberty to discuss another patient's care," Richard replied, never so grateful for HIPPA.

"Dale Reichter told us everything we needed to know, starting with how he approached you directly regarding the care his wife received here."

Richard shifted. Henry took over. "What would you like to get out of this meeting?"

"We'd like for you to stop morcellating women. It's a barbaric practice that has no place in medicine," Russell replied.

"That's your opinion," Henry replied.

"It's the truth," Russell said. "What other field of medicine uses morcellators for removing masses? Would a breast surgeon ever remove an undiagnosed mass from a woman by cutting it up inside the breast?"

Richard and Henry didn't respond.

"I can tell you the answer, which you already know. They wouldn't. No respectable surgeon would cut through anything with the chance of it being an undiagnosed malignancy. Not one."

"Contrary to what you are claiming in the media, power morcellators have proven very beneficial to many women," Richard said.

"And to the ones it hasn't?" Russell replied. "Like my wife?" All eyes moved to Emma. "What do you say to her? I'm sorry it happened to you, but it's helped a lot of other women? You have the chance to do something good here. Kendal Slate has the chance to instill positive change in the gynecologic community."

"Every story has two sides," Henry said. "What do you say to the women who would be harmed by open laparotomy if laparoscopic power morcellation is no longer available?" It was Russell's turn to remain silent. "LPM has benefited a large majority of women in this country. Obese women, in particular, who are at an increased risk of complications from open surgery have benefited greatly."

"We're not asking you to stop laparoscopic procedures," Russell said. "Just halt the use of power morcellators. Start the trend. If Kendal Slate does it, other hospitals will follow suit."

"Since Emma's case was brought to our attention, we've started using containment bags around the morcellators to keep the fragments contained," Richard offered proudly.

Emma shook her head. "That's not good enough. Containment bags can leak, break. You're still cutting up potential malignancies inside an open cavity with ample blood supply."

"It's a step in the right direction," Richard said.

"It's not good enough," Russell echoed his wife. "We came to Kendal Slate because we believed in this hospital. We believed the doctors here cared for their patients. The practice of morcellation is careless."

"I understand your feelings on the procedure based on the outcome it had on your wife," Richard said. "However, I think if you take a step back and look at it from a medical perspective you'd be able to see the benefits of its use versus the risks, which, until you brought it to our attention, were unknown and misunderstood."

"Take a step back?" Russell huffed. "I don't have that luxury. This is my life. This is my wife, the mother of my children. There is no benefit to upstaging her cancer for the sake of a quicker recovery time."

"We are committed to our patients," Richard said. "And we're committed to our employees. We've implemented the use of containment systems in cases involving power morcellators until we can get a better grip on the risks associated with its use. We are all very sorry for your diagnosis, Emma. But we can't halt a practice that has proven very effective without further evaluation because of one claim."

"And Cindy Reichter?" Russell asked. "What about her? The same thing happened to her prior to Emma's surgery."

"We are not at liberty to discuss patient history," Henry reiterated.

"You didn't agree to this meeting to talk about stopping morcellation, did you?" Russell asked.

Richard shook his head. "We're currently evaluating the risks of using power morcellators here at Kendal Slate. In the meantime, however, we'd like you to take some time to be with your family as Emma heals before coming back to work."

"So, you're not going to stop?" Russell asked.

"We are evaluating our procedures to ensure their safety," Richard replied.

At that Russell rose from his seat, helped his wife up and walked toward the door. Before he walked through the threshold, he turned and looked Henry and Richard directly in the eyes. "Every day that morcellators remain common practice, more unsuspecting women are being sentenced to death. By standing by and doing nothing, you are delivering that sentence."

ADDISON

When Addison returned home from Dr. Yorker's office, she searched online for successful hysterectomy stories. To her pleasant surprise, she came across plenty. They weren't nearly as descriptive as the negative stories, but they offered Addison a ray of hope. Many of the women who wrote of their successes were much older than she was and some even lucky enough to have had children before opting for surgery.

There was one story of a woman who had made peace with the fact that she was never going to have children only to find out she was pregnant from the pregnancy test administered at the hospital the morning of her surgery. Addison so badly wanted to contact her, not for information about the hysterectomy she ended up having, but how she came to peace with the idea of never having children.

Throughout the course of their many attempts at conception, Addison read practically everything ever written about dealing with infertility. Acknowledgement was a big step in overcoming infertility issues. She had no problem acknowledging her condition. It was the guilt of not being able to conceive, feeling as though God must've thought she would be a bad mother. There were days when Addison was angry. Angry at the world, at her mother, Keith, basically everyone. A lot of the literature pointed toward talking openly about her fertility problems. But she didn't want to talk. Because if she did, she'd have to admit that she didn't see herself ever coming to terms with her infertility.

"You're back on the computer," Keith said, concerned, when he came in from work.

"Yes," Addison closed her laptop. "Just some more research."

"How did it go with Dr. Yorker?" he asked.

"She's so nice," Addison said. "She didn't make me feel crazy at all even though I'm pretty sure I was acting kinda loony."

"She's a female doctor who specializes in gynecology and obstetrics. I'm sure she's seen a lot of loony behavior in her dealings with hormones," Keith jested.

"Very funny," Addison said.

"What did she recommend?" Keith asked.

"She didn't recommend anything. She told me to do more research and if I had second thoughts to think about postponing the surgery."

"Is that where you're at, putting it off?"

"I didn't say that," she replied quickly. "You asked me what Dr. Yorker said and I'm telling you."

"Did you ask her if the surgery was risky?"

"She said having another ectopic pregnancy was riskier than the surgery."

"Seems pretty clear, then," he said.

Addison rolled her eyes and walked into the kitchen.

"What?" Keith followed behind. "What did I say?"

"You make it sound so simple," she replied, annoyed. "Like it's no big deal."

"I never said it was no big deal," he refuted.

"The risks of surgery might not be as bad as having another pregnancy develop outside of my uterus, but there are still risks. Dr. Yorker even said that."

"She said those exact words," Keith asked, a hint of disbelief in his voice. "She said you are at risk if you have this surgery?"

"She said there are risks associated with every surgery."

"We already knew that," Keith said. "What did she say about *you* and this surgery?"

Addison inhaled and exhaled a long breath before answering. "She said I'm a prime candidate for the surgery. That my risks are lower because of my age and overall health."

"And there it is," Keith said, shaking his head. "You don't have to have the surgery if you don't want to, but please don't turn into your mother in how she sees the bad side to everything."

"I'm scared," Addison admitted. "What if I make the wrong decision?"

"The only way you can make the wrong decision is if you base it out of fear. I read the article. It has very little, if anything, to do with you. It's sad what happened to that woman but she's not you. You're not having the procedure for whatever those things are that she had. You are electing to have this done because you almost died. And unless Dr. Yorker is suddenly concerned you might have cancer, I really don't see the connection."

"That woman is a doctor, Keith. And yet she ended up worse off because of a surgery she chose to have. And Dr. Yorker wants to use the same tool on me. That's the connection. If Emma Speck didn't know the bad stuff that could happen to her, what does that mean for someone like me?"

"Isn't that why you went to Dr. Yorker?" Keith asked. Addison didn't reply. "Look, Addy, ultimately this is your decision. But for what it's worth, I don't see the downside in you having the surgery."

"But what if—"

"Since when do we live by what-ifs?" Keith interrupted. "When you went into surgery, I had to sign your medical release. I read the risks associated with the surgery you were about to have and signed off on them. I didn't focus on all the bad things that could happen to you. If I had waited, or hesitated, who knows what would've happened to you?" He paused and shook his head. "Do you know the kicker of it all was that one of the risks of repairing your fallopian tubes was the potential for a hysterectomy?"

"That would've been so much easier," Addison said.

"Why?" Keith asked. "Because you wouldn't have had a say? You would've been miserable if you woke up and they told you they removed everything."

"But at least it would've been done."

"No," Keith said. "This way you can take control, make a decision for yourself. Don't be bullied by your mom, confused by articles or intimidated by the what-if's. Do what you want to do, what you feel is right."

Addison thought about what she wanted. When the image of a baby flashed through her mind, she immediately pushed it out. It wasn't time to think about what she wished for. It was time to think about what she wanted and decide. No more going back and forth.

"I'm going to do it," she said after a couple of minutes of reflection. "Have it done, get it over with. Spring break, like I planned."

"You don't have to make a decision tonight," Keith said.

"Yes. I do," Addison said. "And I have. I'm not one of the lucky ones who can have children despite endometriosis. I am tired of surrendering my body for a week every month to a chronic condition with zero upside. For what? The pain of surgery is temporary. The pain of having my period every month will continue until I hit menopause. Why would I do that to myself?"

Keith nodded in agreement.

"I'll call Dr. Yorker's office tomorrow and let them know I've made my decision."

"If that's what you want," Keith said.

"It's what I want," Addison confirmed. But they both knew there was a lot of time before then, giving Addison's mom plenty of time to talk her out of it.

DALE

"There once was a town terrorized by a dragon," Carmen began. "Every day the dragon took a young maiden. Some say the villagers offered the women for sacrifice to keep the dragon at bay. Either way, an innocent woman fell victim daily."

"How fitting," Dale said. "Was the dragon ever defeated?"

"Yes, by St. George. He happened to be traveling through the village the day the king's only daughter was offered up. Bravely, St. George took on the dragon and won."

"So the princess was spared?"

"Yes," Carmen said.

"If only it were that easy," Dale said.

"We all know you would have done anything to save Mom."

"She should've never needed to be saved," Dale confessed.

"She had cancer. You did everything you could and now you're helping other women so they don't have to go through the same thing."

It had been a full twenty-four hours since Dale had contacted Dr. Clayton's office and left a message for the nurse. Although they told him it could take up to forty-eight hours to get back to him, he didn't really think it would take that long. Part of him felt the delay was on purpose.

"We'll see," Dale said. "Russell Speck is the only doctor making noise right now. No one else appears to be joining his fight."

"I'm not surprised," Carmen replied. "The medical community is pretty tight-knit. Russell Speck is basically calling out the entire field of gynecology. He's going after his own hospital. I can't imagine that would be looked at with favor."

"If it's the truth, what does it matter?" Dale asked.

"Because it means money," Carmen said. "If Russell Speck is right and women have had their stage one cancers catapulted to stage four from a surgical oversight, there are going to be lawsuits. Wrongful death, negligence, all amounting to millions of dollars. People might not respond to right and wrong, but they sure as heck respond to money."

"It's a lot to prove," Dale said. "I'm sure the hospitals have a bunch of lawyers protecting them."

"I'm sure they do," Carmen said. "But with one of their own doctors leading the fight, they might not be as protected as they'd like to be."

Dale was about to respond when his cell phone rang. He pulled the phone out of his pocket and, recognizing the number, held his finger up to his daughter signaling for her to wait a minute.

"Dale Reichter," he said.

"Hi Dale," a familiar voice said. "This is Susan returning your call from Dr. Clayton's office."

"Hello, Susan," he replied.

"I'm calling to let you know Cindy's records are ready to be picked up."

"Thank you," Dale said. "Did you have a chance to look through them?"

"I reviewed them, yes."

"Can you tell me whether or not a morcellator was used in her procedure?"

"Yes," she said and paused. "A power morcellator was used to remove your wife's fibroids. They were removed without incident or damage to the surrounding organs. Your wife had a routine and successful laparoscopic hysterectomy."

"Successful except for her cancer, right?" he asked.

"Mr. Reichter—"

"Thank you for calling," Dale replied and hung up.

"Who was that?" Carmen asked.

Dale slid the phone back in his pocket, shaking his head.

"What is it Dad?"

"That was the nurse from Dr. Clayton's office," he replied. "Turns out your mother's cancer was morcellated. This just became more than a coincidence."

EMMA AND RUSSELL

"I'm starting with the FDA," Russell said to Emma. She was resting in bed after a morning of playing with the girls. Russell sat beside her, typing feverishly.

The information was readily available, giving Russell a feeling he would be heard, his claims not rejected. The Food and Drug Administration was an agency to protect the public. Unlike a privatized hospital like Kendal Slate, the FDA was run by the government. His tax dollars paid for their protection. The website listed a method for reporting non-emergencies, which he quickly bypassed. Russell considered upstaging cancer a definite emergency and adverse reaction to the use of power morcellators which were, in fact, regulated by the FDA. For those cases, a number was provided for direct assistance.

"Four hundred thousand," Russell told Emma. "Four hundred thousand hysterectomies are performed each year in the United States. Forty percent of them are done by minimally invasive techniques."

"How many of those women have had their cancer upstaged?" Emma asked.

"That's what I can't figure out. Everything I've come across says the odds are one in ten thousand."

"Not if it happened to me and Cindy Reichter within six months at the same hospital," Emma said. "They have to stop. This can't keep happening."

"It won't," Russell said. "They know we're on to something. It's only a matter of time before Kendal Slate sees the error of their ways and changes course."

"How was nothing reported before?" Emma asked. "How did no one see a correlation?"

"There appears to be some literature on adverse events with regards to power morcellation, but nothing as serious as the spread of cancer. Abdominal hyperplasia has been reported, bowel adhesions, organ perforations."

"They've known about these complications?" Emma asked. "I know adhesions and perforations are standard any time you cut into someone, but hyperplasia? Didn't anyone stop to question why benign cells were multiplying abnormally inside women's abdomens post-op?"

"The literature is sparse," Russell said. "I don't even see how they came up with the denominator of ten thousand."

"It's a nice big number," Emma said through a yawn. "Makes is seem less likely to happen, so when it does, it can be just one of those unfortunate things."

"Yeah, well, you're not just one of those unfortunate things." Russell leaned over to kiss Emma on the forehead.

Emma smiled weakly and closed her eyes. "They have to stop this," she said, her voice slightly above a whisper.

"If they don't," Russell said, rising from the bed and tucking his wife in. "We will."

Elaine sat at the kitchen table with her large cup of coffee and iPad in hand, looking confused and slightly annoyed when Richard came in from the gym.

"Did you read the paper?" she asked.

"Always do," he replied. "What has you offended this morning?"

"Did you read the latest article about Kendal Slate?"

Richard poured himself a large glass of orange juice. "Yes."

"Can you explain this whole thing about informed consent?" she asked. "Because it sounds like you guys are lying to your patients."

Richard turned his back to Elaine, putting the orange juice back in the fridge, so she couldn't see him roll his eyes. "What do you want to know?"

He'd had a great workout, ridding his body of more tension than he'd been able to in a long time. Why did Elaine have to read the article? Normally, she wasn't one to get caught up in current events outside her inner circle. Before the Specks started trashing the hospital in the media, Elaine had never once considered Kendal Slate or Richard's job part of her world.

"Did you know your doctors haven't been informing patients of specific risks of surgery, like cancer?"

Richard held his breath, hoping to suppress the steam rising from within.

"Could you lose your job over this?"

Of course, Richard thought. She read the article, saw "lawsuits" and figured her livelihood was at stake. That brought it right into her inner circle.

"I'm not going to lose my job," he said, staying at the counter to keep his distance.

"How do you know?" she demanded, more so than questioned.

"One, you can't believe everything you read. Two, Kendal Slate hasn't done anything wrong. And three, this isn't as big of a deal as the papers are making it out to be. It will blow over."

"It says the hospital is sentencing people to die."

"Cancer sentences people to die," he barked back. "Not a signed document."

Elaine dropped the tablet on the table and looked at Richard with disbelief. "Lack of knowledge can be a deadly thing, Richard."

The way Elaine pronounced his name when she was upset with him, cutting the second syllable short, annoyed Richard like nothing else.

"Madeline said her neighbor was scheduled for a hysterectomy but luckily read the paper and decided to cancel. She said she wasn't going to be touched until she knew she was informed correctly. She said her doctor never mentioned anything about cancer."

"Maybe because she was having surgery for something unrelated to the possibility of cancer," Richard said, regretting his response, but unable to keep quiet.

Elaine shook her head, her blonde, uncombed hair flopping from side to side. "You see, that's what got Kendal Slate in this mess to begin with. Cancer can be found in anyone at any time. It's foolish to think otherwise."

"Foolish, is it?" he asked, refusing to let it go. "So, if a patient presents in the ER with a fractured arm because they fell from a tree, should they be treated for a fractured arm or should it automatically be assumed they have osteosarcoma?"

Elaine rolled her eyes. "Don't be ridiculous. I'm just saying you can't rule anything out. And in any case, a broken arm is different from uterine cancer."

"So now you're a gynecologic oncologist?" he spat. "Tell me, doctor, what is it you know about uterine cancer?"

"I know your surgeons shouldn't be chopping up masses that could be cancer inside of women. I know women deserve to know what you're doing to them and how it's being done while they're unconscious."

"Now you're the one being ridiculous," he said. "You make it sound like we're…" Richard paused, remembering a part of the article in which Russell Speck used the word assault with regards to what happened to his wife.

"Go on," Elaine egged him on. "You can say it."

"Forget it." Richard chugged the rest of his juice, leaving the cup on the counter next to the sink just to spite Elaine.

"No, Richard. I won't forget it. Say it. Say the word, because maybe then you'll get what's going on. It sounds like your doctors are assaulting women against their knowledge."

"They're surgeons," Richard yelled.

"What?" Elaine barked.

"Surgeons," Richard replied. "They are surgeons, not doctors."

"Same thing," Elaine said, tossing her hand in the air to show how little she cared about any differentiation.

"No, it's not," Richard said. "Surgeons put in way more time than doctors. We perfect our craft by putting in countless hours in the OR. Doctors study, do rotations. If you're going to claim to know everything about what's going on at the hospital, the least you can do is use the correct terminology."

Elaine didn't respond.

"And furthermore, if you want to get technical, gynecologists aren't surgeons."

"But they do surgery," she retorted.

"Yes, but they aren't trained as surgeons."

"Potato, potahto," Elaine said. "That's what's wrong with all of you. You're so caught up in titles and training you're not even looking at the patients."

"Why did you ask me to explain informed consent if you have all the answers?" Richard asked, mad he'd replied to her initial question. He should've known better. "I told you before and I'll tell you again. Russell Speck is mad because his wife was diagnosed with a highly aggressive, often fatal, cancer. He's looking for someone to blame, so he's blaming the hospital. He is a surgeon, his wife an attending. They knew what they were signing up for."

"So you're admitting they weren't told?" Elaine asked.

Richard just about lost it. "I'm not admitting to anything and you better not tell anyone I have. I'm just saying I don't buy two doctors claiming to be completely ignorant when it comes to a routine medical procedure they both have undoubtedly witnessed."

"So now it's their fault?" Elaine wouldn't let up.

"It's no one's fault. Cancer happens. It is diagnosed and treated every day. Uterine cancer has no cause. Hell, even people who don't smoke get lung cancer. Bad things happen. The Specks should know that better than anyone."

"I don't think this is going to blow over, Richard."

"It will," he said. "People are going to get caught up in the headlines, talk about it at work. We'll have to change some things at the hospital as a result, but nothing major. Laparoscopic hysterectomies are a good thing. Power morcellators have done good things."

"They sound barbaric," Elaine replied. "I watched a video online. It's disgusting."

"All surgeries are," Richard said. "But no one is saying that. Every time we go into someone's chest and crack it open, do you think it's done nicely? Cardiac surgeons use a saw to cut through the sternum to get access to the heart. Is that something you want to see? Did you want a play-by-play of your C-section? Did you want Dr. Allen to give you every detail? Or were you fine with the overview? The surgeons at Kendal Slate are not assaulting women," he felt the need to clarify. "They're not lying to their patients. We are looking into the Speck's claims, but Christ, Elaine. I need you on my side. I'm dealing with enough of this shit at work. I don't need it at home too."

Elaine made some kind of noise, Richard wasn't exactly sure what it meant. In any case, he considered it a success since she had stopped talking and gone back to reading her tablet. Sometimes Richard wished he'd been on a different rotation the night she showed up in the ER flashing skin and offering a good time. Sometimes it just wasn't worth it.

ADDISON

"Did you read the latest article?" Addison's mom asked before Addison could finish saying hello.

"Yes, Mom. I read it when you sent it at six o'clock this morning."

"Do you still think surgery is a good idea?"

Addison rolled her eyes. It wasn't even seven in the morning and her mother was already at it. Maybe it was a mistake to tell her she'd made up her mind about the surgery. She had four months until spring break, she could've waited until, say, the night before…or maybe not at all.

"I've read the articles, Mom. I've talked with my doctor. You may not agree, but this is what's best for me."

"You're okay putting yourself in the hands of doctors who base their surgical decisions on statistics? That it's somehow okay for them to risk killing someone if it benefits someone else? The fact they consider even one human life an "acceptable risk" is sickening. We're talking about living, breathing people. How can they be so callous?"

"It's not that easy," Addison said.

"Are you saying you're expendable?" her mom said with a huff.

"No, Mom," Addison replied. "Of course I'm not expendable. Everyone has people who love them, who value their lives. I don't think the medical community is pointing to you or me specifically and saying we don't matter. What they're trying to get across is that they are trying to treat the greater good. Doctors are human, just like you and me. When I'm doing my lesson plans, even though I try to make it so that everyone understands and participates, there are going to be some kids that don't respond. No matter how hard I prepare or try, certain children are not going to get it. Does that make me a bad teacher?"

"Addition is hardly the same as death."

"But it's the same idea. I believe that Dr. Yorker genuinely cares about me and my outcome. She agreed there are risks to my procedure. There are risks to everything. And if the worst were to happen, I'm sure she'd feel horrible. But I wouldn't blame her for trying to help me."

"Oh, Addison. I certainly didn't raise you to be so gullible. Dr. Yorker might be a nice woman, but make no mistake about it, she makes a very nice living from what she does."

"She went into medicine, into gynecology because she cares about women. Trust me, Mom. I've had gynecologists in the past who barely even noticed I was alive. I've been treated like a patient plenty of times which made me feel like nothing but a number. Dr. Yorker treats me like a person."

"How would her life change if anything happened to you during the surgery?"

Addison thought for a moment. "She would feel awful."

"Yes, but how would her life change? Day-to-day, how would she be affected?"

"I guess she wouldn't," Addison admitted.

"Exactly. No matter how much she cares and treats you like a person, you are just a patient to her. At the end of the day, if the worst were to happen during your surgery, she would feel bad, yes, but her life would go on. She'd even keep doing the surgery that killed you."

"Can we not say the surgery is going to kill me, please?" Addison asked. While she was certain in her decision, she didn't want to jinx anything.

"I'm being realistic," her mom said. "It may seem a bit harsh, but you need to hear it."

"I'm young and healthy," Addison replied. "I'm what they call an ideal patient."

"So why do anything that could change that?" her mom pleaded.

"Because it's what I want to do!" Addison yelled. Addison's tone took them both by surprise and she immediately recoiled. "I'm sorry, Mom. This has been a really tough year for me. I'm only trying to do what I feel is right, but it's really hard to feel good about my decision when all you do is question my reasoning."

"All I've ever wanted to do was keep you safe," her mom said softly, clearly hurt.

Addison sighed. She wasn't going to let her mom slide by on guilt. "I get it, Mom. I do. But this has to stop. You need to stop."

"What exactly am I supposed to stop, Addison? Loving you? Wanting what's best for you?"

"I don't want you to stop loving me," Addison said. "I just want you to support me and the decisions I make as an adult." Addison's mom remained silent. "I've got to get to work. Can I call you later?"

"Whatever you want," her mom replied.

"Ok," she said. "I'll talk to you later."

Addison hung up the phone, gave herself a last once-over in the mirror in the hall and rushed out the door.

Four months was a long time to wait for surgery when it was all Addison, and apparently her mother, could think about. Part of her wanted to squeeze in the procedure between Christmas and New Year's, but that was her and Keith's special time and she didn't want to infringe on that. She was going to make this Christmas one to remember, especially since her mom was betting against a successful procedure come the spring.

Sophia practically jumped from her seat behind the counter at the library when Dale walked through the automatic glass doors.

"This story keeps getting bigger," she said through a huge smile. "Every day I'm reading something new. You have to be so excited."

Dale shrugged and walked past her toward the computers.

"What's wrong?" Sophia asked. "Did I miss something?"

"No," Dale replied. "The articles are great. I guess I thought I'd feel better once I found out what happened to Cindy. But I don't. The fact that there's no information about it makes it more frustrating."

"Usually it's all about how you search," Sophia said, taking a seat next to Dale. She explained how to use key term searches in the hopes of finding more about the downside of power morcellators and the upstaging of cancer. Unfortunately, her search results only yielded articles dating back a couple of weeks. "Could it be that no one knew?"

Dale shook his head. "No. We're talking about smart, educated people whose job is to know the human body. If I had a staple gun that shot sideways or backwards, hell, even if it constantly jammed, I'd return it. If enough contractors returned the same product, or stopped using it, the manufacturer would take notice. All professions, white jackets or jeans, have a community where word of mouth travels."

"One of these articles interviewed a doctor who says morcellation is a safe practice," Sophia said. "Do you think it's safe?"

"I think it's about as safe as smoking," Dale replied.

Sophia left Dale to his scouring of the internet, promising to let him know if she came across anything. But after two and a half hours of pounding away on the keyboard left him empty handed, Dale found it hard to believe Sophia could come up with anything different.

"What do you mean doctors don't have to report adverse events?" Carmen spat in disbelief when Dale told her about his fruitless afternoon.

"It's completely voluntary," Dale said. "At least by the doctors."

"I don't understand," Carmen said. "How does that even make sense?"

"It doesn't," Dale said. "If there's no suspected negligence on the doctor's side, they don't have to report anything."

"And if they see a device harming patients?" Carmen questioned.

"Well, that's the thing. The doctors don't see morcellators as harming the patients."

"That's just ridiculous."

"It's easy to say that now, knowing what we know," Dale said. "But if nothing was being talked about, how would they know?"

"There had to be some level of discussion," Carmen replied.

"Well if there was, there's no record of it, at least what I can find anyway."

"And Russell Speck, what is he saying?"

"He's saying the hospital ignored what was happening. That they didn't want to see the relationship between their highly lucrative, cash-cow procedure and an aggressive, fatal cancer."

"Well just because they chose to ignore it doesn't mean it didn't happen. You've already talked to men who lost their wives the same way. I'm sure more will follow."

"Let's hope so," Dale replied, holding onto a little bit of optimism. "We need numbers and proof on our side. Right now, we don't have either."

EMMA AND RUSSELL

Numb. Numb would be ideal if Emma could still love her children and Russell while feeling absolutely nothing for anything else. Unfortunately for her, life didn't work that way. Yes, she was home and recovering from a procedure that easily could have killed her. And yes, Dr. Sauer had claimed to remove all evidence of disease. But there was so much more to her health than a successful surgery.

Leiomyosarcoma came back. It was angry and ugly and unforgiving. Dr. Sauer did his best, but he couldn't see the microscopic seeding that had taken place during her hysterectomy. He couldn't see inside her blood cells to see if LMS was flowing freely. He couldn't promise her a disease-free future any more than anyone else, and he was the specialist.

Emma would be destined to suffer in the world of unknowns the rest of her life. As such, she and Russell would take no chances, make no assumptions in preventing the cancer from returning.

"It can't come back," she'd broken down to Russell one particularly bleak morning.

Kaitlin had been talking during breakfast about her friend's sister who turned ten and the amazing birthday party she'd had. When she asked Emma if she could have a similar party for her tenth birthday in a year and a half, it was all Emma could do not to lose it.

"Three-year median survival after recurrence," Emma said above a whisper. "Some go before. How can I tell Kaitlin I might not even be around for her tenth birthday?"

"Because you will be," Russell replied sharply. He refused to entertain any of Emma's thoughts of death. "You will be here for her tenth, her twentieth. Right now we're ahead of this thing and that's how we're going to stay."

Emma curled up in a ball on her bed. Most, if not all, of her rest times throughout the day were less for sleep and more for breaking down. She tried her best to smile and feign normalcy around the kids. But in the privacy of her bedroom, she let it all go.

"You don't know that," she said.

"I do," he replied. "We have a plan, a good one."

"We had other plans, too," Emma replied. "Look how well those turned out."

Russell curled up behind his wife on their bed. "Em, we're going to get through this. In two weeks you'll start chemo and rid your body of any remnants from the surgery."

Emma closed her eyes, trying to suppress any more tears from falling. Why did her body turn on her? Why had any tumors grown? She remembered the day things started feeling different and the subsequent conversation she had with Nicole Stein.

"Something's different," Emma had said. "Something's changed."

The fibroid Emma had in her uterus had grown to where she could feel it by just touching her stomach.

"This is very classic fibroid behavior," Nicole Stein had explained. "I've seen it before."

"Even the anemia?" Emma pushed her concern. "The bleeding has gotten so heavy. It just doesn't feel right."

Dr. Stein didn't share Emma's concern but, sensing Emma's unease, ordered a biopsy and imaging to be done. Emma knew the biopsy was a glorified PAP smear that didn't sample the fibroid itself. But still, when the results aligned with what Nicole Stein had said, Emma had allowed herself to believe the same. The mass was benign.

She had one week of relief, the week after the hysterectomy. For those seven days, Emma's energy levels increased. The constant pressure in her pelvis had been alleviated and her bleeding stopped. For seven days she felt better. Now, Emma was tortured with the knowledge that despite feeling better, there was something occurring in her body more sinister than a fibroid. It was cancer.

RICHARD

Tis the season, Richard thought, rolling his eyes as he passed the twelve foot Christmas tree in the main foyer of the hospital. The extravagantly decorated tree was a staple of the holiday season at Kendal Slate, erected to put a smile on the face of the people coming into the hospital. *Who are they kidding?* He'd thought the first time he'd seen it. People didn't want to go to the hospital. If they worked there it was a place to make a living. If they needed to be there it usually meant pain and discomfort. Even something as glorious as childbirth hurt, and Richard knew better than anyone else that people absolutely dreaded visiting others in the hospital.

When his mother's cancer had metastasized to her bones, forcing her to stay in the hospital, his father made him visit her every day. No matter how tired he was, how much homework he had, Richard had to sit with his ailing mother for two hours a day. In the beginning she'd been happy to see him and coherent enough to carry on a conversation. By the end, he doubted she even knew he was there.

It was a sore time in Richard's life and not one he liked to think about, much less discuss. In fact, he'd never talked to Elaine about it at all. When she'd asked, he told her his mom died when he was little and didn't remember much. That was far from the truth. Richard was a sophomore in high school when his mother was diagnosed and a senior when she died. He remembered plenty, especially the festive decorations around the hospital in the days leading up to her death and the never-ending holiday music playing on repeat.

"Fourteen days," Nancy said as Richard walked past her desk. "Are you ready to be Santa?"

"I let Elaine take care of that stuff," he mumbled. "She's better at it."

"I meant here," Nancy replied. "It's bonus day."

Richard nodded. "Right. I assume everything is taken care of?"

"Yes," Nancy said. "I guess I'm better at being Santa too."

Richard managed a chuckle and walked into his office. Twice a year the hospital issued out bonuses to its employees, which meant that twice a year he had to look at the successes and failures of the department, rewarding those who performed and making note of those who did not. Doctors were in business to help people; Kendal Slate was in business to make money. Being the department chair, Richard needed to keep his surgeons incentivized while keeping the revenue up.

Every surgeon, from cardiothoracics to neurology, believed their specialty to be the most important and vital element of surgery at Kendal Slate. He was routinely inundated with research funding requests from each specialty wanting every new advancement to come to Kendal Slate. It got so competitive that sometimes he felt as though he was dealing with his own twins. No matter what Richard supplied them with, no matter how generous, they always wanted more.

A large portion of Richard's job was managing surgical costs. The time of a procedure versus what the insurance companies would pay, if they paid. Of course, the more surgeries the better. But he had to be careful the surgeons' hubris and their abilities to perform multiple surgeries in a day didn't get in the way of quality. If he focused too much on the bottom line, the quality of patient care inevitably suffered. Yet if he focused solely on patient care, the hospital wouldn't be able to stay in business. All he had to do was let the department slip a little and the sharks would circle in the water, quick to take his job.

There was no true loyalty in the position he held. His surgeons, even the ones he hand-selected, would gladly take his title if given the opportunity. Nicholas Darboh, the chief of cardiothoracic surgery, to name one, wouldn't hesitate to place a scalpel in Richard's back if it meant assuming the role of department chair. If Darboh had his way, Kendal Slate would shed the excess weight of elective surgeries and focus solely on hearts and lungs. He didn't understand that elective surgeries funded the deficiencies stemming from his specialty. Elective surgeries, to include laparoscopic hysterectomies, were often quick and efficient with very little downside. They were the money maker.

Even with the bad press, Kendal Slate continued to schedule and perform minimally invasive surgeries. Laparoscopic hysterectomies wouldn't stop. People fell for sad stories only until it took away the freedoms they enjoyed. Minimally invasive surgery was too easy for the patient and too lucrative for the industry. It was a win-win.

"Happy holidays," Rachel sang merrily on the phone.

"I'll be happy in two weeks when I'm on break," Addison replied.

"What if I had a little info to brighten your day?" Rachel asked.

"I'm listening," Addison said.

"Tina is officially fat," Rachel said.

"Tina is pregnant," Addison replied, defeated.

"That doesn't matter, Addy, she's fat. And she's got acne. All over her face."

"She's growing another human," Addison defended.

"So?" Rachel said, clearly disappointed by Addison reaction. "It's Tina. And she's fat. She's let herself completely go. That has to make you a little happy."

A tiny smirk found its way to the corner of Addison's mouth. Picturing Tina fat because she was pregnant made Addison envious. She wanted to be fat because of a baby. But picturing Tina's perfect face broken out was a different story. Tina, who never left the house without lipstick and mascara. That was cause for a little joy.

"How bad is her acne?" Addison asked.

"It's bad," Rachel said. "Not as bad as her attitude, but pretty close."

"How is the shower planning?"

"It's fine. We're just in the initial phase right now. She's only three months. We've got five until the shower. But of course she wants to know everything we're discussing. Her food aversions have already started. Tracy sends me texts with random food items not allowed at the shower. Today was avocados."

"Why do you do this to yourself?" Addison asked. "I couldn't deal with people barking orders at me like that."

"Because it makes me feel normal," Rachel confessed. "For all the times I thought I was high maintenance, difficult, I get completely vindicated when dealing with people like Tina and Tracy."

Addison laughed. "I never thought about it that way."

"Seriously, Addy. I don't get how Keith stayed with her for as long as he did. She's intolerable."

"He was young and stupid," Addison said, feeling better. "Besides, he hadn't met me yet."

"Very true," Rachel said. "He better be grateful he married you instead of that pregnant psycho."

Rachel couldn't have just said that Keith better be grateful to have married Addison. She had to throw in the pregnant psycho bit. She could've even called Tina a psycho, just omitted the pregnant part. But she didn't. And no matter what he said, Addison didn't fully believe Keith when he said he was happier with her than Tina knowing that Tina could have his children and Addison couldn't, ever.

DALE

"I've been thinking," Carmen said, walking through Dale's front door.

"Hi Car," he said, startled, rising from his recliner to greet her.

The girls and their husbands had always been welcome in Dale and Cindy's home, unannounced and at all hours, no knocking required. Carmen hugged Dale and quickly walked over to the fireplace. Cindy had loved nothing more than fires in the winter and as such, the girls grew up to love them as well.

"It's cold out there tonight. What are you doing here?"

"I was talking with my friend Danielle about the whole morcellation thing and how I wanted to help make it stop and she suggested doing a run."

"A run?" Dale asked.

"Yeah," she said. "Apparently that's what people do to raise awareness and money for good causes."

"I wouldn't know the first thing about organizing a run," Dale said.

"Me neither," Carmen confessed. "But Danielle said it's not that hard. And besides, I'm sure Becca and Gail would help."

"What kind of run?" Dale asked.

"Maybe a 5K. I did a quick search after I talked to Danielle and there are a lot of 5Ks around here. I figured maybe we could go to one to get a feel for how it works and see if it's something we can pull off."

Dale knew Carmen could never pull off any kind of run on her own, she wasn't organized enough. However, with Gail's detail-oriented help and Becca's social grace, the idea wasn't that crazy.

"Please, Dad," Carmen continued. "Let me do this for Mom."

"If you want to look into it, I'm not going to stop you," Dale said.

"You know I'll support you any way I can."

"Then it's settled," Carmen said, a broad smile forming on her face. "Next year we'll host a run in remembrance of Mom."

Emma and Russell

"The data is weak, to say the least," Russell admitted to Emma. "I have no idea how they came up with the numbers they did. How can they claim to have a number if no one reported anything before us?"

While Russell continued fighting the medical community and manufacturers of the power morcellator, Emma chose to focus on making Christmas special for the kids. She had never been so grateful for online ordering and free delivery. Prior to her surgery, she'd enjoyed handpicking gifts. Shopping was a fun date for her and Russell, a chance to break free from unrelenting schedules. She loved imagining her kids' reactions when they unwrapped the presents Christmas morning. This year, however, she couldn't bring herself to go to the stores.

It wasn't that she didn't want to. But for starters, Emma wasn't sure she had the stamina to endure holiday shopping. Getting gifts for four children, ensuring they all got what they wanted and that the distribution was fair was not an easy task. Emma also couldn't afford to get sick. She was scheduled to start chemotherapy two days after Christmas, meaning her immune system could not afford to be compromised. Plus, it was too emotional for her. Given the grim prognosis of leiomyosarcoma, Emma feared that every celebration with her family would be the last. And if this was going to be her last Christmas, it was going to be the best.

That's what she wanted the defenders of morcellation to understand. Power morcellators had dramatically altered her life clock. Stage one cancer is manageable, stage four a monster.

"This is ridiculous," Russell ranted while Emma shopped for gifts online. "The system has to change. This is all wrong."

"First let's stop morcellation," Emma said. "Then we can address the system."

"How can there be no specific data? There is a clear causal link between the surgery and the spread of cancer."

"Because there is no continued care," Emma said. "Think about it. I went to Nicole Stein for my hysterectomy. From her end, it was a successful procedure. The cancer was an incidental and unfortunate finding, so she referred me to Tyler Wilson in oncology, essentially passing me off."

"But the procedure couldn't then be considered successful," Russell fought.

Emma took a break from looking at a very complex Lego Batman set and looked at Russell. "You don't have to tell me that," she said. "I'm just saying that you can't expect doctors to report something if they don't feel that anything is wrong."

"Adverse reporting should be mandatory. Period," Russell said sternly. "The fact that it's up to doctors to decide what they report and what they don't is ridiculous. People are being harmed, women sentenced to death from a medical system failure."

"Good luck trying to change that," Emma said, though she didn't have any doubt that if anyone could do it, Russell would be the one.

When he'd set out to stop morcellation from her bedside, Emma had her doubts. Russell was taking on one of the largest medical establishments in the country. When the hospital and their fellow colleagues had dismissed and discounted him, she'd lost hope. But Russell persevered. He didn't let a few insults and warnings stop him. The controversy only fueled his fire. Now he had a voice. He had people listening. The topic of morcellation was being discussed, people were asking questions. If Russell could amass that level of awareness in such a short amount of time, there was no telling what he could achieve.

"The FDA is looking into it. They're trying to compile their own data and information," Russell said. "There's no way they can't ban the use of power morcellators. They can't claim to be an agency for the protection of the American people and let this keep happening to women."

"I wish it were that simple," Emma said. "But you and I both know there is a lot of money at stake here. The hospitals are biased by the prestige of minimally invasive surgery. Kendal Slate has an entire building dedicated to the advancement of robotic technique. People come from all over the world to train here for that specific reason. That is hundreds of millions of dollars. Obviously, a few of us are acceptable losses when it means that type of financial gain."

"It's not right," Russell said. "I don't care what the numbers are. Women shouldn't be subjected to suffer the brutality of disease progression when it is upstaged that way."

"I agree," Emma said. "Do you think Jacob is more into Batman or Superman?"

Russell glanced up from his computer with the most perplexed look on his face. He was so focused on morcellation that he couldn't spare a thought for anything else. Emma, however, chose to be fully present in her family, interacting with the kids, experiencing life the way it should've been done this whole time. She was not going to let the disease take her from her family one second sooner than it had to.

"I think Batman," she said to Russell. "Or maybe we'll get him both. Yep. Why should he have to choose?" Emma added both Lego sets to her shopping cart. "Now for Jocelyn. Have any suggestions?"

Russell looked up at her again. She could have been speaking Chinese as far as he was concerned.

"Come on Scrooge," she said. "Have a heart."

Russell's heart was the problem. Every day it broke a little more for Emma and what their life had become. She was his life, his love. Being a surgeon didn't matter anymore. The hospital could disappear for all he cared. Saving his wife was all that mattered. How was he supposed to go back to work in the new year and walk among the monsters who had witnessed and been complicit in the assault of his wife?

RICHARD

"We have to get something for the boys," Elaine said to Richard, panicked. "Something big. I'm thinking maybe sibling puppies."

"What?" Richard's neck snapped quickly in Elaine's direction. "I thought you were done shopping. I don't think the pool house can hold any more gifts."

It was just like Elaine to wait until three days before Christmas to demand something outlandish for the boys.

"I was," she said, looking like she was about to cry. "I had everything here and wrapped."

"So why do we need something big?" Richard asked, thinking of how limited his Christmases had been growing up. "Didn't you get the scooter things? Do the boys not want them anymore?"

"They're electro boards and I did manage to get my hands on two," she replied. "The boys really want them but apparently some of them are catching fire."

"Are they being recalled?" Richard asked.

"Not right now. Right now there's just been a warning issued. I saw a clip of a tree going up in flames because of an electro board. I don't know if it's a good idea to give them to the boys. But they're going to be heartbroken if they don't get them, so I was thinking puppies might help."

"Do you know what kind of work puppies are, Elaine?" Richard had to ask.

"They're probably no different than twins," she replied quickly. "And I managed to do just fine with them."

"How serious is the problem with the boards?" Richard asked. "Are they all catching fire?"

"No, just a couple have been reported."

"So we don't know if the ones you bought will."

"No, but I don't think that's a risk I want to take."

Richard rolled his eyes. One malfunction and consumers were up in arms. "Do you want to throw them out? Give them away? I'm sure you could post them online and get double what you paid for them."

"I don't think it would be nice to donate to a family in need," Elaine said. "Heaven forbid their house or apartment were to catch fire. But I certainly wouldn't want to throw away sixteen hundred dollars either."

"Sixteen hundred dollars?" Richard practically choked on the cost.

"Well, they're normally five hundred," she replied. "But they were marked up to eight."

"You paid almost double?" Richard asked. "Just so the boys could have them for Christmas?"

"They really want them," Elaine defended. "It's all they asked for."

"If that's all they really wanted, then why could our pool house pass for Santa's workshop?"

"Why are you being such a Scrooge? It's Christmas. We can afford the boards and we can afford two puppies," she spat.

"It's not about what we can afford," Richard said. "It's about what makes sense."

"I don't know why I even ask your opinion," she said. "I should've just gotten the dogs, but I thought you'd want to have some input, maybe even help me pick them out."

"If you want to get dogs, get dogs," he said. "But if you already got the boys what they wanted, give them what you got. You don't have to get anything else."

"But what if they catch the house on fire?"

"Then they catch the house on fire!" Richard yelled. Elaine looked at him in what he could only describe as pure horror. He didn't care—he'd reached his tipping point and there was no going back. The medical community was under fire because a doctor and his wife were scaring women into believing that surgery could give them cancer. Now his wife was too scared to give their sons a present because it might or might not catch fire. He was sick and tired of people jumping on a bandwagon they didn't fully understand.

"Isn't that the Christmas spirit," Elaine said. "I don't know what has gotten into you, Richard, but you better snap out of it. We are going to have a good Christmas whether you like it or not."

When had he lost control? He'd thought he had it all, reached his goals, his destiny. Yet, with Elaine scowling at him from across the room and the pressure he was under at work, he no longer felt in control. If he didn't get it together, he'd be on the outside looking in at what once was his ideal life.

ADDISON

Addison climbed into bed, dressed in her favorite fleece pajamas and snuggled up next to Keith. It had been a good final day before the break. The kids weren't well behaved by any means, but it was a half day leading up to a two-week break and Addison had already partially checked out.

After bidding the kids adieu for the holidays, Addison went to the gym and pushed herself to run thirteen miles. The winter break always took a toll on her waistline, she'd yet to try a cookie she didn't like, so she wanted to kick start her metabolism before going into fourteen days of endless eating.

Thirteen miles would've intimidated her before her training, even made her vomit. But since she'd been following the regimen she'd found online, her stamina had increased dramatically, surprising even her. It took a little less than two and half hours to get to thirteen miles, but Addison felt great. That is, until she realized the negative impact the surgery could have on her training. She'd come too far to let it all go to waste.

"Don't be mad, okay?" Addison rested her head on Keith's chest. "But I did something today."

"Okay," Keith said hesitantly.

"And it's really important to me, so I want you to listen with an open mind."

Keith wrapped his arm around Addison, pulling her closer. "This doesn't sound good."

"It's actually really good. At least I think it's going to be good."

"What is it?" Keith asked.

"I signed us up for a marathon," she blurted out quickly. "In South Carolina. February fourteenth."

"What?" Keith let go of Addison and pushed himself up on the bed.

"I know it sounds a little crazy," she said.

"You could say that," he quipped.

"I was thinking about my surgery and how hard we've been training. I'd just hate to see it go to waste."

"So you signed us up for a marathon in a month and a half?"

Addison sat up next to Keith and looked him directly in the eyes. "We can do it. I'll be ready and I know you're already good to run."

"Addison…"

"Please," she begged. "It'll be fun."

"Not very romantic," he said.

"I don't know about that," she replied. "I'm sure we'll both be sore. We might need to treat each other to a nice hot bath and gentle massage."

"I feel like I could treat you to a nice hot bath and gentle massage here, in Pennsylvania," he said. "No need to travel or push our bodies to their physical limit."

"A marathon is hardly our limit," Addison said.

"I don't know why you're trying to convince me if you've already signed us up. I'm guessing there's no refund policy."

"No," Addison said. "That's why I did it. I can't change my mind."

"Or mine apparently," Keith added.

Addison leaned in and kissed him on the cheek. "It's going to be great."

"We'll see about that," Keith said.

"Next year is going to be a great year for us," she said. "I just know it."

DALE

It was hard for Dale to get out of bed on December twenty-fifth. It was hard to find the motivation, the will to do anything other than lie in bed all day. The girls had each invited him to spend Christmas Eve at their respective houses so that he could partake in the Christmas morning magic. He graciously declined, saying it wouldn't be fair to pick one family to stay with. The truth was, he wanted the morning to himself, to wallow in his misery.

When he couldn't stand to stay in bed a minute longer, Dale forced his body to get up. The house was cold and his old bones ached from years of manual labor. Once dressed, he made his way downstairs to the kitchen where he brewed a single cup of coffee. For almost forty years their house had been transformed into a winter wonderland every December. Not this year. Dale couldn't bring himself to open one box of Christmas memories. Besides, Cindy was the creative genius behind the decorations. Dale was just the manpower. There was no tree, no lights, not even a wreath on the front door.

"It's depressing, Dad," Gail had voiced her concern, offering to decorate with him. "I'm sure we could put this place together the way Mom liked."

Dale shook his head.

"She did that for you girls, for the grands. It's a lot of work and I just don't feel like it this year."

"But Mom would've wanted you to decorate, to carry on her Christmas traditions."

"Did she tell you that?" Dale asked. "Did she make it a point to tell you all the things she wanted for me after she died?" Gail didn't respond.

"I'm sorry," Dale said after a couple of minutes of awkward silence. "This is just really hard for me right now. Knowing what I know about her surgery, I just can't help but think that I could've stopped it somehow, protected her. And if I had, she might, she would be here with us right now."

"You can't do that to yourself, Dad," Gail said. "You did the best you could. Everyone knows that."

Dale knew better. Cindy would've been home for Christmas had he taken an interest in her medical care. The house would've been decorated and she would've been with him in the kitchen, where a full pot of coffee would've been brewing instead of a single, sad serving.

After drinking his coffee in silence, Dale bundled up and took Cindy's urn out on the front porch. It hadn't snowed like the weathermen forecasted, but it was a frigid twenty-three degrees.

"Merry Christmas, my love," he said, cradling the silver encasement of his wife. "It's a cold one today but no snow. I'm not going to lie, I was kind of hoping you'd send me some snow today. I mean, if anyone could make magic up where you are, it's you. I know the grands would get a kick out of a white Christmas. We haven't had one for ages.

"I miss you. So much. Especially today. You made my Christmas every year. I guess I never fully appreciated it until today. You were a gem, Cindy. I don't know how much longer I can do this without you."

Dale stayed on the porch until his last toe went completely numb.

"I gotta go see the grands," he said hesitantly. "I promised the girls I would. Don't be mad, but I'm just giving out cash this year. Wasn't much in the shopping mood. Not that I ever was. I love you, lady. Always have and always will. Can't wait to be with you again. Merry Christmas."

The tears streaming down Dale's face felt like icicles tearing up his rough skin as he walked back inside. Every part of him was chilled, right down to his aching, broken heart. Once inside, he kindled a fire and sat in his recliner holding the urn tight. The warm fire lured him back to sleep as it thawed his frozen body.

Sleep was proving to be a cruel novelty for Dale. When he was tired of dealing with the stress of living life without Cindy, sleep offered a break. Yet, often, when he did drift off, he was transported back to life with Cindy. Christmas morning was no different.

In his dream, Dale was walking through his house just as it was when they'd first bought it. The room-to-room wallpaper seemed so real that he reached to touch it. The smell coming from the kitchen as Cindy stood by the stove instantly brought pangs of hunger to his belly.

"God, you're beautiful," he said.

Cindy turned with a smile. "Oh please," she said. "My hair needs a washing and Gail just spit up all over my sweater."

"You wear it well," he replied.

"What has gotten into you?" she asked.

"I just want you to know I love you," Dale said, his voice catching in his throat.

"I love you too, honey," she replied. "Come here and taste this, let me know if I have the sauce right."

The spice of the chili sauce hit Dale's tongue just the way he loved. In all his life he'd never had chili like Cindy's.

"It all comes down to the peppers," she'd said. "You have to be selective to give it the right kick."

Dale took in every ounce of Cindy's beauty, the sound of her voice. Once he became aware in his dream that he was dreaming, he was cruelly ripped out of sleep. Dale awoke in his recliner, facing Cindy's vacant, matching chair. For the first time since Cindy had passed, he sobbed uncontrollably. There was no way he'd be able to make it to brunch today. No way at all.

Dale rose to throw more wood on the fire. Once the flames came back to life, he picked up the phone to call Becca. Before he could dial Becca's number, something caught his attention outside of the window. He pressed the number four. The first flakes drifted slowly past the window. He pressed the number nine. More flakes fell. As he pressed each subsequent number, the soft white snow came faster and harder, almost urgently. Dale hung up, shaking his head.

"Fine, I'll go," he said aloud. "But only because I love you."

She was stubborn, even in death. He'd thought that once he agreed to go, the snow would stop. But it didn't. The snow blanketed Goodnoe that afternoon. As the flakes fell and the temperature dropped, Dale finally felt warm, surrounded by the winter wonderland of Cindy's love.

EMMA AND RUSSELL

"It's snowing!" Jacob yelled as he busted through Emma and Russell's bedroom door, waking Emma, Russell, Hope and Jocelyn who were all snuggled together. "And Santa came!" His excitement was unmistakable and quickly transferred to the younger girls.

Hope popped up. "Santa?"

"Santa?" Jocelyn repeated.

"Can we go open presents?" Jacob asked.

"Where's Kaitlin?" Emma asked.

"She's still sleeping," Jacob said.

"Go get her up and we can go downstairs," Russell said, his voice conveying exhaustion.

Jacob turned toward the door. "KAITLIN!" he yelled loud enough for their whole street to hear. "GET UP!"

"Merry Christmas," Emma said to everyone in her bed. She kissed each of the girls on the top of the head.

"Merry Christmas," they echoed happily, pronouncing it as best they could.

"Merry Christmas," Russell said.

"What time did you come to bed?" Emma asked, noticing the bags under Russell's eyes.

"About an hour ago," he replied.

"She's up," Jacob came running back in. "Let's go, let's go."

Emma sat up and slid her feet into the slippers next to her bed. "If only he could be this animated for school."

It was a cruel joke to have a white Christmas this year. Every December, Emma hoped for snow on Christmas so that the kids could experience a true white Christmas, like the many she'd enjoyed as a child. While some years they got close with a couple of flurries, nothing ever stuck to the ground. Of course this year, when her world was anything but perfect, the snow fell abundantly.

RICHARD

"Puppies!" the boys exclaimed in unison.

"What?" Elaine feigned surprise.

"We got puppies!" Ethan said.

Elaine turned to look at Richard as if to say, "I told you so." He turned his attention out the window to the picturesque landscape of white hills.

"If it keeps falling like this, we may not be able to go to your sister's."

"It'll be fine," Elaine said. "That's why we have an SUV."

"Yes, for the one time a year the snow accumulates to anything more than an inch. That's why you wanted the SUV."

"Not on Christmas," she said. "Please."

Richard stood up and walked toward the kitchen as the boys began fighting over the puppies, each wanting the same one. *You had to get two*, he thought. *God forbid they're forced to share.* In the kitchen, he poured himself a large cup of coffee. Elaine had been at odds with him lately, but that didn't stop her from making a good pot of coffee.

"Electro boards," he heard Eli exclaim from the family room.

He knew Elaine would cave. There was no way she wouldn't give her boys the gift that everyone wanted because of a potential safety risk. Besides, if they did happen to catch fire and damage anything of hers, she'd be the first to sue.

"You have to ask your father," he heard her say to the boys.

Richard took a long, warm sip of coffee, enjoying the temporary silence before the boys bounded in the kitchen, each holding what appeared to be a glorified skateboard.

"Mom said we can try these in the house," Eli said.

"I said if it's okay with Daddy," she walked in behind the boys.

"Where are the puppies?" Richard asked.

"I put them in their crate," Elaine said.

"Can we, Dad?" Ethan pleaded.

"Aren't they meant for outside?" Richard asked.

"But it's snowing," Ethan said. "Come on, please?"

"Fine," Richard said. "But if anything breaks, including your bones, they're going in the trash."

The boys were out of the kitchen before Richard even finished talking. He turned and looked at Elaine.

"Don't even," she said. "I spoke with Maddy and she got one for Doug and Mary."

"And you couldn't have her show you up on Christmas?" Richard said spitefully.

"I didn't want the boys feeling bad," she said. "Besides, Maddy said they're not that dangerous."

"Did she get an engineering degree between Thanksgiving and now that I didn't know about?" Richard asked.

"Very funny," Elaine said.

"I'm serious," Richard said. "Guaranteed the ER is flooded with injuries from those boards today."

"Well let's be grateful you're not working," she quipped.

"Yeah," Richard said. "So grateful."

ADDISON

"Looks like Mom's not coming tonight," Addison said, putting her cell phone on the nightstand and rolling back into Keith. "She doesn't like traveling in the bad weather."

"What I hear is that we have absolutely no reason to get out of bed today," Keith said.

"Pretty much," Addison replied. "Unless you want to go out and play in the snow."

"I kind of like where I am right now," Keith said. "Unless you have any objections."

"None at all," Addison said. "This is probably the best way to spend Christmas that I can think of."

"What do you think about grilled cheese and tomato soup for dinner?" Keith asked.

"Beats the chicken, mashed potatoes and salad I had planned," Addison said. "But I still want the mousse I made for dessert."

"Absolutely," Keith said with a chuckle. "We'll get into that tonight for sure."

"Do you think she's using the weather as an excuse not to come?" Addison asked.

"How did we go from chocolate mousse back to your Mom?" Keith asked.

"Sorry," Addison said. "She still sounded a little upset with me and I wonder if she's avoiding me."

"That might not be the worst thing right now," Keith said.

"Keith," Addison shot defensively.

"I'm serious," he said. "I'd like to have a nice holiday with you. Things are going good right now. It might be kind of nice not to have your mom casting doubt on everything you do. Have you told her about the marathon in South Carolina?"

"Not yet," Addison said. "Like I said, I think she's avoiding me."

"You know she'd probably try to talk you out of that too," Keith said. "Tell you you're not ready. Find some obscure statistic or thing that could kill you as a first-time marathon runner."

He was right. Addison loved her mother dearly, but sometimes it felt like her mom feared the world—and Addison's resolution for the upcoming new year was to stop making decisions based on fear.

DALE

The girls were all on board to do a run in Cindy's honor. Carmen, leading the charge, ignited their desire to take a stand and spread awareness about the dangers of morcellation. Becca loved the idea and was all about heading up the organizational aspect. Gail, always the most sensible daughter, had asked if an organized run was a bit much.

"I'm not saying not to do a run honoring Mom," she'd said over Christmas dessert. "I'm just saying that I've run a couple of races and they're a big production. You need a place to do it, a person to time it, cops."

"We can make it however laid-back we want," Carmen replied, a bit defensively. "I doubt we'll have to worry about too much."

"It'll be fine," Becca reassured. "Between the three of us, I don't see it being a problem."

Dale smiled at his girls, knowing it was going to be an interesting couple of months. Like any children close in age, Becca and Gail often butted heads. There was a level of competition between the two of them that didn't exist with Carmen. And because Carmen was so much younger, Becca and Gail habitually discounted her ideas.

"We'll see what happens," Dale said. "If we can do it, great. If it gets to be too much, we'll think of something else."

"We're doing the run, Dad," Carmen said. "I've already selected a date, May twenty-second. I want to do it on Mom's birthday."

He should've known that once Carmen was set on a track it was difficult, if not impossible, to derail her. He admired her tenacity and meant what he said about doing everything possible to support her. For nearly forty years he'd put everything into Cindy, making sure she had what she needed to consider her life a success. With her gone, he planned to dump whatever he had left into his daughters, feeling culpable in robbing them of a mother for the rest of their adult lives.

EMMA AND RUSSELL

Emma stood in front of the bathroom mirror, looking at her long, sandy, thinning hair. No matter how well she'd mentally prepared for chemotherapy, nothing could prepare her for waking up and seeing clumps of hair on her pillow.

Russell walked into the bathroom and stood behind her. "You ready to do this?"

"I guess so," she replied, running her fingers through her hair one last time. "Can you call the kids in?"

"Why do you want them in here?"

Emma opened the bottom vanity drawer and removed the hair clippers. "Because I don't want them to wake up tomorrow and be scared."

"Okay," Russell replied with hesitation.

It was important for Hope and Jocelyn to see Emma's transformation more so than Jacob and Kaitlin. Jocelyn still twirled Emma's hair at night when Emma rocked her. What was she going to do to soothe herself when Emma didn't have any hair to twist around her tiny fingers? In all of her worrying about how chemo would affect her, Emma hadn't stopped to think about how it might affect the kids.

Emma had dreaded starting chemo since she heard the words, "you have cancer." She'd seen plenty of what cancer did to its many victims, witnessed how the treatment often wreaked as much havoc as the disease itself. Sometimes, in her darkest of moments, Emma wished she didn't have the medical knowledge she possessed. The hours of study and practice so that she could be the best physician possible also made it hard for her to hope for a cure. Had she been a financial analyst like her one sister or a teacher like her mother, she'd be able to hold on to some level of hope because she wouldn't be able to fully grasp what she was up against. But she did. And so did Russell. LMS didn't typically respond to chemo, but what other option did she have? She'd poison her body, lose her hair, anything to give her a chance at survival.

Emma heard the ruckus before she saw the kids. They traveled as quietly as a stampede of elephants as they came barreling into the bathroom.

"You sure you want to do this?" Russell asked. "Tonight?"

When Emma had told him she wanted to shave her head on New Year's Eve, he thought it was a bit hasty. But Emma insisted.

"If I'm going to go bald, it's going to be when I decide."

Russell didn't put up any resistance after that. Whatever she wanted.

Emma looked at her reflection, the reflection of her beautiful children and husband. It was so unfair. She put her hair in a ponytail one last time and handed Russell the scissors. Kaitlin watched in horror as Russell cut fifteen inches of long, once-vibrant hair in one swift clip.

"Oh, no," Jocelyn exclaimed.

This is really happening, Emma thought as the clippers vibrated against her skull. *I have cancer.* Emma bit down hard on her lip as her scalp felt the cool air. If she cried, she'd upset the kids. They couldn't start their new year seeing their mother lose it, so instead she smiled.

As the ball dropped in Times Square at midnight, Russell closed his eyes, vowing to see his wife recover in the new year, no matter what it took. Emma said a silent prayer that she'd survive the year and be around for next year's New Year's Eve. At the stroke of midnight they kissed, both holding it a little longer, both afraid of the possibility that it could be their last.

JANUARY

RICHARD

The new year brought a slew of new emails from Russell Speck. The most recent, a link to an article about a hospital in Philadelphia that decided to stop morcellation altogether.

"Unable to guarantee the safety of our patients, even with the utilization of containment bags, we have decided to stop using power morcellators until further research can be done," the Chief Operating Officer was quoted as saying.

It was only a matter of time before Kendal Slate would have to change their practice of morcellation, no matter how foolish Richard believed the decision to be. The FDA was in the midst of organizing an official hearing to review the approval status of power morcellators, and the risks they posed during laparoscopic abdominal procedures. They'd already issued a statement advising against the use of morcellators when malignancy was suspected or could not be ruled out.* The cards were beginning to fall, and not in favor of Kendal Slate's position.

The insurance companies were the next to take notice of Russell's campaign. They, too, were questioning their costs associated with power morcellation, some even refusing coverage for laparoscopic procedures involving power morcellators. Money was the driving force behind the decisions being made, not ethics. The hospitals jumping on board didn't want to deal with lawsuits and the insurance companies didn't want to incur any additional costs if, in fact, cancer was upstaged. Russell's smear campaign was working and with the FDA involved, there was nothing Richard could do to stop it.

Richard was reading Russell's latest email when Nancy tapped on his door.

* The FDA issued an advisory against the use of power morcellators on April 17, 2014, stating the risk of spreading undetected malignancies in women to be 1 in 350.

"Yes," he said, annoyed.

"I have a Janine on the phone for you."

"Janine?"

"She said you'd know who she was."

Richard rolled his eyes. Why wouldn't his ex-wife pop up out of blue and decide to call him?

"Tell her I'm not available and ask her if she wants to leave a message," he instructed.

"I did when she called before," Nancy said. "But she's insisting on talking to you directly."

"Tell her I'm not available," Richard repeated. "If she doesn't want to leave a message, that's on her."

"Okay," Nancy replied with a tone conveying her disagreement.

Janine didn't leave a message, just as Richard had expected. Whatever she was dealing with would pass and she'd give up. However, he'd also thought that about Russell.

ADDISON

For five days, Addison eluded the stress of her mother, work and her health, enjoying a much-needed break on the ski slopes. Physically, she'd never felt better. And when she was on top of the mountains, she'd never felt so free.

"Maybe we can quit our jobs and move here," she'd said to Keith on the last day of their stay. "We can be instructors."

"Do you think we're that good?" he asked. "I'm not sure I want to be responsible for getting someone down the mountain."

"You have no problem dealing with people's entire life savings, but teaching them the basics of how to ski is what makes you nervous? I'm just thinking how amazing it would be to work outside every day, in the fresh air."

"And what about the summers?" he asked. "You know the slopes are only open a couple of months a year."

"We could find some seasonal work somewhere else, like the beach," she offered.

"So what, we'd live like the retired people who spend their winters in Florida?"

"Exactly!" Addison exclaimed. "Except we'd be the opposite. We'd stay where it was cold."

Keith laughed and shook his head. Addison was kidding—she'd never move that far away from her mother despite their many issues—but he was also a little concerned. Since deciding on the surgery, she'd made a couple of rash decisions. Plenty of people wanted to run a marathon. But to train like crazy, and then sign up for one states away, all in four months? Just before they'd left for the ski trip, she'd talked about getting a dog.

It was obvious Addison was attempting to fill the void of children in her life. A marathon, a dog, and now she wanted to forgo her tenure to teach ski lessons. He was familiar with what discontent looked like. He'd experienced plenty in his past relationship. Nothing was ever good enough for Tina. That's what had been so appealing about Addison when they'd first met. She was happy with life. Despite growing up with just her mother, Addison never complained. She didn't blame her shortcomings on not having a father around. In fact, she often said it was what made her who she was.

"If he'd been around, I might be a completely different person. And who knows, maybe we wouldn't be together," she'd said. "So if not having my father around led me to you, I wouldn't change it for the world. Besides, based on what my mom said, he was quite a jerk."

That was her attitude before the miscarriages, before she knew life wasn't going to pan out the way she'd envisioned. Not having a father was a misfortune at best, not having children, unthinkable. Deep down, Keith feared that her dissatisfaction with how life was turning out would eventually point to him. He was happy when Tina finally admitted he couldn't give her the life she wanted. Having those words come from Addison would devastate him.

"A run?" Russell asked.

"Yes," Dale said. "My daughter says it's a good way to raise awareness."

"We could raise more than awareness," Russell replied. "We could raise money for research. You know, there's no federal funding for LMS research."

"I don't know anything about funding," Dale said. "I told my daughter that the hospital did wrong by Cindy and she said we had to do something, tell people. So she wants to do a run."

"That's a great idea," Russell said.

"I see the FDA is warning against morcellation," Dale said.

"A warning is nothing," Russell said. "Women are still getting morcellated every day. We need to stop the assault."

"Seems like you're on the right path," Dale said.

"We'll see," Russell said. "The word is spreading. If we can get a big turnout for the race, maybe some media coverage."

"I wouldn't expect much. It's just my girls' way of doing something."

"It's a great idea," Russell said. "I think it could turn into something big."

Dale hung up with Russell feeling more pressure about the race than he'd wanted to. Maybe he shouldn't have told Russell, kept it a small family thing for the first year. Who knows if it would even go past that, if they would raise any money? Now he'd included Russell who was all about funding LMS research. Dale didn't know the first thing about charity and donations.

Cindy was always good about donating money and time. "We're so blessed," she'd say. "It only makes sense to pay it forward." It was Dale who was the crabby one, always making excuses why others didn't need his handouts or why he didn't have an extra hour a week to help strangers. For years, Dale had hung up on callers, ignored petitioners at his door. What a strange twist of fate that he would be the one asking strangers to join his cause.

Emma and Russell

"You sure you're ready to do this?" Emma, nauseated in bed, asked Russell as he got dressed. It was his first day back to work after taking leave to care for Emma, and the way he was moving showed his apprehension.

She'd hoped to feel well enough to get up with him, cook a nice breakfast, send him off. But the effects of the chemotherapy and the treatments that went along with it had worn her down. Today was nausea day. Nausea day was not to compare to the day after the injection she was given to help promote the growth of healthy white blood cells in her body. Those days she swore she could feel the white blood cell stimulation occurring inside her bone marrow. The constant reverberation within her bones was unrelenting. And just as the bone pain would subside, came the onset of the nausea, only to be replaced by neuropathy in her hands. She loved braiding the girls' hair. But since starting chemo, Emma was lucky if she could manage simple ponytails.

"Not especially," Russell said. "How can I go back and work with these people after what they've done to you, to us?"

"Because you're better than they are."

Russell knew the only reason the hospital hadn't fired him was legal risk and bad press. He could only imagine the headlines Alyson Baker would write about a hospital firing a promising surgeon after they'd upstaged his wife's cancer. The media would be all over that. He kind of wished they would fire him, but at the same time he wanted to operate, show the hospital he wasn't crazy.

"Are you sure you're okay here?" he asked. "I can postpone another week or so."

"I'll be fine," Emma said, knowing exactly how the next seventy-two hours would play out. She'd stay in bed during the worst of the nausea and force herself downstairs to endure the rest with the kids. She was stronger, braver with her babies around, pulling her strength from their love.

Sara was a Godsend. Between her and Emma's parents, the kids weren't neglected one bit. Russell's parents came on the weekends to help, but during the week, when Emma's symptoms were the worst, she was very selective about who she wanted around.

The social awkwardness associated with having cancer continued during Emma's chemotherapy treatments and was made worse by her physical appearance. When she'd first been diagnosed, the friends and family who came to support her might not have known what to say, but they could look her in the eyes. Once she'd shaved her head and lost her hair, eyebrows included, she noticed people were more hesitant to look directly at her.

Russell walked over to the bed and kissed her on the forehead. "Do you need anything?" he asked. "Have you taken the Zofran?"

Emma nodded.

"Not helping much?"

She shrugged.

"Call me if you need anything. I love you."

"I love you," Emma whispered.

Russell wasn't out of the bedroom before Emma's eyes closed. In the doorway, he stopped and looked back at her.

"Stop it," she said with her eyes still closed.

"What?" he asked.

"Staring at me like it's the last time you're going to see me."

"I'm admiring your beauty," he said.

"You're full of it," she said, a small smile forming on her face. She opened her eyes for a quick glance. "Now go to work. Good luck."

"Surgeons don't need luck. We have skill," Russell said, heading towards the stairs. If only he believed that.

Russell's apprehension increased on the drive to the hospital. He couldn't think of a time he had ever been nervous walking into Kendal Slate. The hospital was his playground. Even during residency he knew he belonged there. Today, however, he was anxious.

For the most part, he hadn't seen anyone since his last shift. When he and Emma met with Richard Oakley, they'd essentially been escorted directly to Richard's office and then back out of the hospital. Hell, Richard Oakley had a representative from legal sitting in his office. What was to await Russell when he returned?

I'm not on the surgical board was the first thing that hit Russell when he checked his schedule for the day. The surgical board kept track of all surgeries taking place at Kendal Slate on any given day. The OR time blocks, surgeons scheduled to operate, and patient names were all organized and updated in real time throughout the day. *What am I supposed to do if I'm not on the board?* Not being scheduled to operate was a low move and one that could have only been orchestrated by Richard Oakley. Taking the operating room away from a surgeon was an act of aggression. Russell wasn't about to let it slide.

RICHARD

"I'm not on the board," Russell stated as he walked into Richard's office, unannounced.

Richard looked up from his desk. "Russell. Welcome back."

"You can save the pleasantries, Richard. I know what you're doing."

"And what is that?" Richard asked. He'd be lying if he said he didn't enjoy seeing the flustered look on Russell's face.

"You're forcing me out," Russell said.

Richard laughed. "Forcing you out?"

"Yes," Russell spat. "How else would you explain not having me scheduled for any surgeries?"

"A strategic one for the hospital and a safety one for our patients. You, of all people, should understand our concern for patient safety."

Russell appeared too furious for words.

"For starters, we weren't sure if you were going to make it in today. Secondly, you haven't operated since taking leave in October. Given the scrutiny the hospital is under for patient care, it was decided to let you work your way back into the surgical rotation."

"You've got to be kidding me," Russell said.

Richard didn't respond.

"You can't do this."

"Technically, I can. Furthermore, I don't have to explain my decisions to you. If you don't mind, I have a department to run."

As if on cue, Richard's phone rang. Russell stared Richard down as he reached for the phone.

"Richard Oakley," Richard said and pointed to the door. Russell shook his head and stormed out. Richard smiled until he heard the shrill come through the phone.

"She called the house looking for you, Richard."

"What?" he asked.

"She called the house, *my* house."

"Janine?" Richard guessed. There was only one person Elaine would refer to as *she* with such contempt.

"Yes," Elaine replied. "Why is *she* calling *my* house?"

"How should I know?" Richard asked.

"Have you been talking with her?" Elaine asked. "Are you sleeping with her?"

"Elaine, please," Richard said. "Don't be ridiculous. I have no idea why she's calling, probably because she knew it would get a rise out of you."

"How would she know that, Richard?"

Richard knew better than to fall into that trap. "I don't know why she's calling. Just ignore her and she'll go away."

"That's your answer for everything, isn't it? Things don't go your way, just ignore it?"

"What are you talking about?" he asked, getting annoyed.

"Forget it," Elaine spat. "You better not be lying to me. You better not be talking to her. You promised."

Richard sighed. "I haven't talked to her in years. If she calls again, don't answer. Or answer and ask her what she wants. I really don't care."

"Of course you don't," Elaine said, slamming the phone down.

When Richard had left Janine, it was a clean break. Elaine didn't want any competition, especially from a baby, and he didn't want any baggage.

"It'll be easier," Elaine reasoned when she encouraged him to walk away from his daughter. "My parents were divorced, and I wished my dad had just left instead of them constantly fighting over me."

It wasn't his proudest moment, but Richard fell for the justification. He didn't want complicated. He wanted the freedom to practice medicine and come and go as he pleased. A wife and kid weren't freedom. He'd actually been foolish enough to believe that Elaine was, his first in a line of many mistakes.

ADDISON

"Less than a month to go, baby," Addison jumped on Keith to wake him up. "Time for the eighteen miler."

"Eighteen miles?" Keith whined. "Today?"

"Don't act like I didn't tell you last night," she said.

Keith rolled over, pulling the comforter up around him. "I didn't think you were serious."

"I've never been more serious in my life," she said. "Let's go. Get up. Get up. Get up."

"Addy, what time is it?"

"Nine o'clock."

"Oh," he said. He'd hoped she'd say something ridiculous like seven a.m. so he could mount a defense as to why it was absurd to wake up so early on the weekend, especially to run eighteen miles. Nine left him with no rebuttal.

Four hours later, Addison and Keith returned home, sweaty and exhausted. She'd wanted to keep their pace to an eleven-minute mile, similar to her runs on the treadmill, but outside, first thing in the morning was rough. Not being able to set their speed mechanically made it easier to fall behind.

It was cold, but not bad for the middle of January. The weather this winter had been so bizarre. It went from snowing on Christmas day to being close to sixty a week later. Since then, the temperature had declined steadily, but never dropped to anything too unbearable.

"How are you feeling?" Addison asked as they stretched on the floor of the living room.

"Let's see—my hands are frozen, my lungs are burning, and my legs feel like Jell-O. I feel great. How about you?"

Addison laughed. Her frozen hands were the color of raw salmon. "I feel terrific," she boasted. "We just ran eighteen miles. Eighteen! You know, I had my concerns about running a marathon, but not after today."

"Is there a time limit?" Keith asked.

"I think it's six hours," Addison said.

Six hours of running made Keith want to throw in the towel right then and there. They'd just run for close to four. He couldn't imagine adding another mile after that, let alone eight. Honestly, he only agreed to train with Addison because he figured she would stop once she realized how long it took. But watching her as she sat on the floor with her dry, pink hands and runny nose, he saw only pure joy and excitement. She wasn't giving up at all. He was going to have to run the marathon in less than a month, all twenty-six point two miles.

Dale was enjoying a cup of coffee on his front porch when Carmen pulled up.

"What are you doing out here? It's freezing," Carmen said, tightening her coat around her neck as she got out of the car.

"This?" Dale said. "This is nothing." He thought of his days building houses after snowfalls. Forty degrees and a warm cup of joe was enjoyable compared to freezing temperatures and ice-slicked wooden beams. "What are you doing here?"

Carmen took a seat besides Dale. "I was out running errands and figured I'd stop by."

"Still concerned I'm going to forget how to care for myself?"

"Always," she said with a smile. "But that's not why I'm here."

"Ok," Dale said, bracing himself. Raising three daughters taught him to be suspicious of the casual drop by. "What's up?"

Carmen shivered and looked toward the house. "Do you mind if we go in?"

Dale smiled. "Of course not." He pushed himself up and walked to the storm door, holding it open for his daughter.

Once inside, Dale walked over to the fireplace and got it going, knowing how much Carmen enjoyed it. She snuggled up on the couch across from the glowing flames, pulling Cindy's quilt around her shoulders. Although she was full grown, Dale still saw Carmen as a baby girl cuddled up on his couch.

"We need to change Mom's webpage," Carmen said.

Dale furrowed his eyebrows. "Change it?"

"Not change it," Carmen corrected. "More like update it."

"Update it how?"

"To talk about the race."

"What do we have to say?" Dale asked.

"Well, we have a date and a location," Carmen said. "I was just thinking it would be a good idea to have a place online where people could go for information."

"So why don't you make your own page for the race?" Dale asked, the thought of messing with what he created not sitting well with him.

"Because we're doing it for Mom," Carmen answered.

"I don't know, Car," Dale said. "I like it the way it is."

"I know you're not a fan of change, Dad," she said. "But we need to get the word out about the race if it's going to be successful. If you already have something set up for Mom, it would be easier to add to it, show what we're doing to remember her."

Dale thought for a moment. The girls were constantly trying to get him to move forward, like his time of grieving was supposed to have come to an end with the new year. Every other week or so, one of them would bring up going through Cindy's belongings or the idea of selling the house. He was pretty sure they'd convinced themselves that he was going to go crazy and start living on cat food. They didn't understand that he didn't want to move on or past his life with Cindy. He was going to live out his years in their house, like he and Cindy were supposed to have done together.

"Okay," Dale agreed, hoping it would show his ability to adapt so that they would back off a bit. "Whatever you want, honey."

FEBRUARY

EMMA AND RUSSELL

One more treatment, Emma thought. One more day of going in, feeling like she was in a sci-fi movie along with the other patients in the treatment room who were attached to machines, receiving their chemotherapy. They were all at different stages, the beginners easily identifiable with their locks still intact and the veterans, like her, sporting different colored bandanas to cover their smooth scalps. Most of the patients were older than Emma. Some of her treatments, she appeared to be the youngest one, which made the ordeal even harder for her. She'd questioned God on those days, asking why he couldn't have waited until her children were grown before turning her body against her. She'd even bargained with him, saying that if he could cure her now, keep her in remission, she'd accept her fate later in life, perhaps in her seventies. Hopefully by then, there'd be a cure for LMS. But at least her babies would be grown.

Viruses, such as HIV, were easier to treat because they were foreign to the body, easier to identify and attack. Cancer, on the other hand, was part of the body. Cells that once functioned normally gone astray and multiplying quickly. How could the body not identify the rogue cells and fight them when it was capable of such incredible things? How had it not been discovered, in all the years of research, how to fight the bad cells without wiping out the good ones?

One more time, Emma thought as she rose from bed. At least she hoped it would be the last time. She hoped the dramatic damage control they'd attempted would be successful in keeping the cancer from returning. Despite the initial reports after her surgery, that there was no evidence of remnant disease, Emma wasn't free. She would be held hostage for the rest of her life by the fear of recurrence. Every three to four months she'd have to have scans, then wait, anxiously, for the results. Her life, once arranged by call schedules and child events, would be partitioned in three-month increments.

"Do you want to ride in with me?" Russell asked as he scurried about the room getting ready.

"No, thanks. My mom is going to take me."

Russell straightened his tie in the mirror, turning to Emma as she made her way to the bathroom. "I'm proud of you," he said.

"There's nothing to be proud of," she replied.

"There's plenty," he said. "You've been through so much, put your body through so much and you've done it all without complaining."

"I've complained plenty," she admitted.

"No you haven't. You're amazing."

"Please," Emma said. "Who are you and what have you done with my husband?"

"I just wanted to let you know I'm proud of you," he said. "What's wrong with that?"

"Don't you have to get to work?" Emma asked, feeling like a fraud. If Russell knew how she thought about her disease, what she felt most days, he might think differently.

"What for?" Russell asked. "To be ignored? Maybe today I might be lucky enough to close a patient."

"I'm sorry," she said, feeling bad for bringing up the hospital. She gave him a lot of credit for not walking out. "I admire you."

"Stop."

"No, I'm serious. Your dedication to women's health should be applauded by the hospital, not discouraged."

"The adversity only reinforces what we're doing. They can do whatever they want to me, but I won't stop until every institution in this country bans power morcellation."

RICHARD

Another one bites the dust, Richard thought as he read yet another article about a renowned hospital abandoning morcellation. Richard felt the pressure. Rather than be forced by the board who would be forced by public perception, it would be better for him to make the decision, retain some level of authority.

He wouldn't ban the practice—he still believed it had a place in gynecologic care. His advisory would be to limit the procedure substantially and ensure containment bags were used at all times. The hospital had already updated its informed consent considerably, but he would also have all patients counseled extensively about power morcellation and the potential for adverse effects prior to surgery.

While Russell liked to paint the picture of morcellation as being black and white, there was a large gray area he neglected to acknowledge. Yes, there were women negatively impacted by power morcellation, but there were also women who wanted the choice. Over the course of the debate, power morcellation had risen to be not only a question of medical procedure, but also women's choice. Who were the hospitals or medical industry to dictate a decision women should be able to make for themselves?

In the beginning, the risks might not have been properly outlined for women to truly understand what could happen if an occult cancer was disseminated in the peritoneum. But now the risks were known. They were even being discussed on talk shows. Women's rights were a hot-button item and Richard, unlike Russell, knew to walk that line with extreme caution. Even though limiting the procedure was the right call, Richard felt like he was losing. And Richard didn't like to lose.

ADDISON

"We're in corral twenty-six," Addison said excitedly, pinning her race bib on the front of her shirt. "Can you believe all these people?"

Her radiant happiness was contagious. Although Keith wasn't looking forward to what they were about to undertake, he was happy to be doing it alongside Addison. He scanned the massive crowd. "It's definitely more than I expected."

"It's great, isn't it? Can you feel the energy?"

"I feel something," he said, talking more about his nerves than energy.

"How many people do you think are here?"

"Well, we're one thousand twenty-six and seven, so maybe fifteen hundred?"

Addison smiled.

The runners were called to their corrals shortly before eight in the morning. Addison prepared her watch so that she could keep track of their pace. Together, they watched as the corrals emptied ahead of them, one at a time, hundreds of people choosing to run twenty-six point two miles on Valentine's Day.

"I love you," Addison squeezed Keith tight as corral twenty-five dispersed.

Keith kissed the top of her head. "I love you," he said. "Now let's do this."

The first three miles went by quickly. Addison and Keith both kept a steady pace behind the five hour pace runner.

"You think we can catch up to the four and half hour pack?" she asked.

"It's worth a shot," Keith said, thinking he'd do whatever it took to finish quicker.

Addison increased her pace until the sign marked four and half hours was within sight. Keith naturally assumed they could settle into that pace and follow it out. He was sadly mistaken. After only two miles in that pack, Addison suggested they bump up to the four-hour pacer. Keith followed her lead, counting down the miles in his head.

At ten miles, they were still on target to finish in four hours. Addison was loving every second of the run. Keith was comfortable in their pace. When they hit the halfway-way mark, thirteen point one miles, they both got excited. They were two hours into the run and felt no pain.

They ran by a water table, grabbing small cups without stopping. They'd made a pact that no matter what, they wouldn't stop. Run the whole way, they'd promised each other. Addison threw the cup on the side of the road with all the other discarded cups.

"This is so fun!" she exclaimed. Keith smiled. "Let's bump up to the next group."

"Let's not overdo it," Keith cautioned. "I like this pace."

"Come on," Addison said. "One more, that's it."

Keith knew better than to let the excitement get the best of him. The back half would be tougher than the first and he wanted to stay where they were comfortable, but Addison wanted to push it. Who was he to stop her?

It took them a bit longer to catch up with the group aiming to finish in three and a half hours, but they did. And the good news was that by the time they did, they only had ten miles left. What was ten miles when they'd already run sixteen?

The excitement and determination to finish at three and half hours was quickly overrun by the effort required to keep an eight-minute mile pace. They were already out of their comfort running a nine-minute mile.

Addison fought to keep up as long as she could—about three miles. When they hit the twenty-mile mark, the reality of their undertaking sank in. Each subsequent mile felt longer and longer, and the pacer for three and a half hours was quickly replaced by four hours and soon after, four-and-a-half.

"We must have missed the twenty-three mile marker," Addison said, out of breath. "It's been too long between markings."

"I don't think so." Keith said, knowing they'd wasted precious energy trying to finish faster than their plan.

Addison pointed ahead. "Oh, there's a marker. It's gotta be twenty-four. Only two point two to go, Babe. We got this."

"We got this," Keith panted.

As they approached the white board with black numbers, Addison's face and pace dropped. "What?" she said in disbelief. "How is this twenty-three?" Keith didn't reply.

The pain in Addison's feet had moved up her legs and was now at her lower back. How could they possibly have three more miles? Suddenly, she was overwhelmed with the urge to cry. Three miles, which used to be nothing, felt undoable, impossible.

"We got this, Babe," Keith said, sensing her falling spirit. "We trained for this."

"It hurts," Addison admitted. "I hurt."

"I know," Keith replied. "I do too. But we can do this."

The five-hour pacer ran past them and Keith could see Addison's resolve diminish. He needed to find something to get her going, to push her forward to the finish line.

"Maybe your mom was right," he said. "Maybe this was too much." Addison, too tired and out of breath to talk, turned and looked at him. Keith shrugged. "I'm just saying."

He wasn't sure if it had worked at first, but after a couple more steps, Addison picked up her speed. In no way were they going to increase their time beyond their current pace, they just weren't going to fall behind any further.

Addison felt struck by lightning from the ground up each time her foot hit the pavement. The pain was excruciating but if she stopped, there was no way she'd finish. People in their sixties were passing them, she didn't care. Her only goal was to cross the finish line.

With a half mile to go, Addison and Keith could hear the applause from the crowd cheering the racers as they approached the finish. Instantly, they were both reenergized. As the inflated arch of the finish line came into sight, Addison smiled. Mentally, she sped up to cross the checkered line and get her medal. Physically, her body refused to go a second faster.

Funneling into the ending chute, Addison and Keith interlocked their hands and practically jumped over the finish line. They'd completed a marathon, together, and in one piece. Addison glanced down at her watch, struggling to catch her breath. Five hours and seventeen minutes.

"We did it," she panted.

"And they didn't even have to close the course on us," Keith said.

"Thank you," Addison replied. "I needed this."

"We'll see if you feel the same way tomorrow," Keith said. "Now, if I remember correctly, you said something about a hot bath and massage?"

DALE

All his life, Dale discounted the phenomenon of a "broken heart." But after Cindy's passing, his chest ached as it never had before. For years, Cindy, a hopeless romantic, tried her best to warm his cold heart. He'd watched the sappy movies, hugging her while she cried, but never once was swayed to believe they were any more than fiction. But then she died and he felt his heart break. Despite the pain in his chest, he was forever grateful to have had the honor of being her husband, even if it had cost him his best friend.

Mickey had been cool at first when Dale and Cindy had gotten together. Along the way, he made a few comments here and there, but never appeared to be jealous of the time Dale spent with Cindy. It wasn't until after the wedding that things changed. Mickey was constantly trying to get Dale to go out to the bar and leave his woman at home. Dale tried to find an even balance, but nothing was ever good enough for Mickey.

The night things came to a head, Cindy had wanted to go out to dinner with her best friend and her husband. Dale, not knowing about her plans, had arranged to go bowling with Mickey. When the conflict had been discovered, Dale tried to cancel but Mickey was relentless and very convincing.

"Tell her you're going out," Mickey had said. "Don't give her the option to say no. Be the man in your relationship and tell your wife to stay home."

"Easy," Dale warned.

"I'm just saying that you're giving her too much say," Mickey said.

"That's how relationships work," Dale said.

"Not mine," Mickey replied.

"And how long do yours last?" Dale asked.

"I'm smart enough to keep 'em short."

"Yeah, well marriages work a little different."

"You never come to the bar anymore. We barely hang out. Just tell her you're going out tonight," Mickey said. "Or does she run your house?"

"Excuse me?" Cindy glared at Dale. She didn't take kindly to him telling her he was in charge of the house. They stood in the kitchen, Cindy at the sink with rubber gloves on, Dale leaning against the fridge.

"What I meant was—"

"I understand exactly what you meant," Cindy replied calmly.

Dale knew he was in trouble. When Cindy raised her voice, a fight would be short-lived. When she stayed calm, it was a different story.

"I'll tell you what. Being that you're the man of the house, you go out and have a good time. Do whatever it is that men of the house do."

Dale didn't trust her offer. When she insisted, he figured it might be good to leave, allowing her time to cool off. He went bowling, but all he could think of was Cindy. Mickey didn't like when Dale called it a night early, so he said some things Dale hoped he hadn't meant. But Dale didn't care. He wanted to get home and apologize.

When Dale arrived home, the house was dark and empty. Usually when he'd gone out, Cindy would wait up for him with the lights on. But she was not home and she'd left no note. Dale drove by every one of her friends' houses. He was relieved to find her at her sister's house.

"I love you," he'd told her in front of her sister and brother-in-law. "I'll scream it for everyone to hear. I'm sorry."

Cindy remained seated on her sister's couch.

Dale kept groveling. "I should've known better than to listen to Mickey. I had a horrible time. All I could think about was you. Tell me what to say to get you to come home, please."

"You mean to tell me the man of the house couldn't stand to be home alone?" she asked.

"I was a jerk," he admitted.

"You were more than a jerk," she corrected.

"I let Mickey—,"

"Don't blame this on Mickey," she interrupted. "Be a man and own up to your mistakes. Mickey is Mickey. You, however, I'm not sure who you were tonight."

"I didn't like coming home without you there," Dale confessed. "I don't ever want to come home with you not there."

"Then don't ever talk to me like that again," she said.

"I swear," Dale replied.

Cindy rose from the couch, hugged her sister and left with Dale. Apart from a few times throughout their marriage, Cindy always waited up for Dale. Now, if he forgot to turn the lights on before going out, he came home to a dark, empty house. Every time he did, he was reminded of that fight and how stupid he'd been. Every time he came home to a desolate house, his heart ached a little more. His heart was broken and time without Cindy was only making it worse.

EMMA AND RUSSELL

One of the hard parts about being given a cancer diagnosis, Emma was coming to learn, was that there was no finality to anything. She hadn't and wouldn't feel the concept of being done since her hysterectomy. She'd thought removing her uterus, while the sad end of her childbearing, would also be the end of pain and bleeding. She could laugh out loud at the thought. The pain was nowhere close to being done. The end of one surgery brought on the beginning of chemo. The end of chemo brought on the beginning of the wait period. The end of each wait period brought on the dreaded scans. The scans would either bring on another waiting period or another phase of treatment. Either way, it was never going to end.

One particular fear that Emma harbored was that her hair would never grow back. Knowing it was unreasonable, she never shared her concern with Russell, thus allowing it to continually dance around in her mind. Emma had no faith any more, especially in the things that once seemed so certain. However, as a dark fuzz appeared on the top of her head, and the once barren skin above her eyes filled in, she experienced what she could only describe as hope. If her hair could grow back after falling out completely, maybe her body would recover just as strongly and fight. The problem was that chemotherapy didn't discriminate between the rapidly growing cells of her hair follicles and the rapidly growing cells of cancer, thus wiping out any quickly multiplying cell in her body. If, once the treatments were done, things started multiplying again, Emma feared the cancer cells would as well.

Prior to chemo, she'd stayed awake at night wondering if she'd be able to handle the poisoning of her system, if she was doing the right thing.

Now that it was over, she stayed awake plagued by what-if's.

Emma had just nodded off after another restless night when Russell's alarm sounded, marking the beginning of another day. He groaned, hit the snooze button and rolled over, wrapping his arms tightly around her. No sooner did their eyes close when Hope sauntered in the room, quickly finding a place next to Emma. Emma, never one to turn the kids away, pulled Hope close and kissed the top of her head.

"Morning angel," she whispered.

"Morning," Hope replied.

The pain shot through Russell, from his eyes where he watched the love pouring from mother to daughter, to his heart, where the love he felt for his wife and child overflowed. It was so unfair. One senseless act and a daughter was denied the mother she once had, the mother she deserved.

Russell had read the responses to the articles in the paper, the ones where women chastised him for taking a stand against something that clearly should be their choice. What those women failed to understand was that when cancer is upstaged, all choice is gone. It's one thing to know the risk and say you're okay with the chances. It's another thing to have to live with the consequences of the worst-case scenario happening.

There were days he wanted to document it all, the surgeries, recoveries, wounds that were still struggling to heal. He wanted to show the world, scare everyone into seeing morcellation for the atrocity it was.

The second time the alarm sounded, Russell got out of bed and prepared for another day of acting like a surgeon. God knows, he wasn't going to practice like one. Hope and Emma remained behind, snuggled up and content under the covers. As he kissed his two girls good-bye, he tried to take a mental picture of the beautiful image before him.

He didn't want to leave, go to a place he was no longer appreciated. He wanted to stay with his wife and mount his campaign. If only he could quit. But cancer treatments were expensive and if he quit, he and his family would have no income and no insurance. He was without a choice.

The hospital looked different to Russell as he approached it now. It was old and drab, not the beacon of greatness he once believed it to be. The revolving doors at the entrance were a bit obnoxious and rather inconvenient. Why couldn't they have regular glass sliders like many other hospitals? Why couldn't they do things, implement change like so many other hospitals? Many of the things Russell once admired about Kendal Slate Memorial, the things that made it unique, now appeared like blemishes on a once perfect complexion.

Russell waited alone for the elevator. He preferred it that way. When the doors opened on the ground floor, he stepped in and pressed the button for the third floor. Just as the doors were about to close a hand slid in between them, making them retract. Russell looked up with a smile, ready to force a conversation. Immediately his hand clenched into fists.

"Russell," Richard Oakley said before pressing the button for the seventh floor.

RICHARD

Richard's head was splitting from yet another early morning disagreement with Elaine. He wondered how many men had to put up with the shit he did before seven a.m.

"Why is she calling the house?" Elaine demanded. "What are you hiding?"

Plenty, Richard had thought. Just nothing to do with his ex-wife.

"Don't think I don't remember how we got together," Elaine said.

It always came to that. Somehow his indiscretion with her was all his fault, as if she was an innocent bystander who didn't enjoy taking a man away from another woman. That statement was his cue to leave.

When he saw Russell standing in the elevator, alone, he tried his best not to let his disappointment show. They rode for about three seconds before Russell started.

"When am I going to operate again?" Russell asked.

"When I feel you are no longer a liability to your patients or this hospital," Richard replied.

Russell huffed. "A liability? Do you think I'd actually harm one of my patients in retaliation for what this hospital did to my wife?"

"I didn't say that," Richard replied.

"It's bad enough you've made everyone turn their backs on me here," Russell said. "But to accuse me of ignoring the oath I took? To be vengeful?"

The door chimed, signaling the third floor. Russell didn't get out. Two doctors stood at the door, ready to step on until they saw the occupants.

"We'll get the next one," one of them said.

The doors slid closed and Richard replied. "You offended this hospital and the people who work here. I can't help it if you feel alienated."

"Of course you blame me. This hospital could never be at fault. The great Kendal Slate is invincible. Even the great ones fall, Richard."

"Is that a threat?"

"I didn't say that."

Richard thought for a moment. "It's becoming clear that this hospital may no longer be a fit for you."

"Why, because I don't assault my patients?" Russell interjected.

"Go home," Richard said. The words came out before he could stop them.

"Are you firing me?" Russell asked, almost joyful.

Richard shook his head. "No. We'll honor your contract," he said. "I just feel your time would be better served at home."

"I'm not going to stop what I started," Russell said as the elevator chimed on the seventh floor.

"Take care of your wife," Richard replied and stepped off the elevator.

ADDISON

The morning after the marathon, Addison and Keith could barely walk out of the hotel. Originally, Addison had thought that the pride of running a marathon would make the physical discomfort worth it, but she was wrong, so very wrong.

"My whole body feels bruised," she said to Keith during their long ride home. The anticipation of the race had made the trip to South Carolina pass quickly. Returning was a different story.

"Keeping my foot on the gas hurts right now," Keith admitted.

Addison laughed. "It was fun, though, right?"

"Fun? Is that how you're describing it?"

"I mean it was awful, sure, but we did it. And we got these fancy medals." Addison pulled the marathon completion medal from her chest and smiled at it admiringly.

"How long are you going to wear that?" he asked.

"I haven't decided," Addison said. "I think the kids will get a kick out of it tomorrow."

The soreness continued to invade Addison's body overnight and she wasn't walking much better come Monday morning. She couldn't help but laugh as Keith hobbled from the bed to the shower. Just this once, her misery enjoyed his company.

Her students oohed and ahhed over the bright silver medal hanging from her chest as she called their attention to the front of the room.

"What is that?" one of her students called out.

"I ran a marathon this weekend," Addison said. The children looked back and forth at each other. "Twenty-six point two miles," she clarified. "It's like running from here to the aquarium."

That statement, the kids could process. Their eyes widened as they looked at their teacher in disbelief, as if they doubted she could accomplish something so cool. Addison removed the medal and allowed the students to pass it around the classroom before starting the math lesson.

"Mrs. Jones?" Suzy, one of her best students, approached her desk before lunch.

"Yes?" Addison said with a smile.

"Do you like to run?"

"I do."

"Do you want to run a race for my Grandmom?"

"What race is that?" Addison asked.

"I don't know. My mom is making a race for my Grandmom," Suzy answered. "She said it's a 5K. Is that like a marathon?"

Addison chuckled. "No, sweetie. A 5K is much shorter than a marathon."

"So you can do it?" she asked.

Although her body refused the idea of any type of physical activity, Addison couldn't say no to Suzy. "I'd love to," Addison said. "When is it?"

Suzy shrugged her shoulders.

"Well you tell me when it is," Addison said. "And I'll be there. I'll even bring my husband."

Suzy smiled, which made Addison smile. Of course she would run a race for Suzy's grandmother. She'd do anything she could for her students.

"Another race?" Keith groaned when Addison told him about Suzy.

"It's just over three miles," she said. "It's nothing."

"Walking up the stairs is something right now," Keith said. "I don't know if my body will ever forgive me for what I did to it."

"It will," Addison said. "And when it does, we can treat it to a three-mile run for one of my students."

"Is this before or after your surgery?"

"Oh shit," Addison said. "I didn't even think about that."

"Speaking of which, did you finalize the date yet?"

"I'll call first thing tomorrow."

MARCH

DALE

The emails were nonstop. At first he didn't mind, it gave him something to read, kept him encouraged. But since the truth had been revealed about Cindy's procedure and the news was making headlines, Dale didn't see the need to remain so closely entangled in Russell's fight. Dale wanted the hospital to acknowledge what they'd done. He wanted to prevent it from happening to other people. Both items appeared to be checked off his list. He wasn't a doctor, knew nothing about the medical field. Half of the emails, if not more, that Russell copied him on needed to be interpreted. Still, they came often.

Russell's latest was about Kendal Slate's decision to limit the use of morcellators in minimally invasive procedures. While Dale agreed they should be stopped altogether, the hospital now required the use of containment bags, which Dale thought made sense. Russell believed it was a failure at the most basic levels of medicine, whatever that meant.

The same point was argued over and over. Was morcellation beneficial? Should it be stopped? Whose job is it to determine what procedures can be done? What are the odds? The most frustrating part of it all was that no one had an answer. The doctors, it appeared, were just as clueless as the patients. Some claimed the odds of hidden cancer to be one in ten thousand, others one in four hundred. It didn't matter what the odds were. It had happened to Cindy and she was no longer there. That was what mattered. Not statistics and opinions. He was growing weary of it all. He just wanted to be with Cindy.

EMMA AND RUSSELL

Russell awoke at seven-thirty, looked at the clock and went back to bed for another half an hour. Eight a.m. was the latest he'd slept in a very long time. His usual schedule had him getting up at five. A "sabbatical" was how the hospital had rationalized paying Russell for not showing up for work. They could call it whatever they wanted, he considered it a small victory. By not going in, Russell could be home for Emma and continue making his case against morcellation.

Deaths immediately following or during surgical procedures were easy to track and report. Complications resulting from surgery, if not discovered soon after, were not as easily identifiable. Blood clots and infection could be correlated with little doubt if the circumstances were right. Cancer, though, hadn't been tagged as a surgical complication. Surgery didn't cause Emma's cancer. Morcellation didn't cause cancer. In fact, the etiology of leiomyosarcoma was unknown. Morcellation just upstaged it, setting a time bomb in women's abdomens. The shrapnel, tiny bits of cancer that would spread and seed, causing extreme pain that only came to an end with death.

One revelation that came from the media attention which helped Russell's cause was that of a pathologist who'd noticed an increased amount of cancer cells in specimens coming from gynecological procedures. What caused him concern and eventually led him to reporting his findings was the nature by which the samples he was receiving had been removed. Despite his raising a red flag, it didn't cause any investigation or change. It was merely another finding published along with thousands of others.

Hopeful that the FDA would find in favor of banning morcellation, Russell decided to take his fight one step further. He was going to go back to the beginning. If morcellators had never been approved in the first place, they couldn't have done any harm. Maybe the tool wasn't the issue as much as the approval process allowing it to market.

"It's called the 510(k) process," Russell informed Emma over breakfast. He'd made a plate of scrambled eggs for the family, though Emma barely touched it.

"Ok," she said.

"It's a crime in and of itself," he continued.

"So it's not just the hospitals and gynecologists?" Emma asked. "It's the Food and Drug Administration?"

"The whole system is broken," Russell said. "Every step. Basically, power morcellators were grandfathered in by the FDA."

"How does that even make sense?"

"Medical devices can be granted FDA approval without formal clinical trials if there is a current device with the same basic design and functionality already approved by the FDA on the market."

"You're kidding me," Emma said, her pale complexion starting to show signs of pink. "There was no formal testing required?"

Russell shook his head. "None."

"This keeps getting better," Emma said.

"Apparently there was an approved device on the market used in orthopedic procedures that was similar enough to power morcellators."

"So they approved a device to be used in the peritoneal cavity based on something used in knee surgeries?"

"Pretty much," Russell said, shaking his head.

Emma felt like crying. "How is this legal? I thought FDA approval meant something. How many other deadly devices have been grandfathered in that we don't know about?"

"The entire medical community, including the FDA, is putting speed ahead of safety. Do no harm should be changed to do no harm unless it's done quickly.*"

"I don't know how much more I can take," Emma said. "What happened to me, all these other women, was completely avoidable. And for what? More reimbursements for the hospitals? More money for the manufacturers? Has society become so money hungry that we're forgetting about basic human value? Have patients now become a disposable entity?"

It was too much for Emma to process. Perhaps even a formal clinical trial might not have caught the spread of cancer. But they would have shown disseminated tissue, even if it wasn't malignant. Then again, that would have only led to the production of containment bags, which had to have a failure rate.

What she wanted so badly to convey, for everyone fighting what she and Russell were trying to accomplish, was that cancer should never, ever be cut apart. No exception. It wasn't a women's issue. It wasn't them looking to blame someone for her illness. It was to create a standard of care that was correct, every time. If cancer can't be ruled out, it shouldn't be cut up. But if morcellation stopped and laparoscopic hysterectomies took a hit, millions of dollars would be lost. Somehow that made the drastic change of a woman's prognosis and lifespan acceptable.

* The Institute of Medicine (IOM) issued a report brief in July 2011, where it labeled the existing 510(k) process as "flawed."

RICHARD

Nancy tapped on Richard's door and walked into his office when he returned from lunch. "I have another message from Janine." Richard rolled his eyes. "Should I just throw them out?"

Richard sighed. "Do you ever contact your exes?"

"Not if I can help it," Nancy said. "Why?"

Richard didn't want to delve too deeply into his personal life, but with Elaine hounding him at home and Janine stalking him at work, he didn't know what to do.

"It's nothing." Richard decided it was better not to think about it.

"She won't leave a message," Nancy said. "I've tried. But she says she'll only talk to you. That it's really important."

"It is important," a female voice echoed from behind Nancy.

Richard's eyes grew large and Nancy spun quickly to see who was behind her.

"Janine," Richard said, his voice sticking in his throat.

"What'd you expect?" she replied. "You weren't taking my calls."

Richard laughed nervously. "Nancy, would you excuse us please?" He wasn't sure he wanted to be alone with Janine, but he also didn't want Nancy to hear anything that could come out of Janine's mouth."

"You look well," he said when they were alone.

"What? You think because you walked out on me I'd fall to pieces? You always were an arrogant prick."

Richard couldn't help but laugh. Her attitude, her spunk was a breath of fresh air. "What can I do for you, Janine?"

"You could answer my phone calls," she said. "Save me the hassle of coming to this place."

"Well you're here now, so what do you need? What is so important?"

"I need information about your mother."

"My mother?" Richard asked, shocked. Of all the things he thought Janine would ask about, his mother was not one of them. "Why?"

"I know she died of cancer and I know you don't like to talk about it. But I need to know what kind of cancer she had. I don't think you ever told me."

Richard sighed in relief, thinking it was a small miracle Janine hadn't asked Elaine. If Elaine found out that Richard had shared stuff about his mother with Janine and not her, she might have filed for divorce that day. A smile came to the corners of Richard's mouth at the thought.

"Why?"

"I think it's important that my daughter, your daughter, knows what her true family history is so that she can make informed decisions about her health."

"Is something wrong?" Richard asked.

"Would you care if there was?" Janine replied.

"Fair enough," he said. "My mother died of ovarian cancer."

Janine's face went pale.

"What is it?" Richard asked.

"Is there testing that can be done to detect it?" Janine asked.

"I thought you didn't trust us doctors," Richard said.

"I don't," Janine replied. "Is there accurate testing available?"

"Ovarian cancer is a silent killer most of the time, especially back when my mom had it. There really aren't any symptoms until it's too late."

"What about imaging?" Janine asked. "Or biopsies?"

"It's a hard cancer to detect. Though recent studies have found that most ovarian cancers actually start in the fallopian tubes. So having them out may actually decrease a woman's risk of having ovarian cancer later in life."

"Is it hereditary?"

"It can be," Richard said. "Janine, what's going on?"

"Why wouldn't you tell me that before you left?" Janine asked, panic taking over. "A simple, hey, my mother died of ovarian cancer. You might want to keep an eye on our daughter as she gets older."

"Is she sick?" Richard felt a pang of panic in his gut.

"No, well, not yet," Janine stammered.

"What do you mean?" he asked.

"She's set to have surgery here, next month," Janine said. "I don't want her to, but she's insistent."

"Does she have cancer?" Richard asked, annoyed Janine wasn't getting to the point.

"No, Richard. She has endometriosis. She's getting a hysterectomy."

"Oh," he said with a hint of relief.

"Oh?" Janine shot back. "Oh, like that's no big deal?"

"It's not," Richard said. "It's relatively safe, quick."

"Don't give me that load of doctor talk," Janine said. "I don't buy it, especially with what's been all over the news lately."

"That story has been blown out of proportion," Richard said.

"Is that why this hospital, under the advice of Department Chair Richard Oakley, decided to limit the use of power morcellators?"

"Trust me, I didn't want to do it," Richard admitted.

"Why am I not surprised?"

Richard inhaled to keep himself from exploding. Even Elaine couldn't get under his skin like Janine. She knew what to say, how to say it, all while keeping her eyes, as dark as chocolate, fixed on his, like she was reading his mind, examining his soul. "Is there anything else you want to know? I doubt you came down here for an argument."

"I came down here for information and to get your word that this hospital protects its patients. You walked out years ago and I never asked you for anything. I let you go, live your perfect life with your perfect wife. Addison is all I have and I want to keep her safe."

Hearing her name sent a chill down Richard's spine. "This is a good hospital, Janine. With good doctors."

"Well that's not what I've read. I know it's asking a lot, but can you try to be a father instead of a doctor and make sure our daughter doesn't get hacked up like some of your other female patients?"

ADDISON

"You expecting someone?" Keith asked Addison.

They had just sat down for dinner when there was a knock on the door. Addison shook her head. Keith got up and walked down the stairs to the foyer. Addison took the opportunity to pour her and Keith a glass of wine.

"I'm not interrupting anything, am I?" Addison's mom asked when Keith opened the door.

"Of course not," Keith replied. "Come on in. Would you like to join us for dinner?"

"You're eating kind of late," her mom said, her voice getting closer to the stairs.

Addison chugged her glass and poured another.

"Mom," Addison said as pleasantly as possible when her mom came into sight. "To what do we owe this honor?"

"I was going to call but didn't want to upset you over the phone."

"Would you like me to leave you two—"

"No," Addison and her mom said in unison.

"This concerns you too," her mom added.

Keith nodded and sat down at the table next to Addison.

"I don't want you to be mad," Addison's mom began, pulling out the chair across from Addison.

"Just say it," Addison said.

"I went to see your father," she replied.

Addison's mouth fell open. "My father? Why?"

"Well, since you're insistent about having this surgery, I wanted to make sure I knew his family history."

"You told him I was having surgery?" Addison asked.

"His mother died of cancer. I wanted to know which kind, and if it meant anything for you."

"And?" Addison asked.

"She died of ovarian cancer, so I'd say it's relevant."

Addison exhaled. "I see."

"I also wanted to ask him about everything the newspapers have been saying about Kendal Slate."

"I told you it's a good hospital, Mom. I like my doctor."

"He's in charge of the surgical department, Addison, at Kendal Slate."

"Ahh," Keith said, though he'd meant to stay silent. All this time, Janine's rants and anger about the medical establishment were rooted in her hatred of her ex-husband.

"What did he say?" Addison asked.

"Pretty much everything you have," her mom said. "He believes in his doctors."

"I could really care less about what he believes," Addison replied spitefully.

"It's important to know everything going into your surgery. Family history is important."

"It is, but I don't see how that changes anything for me." Addison said. "The surgery is scheduled. The preoperative bloodwork and tests are done. I'm ready for this, Mom. And so is Dr. Yorker."

"It still might be good to let Dr. Yorker know about your grandmother," Keith offered.

Addison shrugged.

"Yes," Janine agreed. "Talk with her, see what she has to say."

"She's going to say the same thing she has all along," Addison said.

"That the surgery is safe, the risk of complications is low. Nothing's going to change."

"She'd be a fool not to take it into consideration," Janine said.

"I'm sure she'll appreciate the information," Keith interjected before Addison had a chance to reply. "Dr. Yorker is a good doctor. Everything's going to work out. Addison is going to be fine."

"Yeah," Janine quipped. "Bad things never happen to good people in hospitals."

DALE

Though he was never one for words, Dale found himself missing the conversations he and Cindy enjoyed. They had a rhythm, a flow that had been perfected over years of banter and arguments. The girls didn't get the difference of being alone and being lonely. How could they? They thought that by calling daily, they'd provide him with the interaction he missed. They failed to understand that while he enjoyed talking with them, their conversations didn't replace the ones he couldn't have with Cindy.

"Hey Dad," Rebecca called right on time with her daily invitation. "I was just about to put dinner on and thought you'd might like to join us."

"Thanks, Becca," Dale said. "But I just had a sandwich."

"A sandwich?" Rebecca replied. "That's not a good dinner. I'm making spaghetti and meatballs, with homemade garlic bread."

"Thank you. I'm okay."

"Are you sure? You don't sound so good tonight."

"I'm just tired," Dale said.

"Gail said you were tired when she stopped by the other day. Is everything okay?"

"Everything's fine. You go and put dinner on. I will talk to you later."

"Okay," she replied hesitantly. "But there's another reason I called. Suzy told me she got her teacher to come to the race. She was so excited."

Dale laughed. "That's great. So we know we'll have at least one non-family member there."

"We're going to have more than that, Dad. Just wait."

"I'm sure," Dale said. "There's nothing you girls can't do when you put your heads together. You got that from your mother."

"I think we got a little from you too."

Dale hung up with Rebecca, went to the refrigerator and fixed himself a ham sandwich, light mayo, little bit of salt. "Just a sprinkle," Cindy used to say. The pain in his chest was real. He never knew he could miss someone so much.

APRIL

EMMA AND RUSSELL

Scanxiety. Emma had read about it during her chemotherapy sessions. She'd seen it on the online discussion boards. She wondered if going to her first scan after chemo would feel any different to her daily anxiety. It did. As she changed into the gown and placed her clothes in locker number three, she was all nerves. Her hands trembled as she removed the key from the lock and slid the purple coil bracelet keychain around her wrist.

Her parents had called, her sisters, all to check in and wish her well. She didn't answer any of the calls. She just couldn't, not today. She barely had the words to talk to Russell.

She took a seat in the waiting room, waiting for the nurse to escort her back. The nurse was pleasant, making small talk as they walked, Emma didn't reciprocate. She followed the nurse into the large, cold room where the CT scanner sat quiet in the corner like an enormous sea creature waiting for prey in the depths of the ocean. She walked over to the machine, sat down on the table attached to its center like a tongue and waited for the test to begin, for the beast to swallow her whole.

Emma closed her eyes as the table slid into the scanner. She'd tried to do it with her eyes open but couldn't escape the thought that she was being buried alive. Claustrophobic at baseline, it didn't take much for Emma to feel confined and short of air.

"Everything okay?" The technician spoke through the speaker in the belly of the beast.

"Sure," Emma replied, the anxiety stinging her nerves.

The table moved, the machine whirred into action and Emma tried to find a happy place. Every happy place took her to her children. The thought of a possible negative result destroyed any happiness she'd begun to feel.

An hour and half later, Emma was sent on her way, no escort needed. "Follow the green line on the floor," the nurse had said. "Have a great afternoon."

Emma smiled weakly. If only she knew. She had to know. But what was she supposed to say? Hopefully your cancer hasn't come back? Emma wanted to have a great afternoon. She wanted to have a great life. The answer, for at least the next three months, was imaged in the computer, awaiting the eyes of the radiologist who would deliver what would either be the best news since she'd heard the words, "you have cancer," or the ones she feared the most, "we found a mass."

Russell rose from his seat in the waiting room when Emma walked out. He smiled, she shrugged. "Since Sara's with the girls, do you want to go grab lunch?"

"Sure."

"We don't have to," he said.

"You need to eat," she replied.

"We need to eat," he corrected.

Emma didn't share Russell's confidence that everything was okay. She had felt so good after the hysterectomy only to find out that she had a very aggressive cancer. There was no way Emma was going to be fooled into thinking she was okay, despite her hair growing back and increasing energy. She needed to hear it from her doctor. She needed to hear the words, no evidence of disease. Until that point, she'd assume the worst and remain scared numb.

RICHARD

There'd been times over the course of his life with Elaine that Richard thought about Addison. He'd considered reaching out to Janine a few times, not so that he could establish a close relationship with Addison, but just to check in, see how she was growing up. Addison was, after all, his firstborn.

Richard wasn't so heartless he could walk out and never look back. At first, he'd missed Addison and Janine. He'd considered going back, begging Janine for forgiveness. The problem was, he was too proud and Janine too unforgiving. He could ask for forgiveness, but even if he was able to muster the courage to admit his faults, Janine wouldn't hear any of it.

When things with Elaine got rough—in the beginning there were many fights—Richard couldn't help but wonder what his life would have been like if he'd stayed with Janine. There was no doubt in his mind that Janine would have stuck by him, she loved him. He might have even become a better surgeon, a better doctor if he had stayed. But he didn't.

As time passed, it became easier to forget about his first family and the way his ex-wife constantly challenged him to be better. Elaine could care less about his personal growth as long as her lifestyle didn't change. Most days he forgot he was ever married before, that he had a child walking around somewhere in the world. He used to wonder if any of the faces he'd see in the halls of the hospital were Addison. Even that faded. But now, Janine had brought his past to his present, demanding him to be a better man, a better father, if he could even call himself that to Addison.

There are laws about looking at patient files without their consent. There are laws protecting doctor-patient confidentiality. However, any doctor with hospital credentials has the power and ease of reading just about any patient's file.

He went back and forth, should he, shouldn't he. Why did he care? Why should he care? Did he care? It was all irrelevant as he found himself in front of his computer, reading Addison Jones' file. Her medical story told of continual heartbreak through failed fertilization treatments, miscarriages, and finally an ectopic pregnancy. No wonder she wanted a hysterectomy.

She's smart, he thought. And courageous. There was no way Janine was on board with the surgery and for Addison to go against her mother made him proud. After discovering her background, the next thing Richard wanted to check on was her doctor.

He'd made claims about all the doctors at Kendal Slate, but the reality was there were a few duds. With Janine's words beating him down mentally, "make sure our daughter doesn't get hacked up like some of your other female patients," he wanted to ensure Addison was under the care of one of the good doctors.

Richard breathed a sigh of relief when he saw the doctor on file as Elizabeth Yorker. Elizabeth was definitely a good one, the best one Addison could've hoped for. If Richard had thought for one second he had a shot with Lizzie Yorker, he would have tried years ago. She had it all, long lean legs, intelligence, and one dimple on her right cheek that was always on display. Lizzie Yorker genuinely cared about her patients. In fact, the only disagreements she and Richard had were over her refusal to turn anyone away.

Janine may have been against the idea of Addison's surgery, but from a medical perspective, it made perfect sense, not that she'd want to hear that from Richard.

There was a notation in Addison's file, documenting her paternal grandmother's history of ovarian cancer. As Richard read through Lizzie Yorker's notes on Addison, it became clear she planned to use electric power morcellation.

It had been a no brainer when Elaine had asked Richard if he would be okay with her undergoing a procedure that used power morcellation. However, thinking about the same for Addison gave him pause.

This is ridiculous. He thought. *Morcellation is safe. Addison will be fine.*

Richard shook his head and closed Addison's file. It was out of his hands. Addison wasn't his responsibility. But if he should happen to bump into Lizzie Yorker, it might be worth a casual conversation. He might even try to dissuade her from morcellation… just for this one case.

ADDISON

The last time she'd had surgery, it was an emergent situation. There was no preparation, only urgency. This time around, Addison had soap to shower with and a set of instructions to follow the night before.

"I'm nervous," she told Keith as they sat on the couch, watching television as though it was an ordinary Tuesday night.

"I'm not," Keith said. "You're going to be fine."

"I hope so," she replied. "Because I love our life together. There's still so much I want to accomplish."

"And you will," he said. "Addy, this is a routine procedure. Women have it done every day."

"And I'm sure there's a woman who dies as a result every day."

"Am I talking with you or your mother?"

Addison nuzzled into Keith. "I'm sorry. It's just, we talked so much about all this and now we're here. There's no turning back."

"We can start a new chapter. Move forward."

Addison was about to respond when her phone rang. A number she didn't recognize flashed on the screen.

"Hello?" Addison asked nervously.

"Addison, hi. It's Elizabeth Yorker."

Addison flashed a surprised look at Keith. "Hi Dr. Yorker."

"I know you're really anxious about the procedure, so I wanted to make sure you were okay and didn't have any last-minute questions."

"That's really nice of you," Addison said. "I'm just really nervous."

"That's actually why I'm calling," Dr. Yorker said. "I've been thinking about your family history of ovarian cancer. While I don't believe there is anything to worry about, I'd like to err on the side of caution."

"Okay," Addison said slowly, not completely understanding what Dr. Yorker was getting at.

"Again, I don't think anything is wrong. I'd just like to perform the procedure a little differently. I'd like to remove your uterus through the vagina, in one piece."

"Okay," Addison repeated.

"Not much will change with regards to anything else. I'd still like to make the incisions in your abdomen that we discussed, but only for the cameras. Because the plan is to leave your right ovary, I want to get a good look at it while I'm in there."

Addison exhaled. "That actually makes me feel a little bit better."

"I am confident in what I do," Dr. Yorker said, her voice as reassuring as ever. "You are going to be just fine."

"Thank you, Dr. Yorker," Addison said.

"I'll see you Thursday morning. Try and get some rest."

Addison hung up the phone and smiled. "That was really nice. She just wanted to check in and make sure I felt ready for Thursday."

"Do you feel better now?"

"A little," Addison said, though she was still scared out of her mind.

At five o'clock on Thursday morning, Keith and Addison set out for Kendal Slate Memorial Hospital to put one part of their life behind them and begin another, better one, free from loss and constant disappointment.

DALE

It was five o'clock in the morning and Dale was wide awake, the words *'til death do us part* repeating in his mind like a broken record. Unlike the younger generation, he knew what records sounded like when they were, in fact, broken. *'Til death do us part.*

They had both vowed to love each other 'til death do us part, never really thinking about what it implied. But as Dale contemplated his love for Cindy and their vows, death didn't release him of any of it. When they promised themselves to each other, he'd promised himself to her for the rest of his life, not the rest of hers. Even parted by death, he wasn't absolved of his dedication.

He had friends who dated again after losing their wives. Some even remarried. Not him. Even in death, he would find her. If he knew Cindy, she was hanging around until he died so they could cross over into the light, or whatever waited for them in the beyond, together.

"Hey Cin, if you're listening, I'm ready," he said into the darkness of his bedroom. "I know you're watching me sleep because you know how much it used to freak me out. So, if you're here, do what you have to do. Talk to your people up there and get them to bring me along. Make it quick, if you can. The girls are good. They know I'd be better with you. I'm ready when you are."

He'd officially become crazy, awake at five in the morning, talking to his dead wife, asking for death. If the girls could only hear him now, they'd have him declared mentally incompetent and force him to move in with one of them.

It was Wednesday morning. He was due at the library. He didn't want to go. Dale felt himself slipping into something, a form of depression maybe. Maybe it was the buildup of finding out that there was more to Cindy's care than previously thought and the letdown that came once he realized it didn't change a thing. Russell Speck had something to fight for, someone. At the end of the day, Dale was left without Cindy, with a broken heart and a bitter spirit.

EMMA AND RUSSELL

Emma had drifted off to sleep sporadically throughout the night, never sleeping for more than a half hour. How could she sleep knowing her films had undoubtedly been read and evaluated? If she didn't hear in the morning, she would call.

Russell passed out sometime after three. He'd been up late researching, commenting on published articles, and responding to emails from women and their loved ones affected by LMS. What started as a fight for Emma had evolved into a crusade for many women across the country and beyond. He'd been contacted by women in Canada and most recently, Germany. His inbox was flooded and Facebook was a never-ending stream of messages.

The stories were mirror images of each other, all including morcellation, dissemination, advanced disease, and, in most cases, death. At the root of all of the messages was hope. Hope that Russell could do something for them, that he had the answers the other doctors didn't. It pained him to admit that he couldn't offer these connected strangers anything more than his condolences and vow to end morcellation. Emma had grown weary of the repeated stories recounted by Russell. She was battling her own malignant demons and each new story provided her with less hope that things would get better.

At six a.m., Emma got up and went downstairs, fixing herself a cup of green tea. Oh, how she despised the taste of green tea. She much preferred and rather enjoyed the aroma and flavor of coffee. Green tea she likened to dirt.

"Try adding lemon," her sister had suggested.

"I did," Emma replied. "It tasted like lemon flavored dirt."

Despite her revulsion of green tea, Emma stuck with it as a major component of her daily food regimen. Upon completion of chemotherapy, she completely revamped her diet. No more red meat, not that she'd eaten much of it before. She bid farewell to processed foods and sugars, tearfully swapping her adored milk chocolate for dark chocolate, and organic at that. Turmeric replaced salt and was sprinkled on just about everything, stopping short at yogurt. The kids turned their noses up at her new diet. She didn't blame them one bit.

"Hi Mom," Kaitlin said, appearing in the door of the kitchen.

"What are you doing up so early? You don't have to be up for another hour," Emma asked.

"I couldn't sleep," she said.

"That makes two of us," Emma replied.

"Are you okay?" Kaitlin asked.

Poor thing, Emma thought. Since Emma's diagnosis, Kaitlin had become overly concerned with Emma's health. Emma couldn't so much as sneeze without Kaitlin coming to her aid, asking if she was all right, if she needed anything.

Emma smiled, taking a seat at the kitchen table with her steaming cup of dirt water. "I'm perfect, honey. Don't you worry about me."

"Are you?" she asked. "Perfect? Are you all better now?"

"For now," Emma answered. She and Russell both agreed it was best to be as open and honest with the kids as they could comprehend.

"What does that mean?" Kaitlin asked, worry flashing across her face.

"It means you don't need to worry about anything right now. We are all here, together. That is what we need to focus on."

"So you're not all better," Kaitlin said. She was smarter than Emma gave her credit for.

"Cancer can come back," Emma admitted. "I hope it won't, but it can. That's why it's important to be happy now." Kaitlin went silent. "Kay, you know you can always talk to me about how you're feeling, right? Or ask me any questions you might have."

Kaitlin kept her head down, looking at the floor.

"What is it, honey?" Emma asked.

"It's just that…" Kaitlin played with her fingers. "I don't…"

"What, honey?" Emma asked. "Just say it."

"I don't want you to die." Kaitlin bit her lip and looked up, tears streaming down her face.

"Oh baby," Emma got up and rushed to hug her daughter. But what could she say to make it better when Emma didn't know herself? "I love you so much."

They were standing in the kitchen, Emma's arms wrapped tightly around Kaitlin when the phone rang. Emma's heart stopped. "I have to take this honey." She released Kaitlin from her tight embrace and rushed to the phone.

"Hello?" she said.

"Emma, it's Cole Teigan."

Emma began shaking. She felt Kaitlin watching her from across the kitchen. "Yes?"

"I've read your report and there's no evidence of disease."

"Oh thank God," Emma exclaimed. She was so elated she felt lightheaded.

Emma hung up the phone, smiled at Kaitlin through the tears falling from her eyes and thanked God for granting her more time.

RICHARD

"Why are you going in so early?" Elaine had asked when the alarm sounded at three thirty in the morning, an unusual departure from his standard four fifteen wakeup.

"I've got a lot to get through today," Richard lied.

He couldn't exactly explain to Elaine that Addison was scheduled as the first case of the day. She'd lose her mind. Part of Richard hoped that Janine would stop by to yell at him for something so that he could perhaps get a little more information out of her or at least reassure her that their daughter was in good hands. It was weird to think of it that way, their daughter, his daughter. Having two boys, he'd never had the need to refer to a daughter. But knowing she was having surgery in his hospital, his house, somehow made him feel responsible for her, for the first time in his life.

ADDISON

Faces hovered over her when she opened her eyes, none of whom she recognized. "Keith," Addison said, her throat tender and voice hoarse. "Where's Keith?"

"He'll be back soon," one of the blurs said. "Just try and get some rest."

The next time she woke up, Keith was by her side.

"Hi there beautiful," he said. He took her hand in his, careful of the IV placed in the middle. "You did great."

Addison closed her eyes and went back to sleep.

"You lost a little more blood than usual," Keith informed her the next time she woke up and appeared a little more coherent. "They want to keep you overnight."

"It hurts," Addison said.

Within seconds a nurse was at her bedside, adding something to her IV. Addison drifted back out.

When she was able to go to the bathroom without being too lightheaded, they moved her to her room where her mom was seated, waiting.

"How are you feeling?" she asked as Addison was wheeled in.

"Not great," Addison admitted, struggling to get out of the wheelchair.

"Are you in a lot of pain?"

"I'm sore," Addison said. "And really tired."

"Well, sleep is the best thing you can do. Do you want a blanket? An extra pillow?"

Addison smiled. "I'm okay. Thank you."

"Okay, how about food? Are you allowed to eat?"

"Mom, I'm okay."

Despite the words coming from her mouth, Addison couldn't get her mother to relax. She talked a mile a minute and paced the room. All the while, Addison was in and out of sleep, the anesthesia lingering. Addison woke up as her mom ranted about the insanity behind March Madness. Thankfully, a gentle knock on the door made her mom pause.

"Knock, knock," Dr. Yorker said, walking in.

"Hi Dr. Yorker," Addison replied.

"Hello," Janine said crisply.

"Hello," Dr. Yorker said, extending her hand to Janine.

Dr. Yorker walked to the side of Addison's bed and looked at her belly, pressing gently and examining her incisions.

"The surgery went fantastic. You did great. I was able to remove your uterus in one piece. You bled a little more than what I like to see, but given your history, it's not unusual. There was a lot of internal scarring to deal with. I'd like to keep you overnight for observation, make sure your blood counts are where they need to be before we send you home."

"Makes sense," Keith said.

"You didn't cut her uterus up?" Janine asked. "You left everything together?"

"Yes," Dr. Yorker replied.

"I appreciate that," Janine said, feeling Richard had something to do with the decision. "Thank you."

"Yes, thank you," Addison replied. "For everything."

"It was my pleasure," Dr. Yorker replied. "Please take it easy. No more marathons until you're all healed."

"How about no more marathons at all?" her mom advised.

Dr. Yorker laughed. "You know the restrictions that we talked about prior to the surgery. No heavy lifting, nothing heavier than a gallon of milk. You can shower tomorrow but leave the bandages on."

Addison nodded.

"Your body has been through a lot," Dr. Yorker said. "You need to give it time to heal."

"You have my word," Keith said.

"And you have my number," Dr. Yorker said. "Please call if you need anything at all."

"I will," Addison said. "Thank you."

Addison watched Dr. Yorker as she left the room, grateful to have such a wonderful doctor. "See, Mom," Addison said. "She's fantastic."

Janine looked at Addison with a smile that quickly turned to a stone-cold glare. Addison followed her mom's gaze out the door to a taller man with graying hair, looking in on them.

"What?" Addison asked her mom. "Is that him?"

MAY

DALE

The sun shone and the April showers had thankfully passed, leaving Stoney Hill Park dry and filled with green, plush grass. It was a beautiful day for a race. Dale watched as the girls divided and conquered the race-day task list, just like he knew they would.

Carmen said they had seventy-five registrants prior to the race, with the potential for more signing up the morning of. Rebecca arranged the registration table, the snack table and the water station while Carmen, with the baby strapped to her chest, directed everyone to the starting line.

"Mom would be proud," Dale said to Rebecca as he entered the registration tent.

Rebecca smiled and looked around. "I think it all came together nicely."

"I'll say," he replied.

Rebecca was about to respond when she got distracted by a couple walking across the field, four children in tow, talking to another woman. "I think those are the Specks."

EMMA AND RUSSELL

"How are you feeling?" Alyson Baker asked as Emma and Russell did their best to keep their children corralled.

"Grateful," Emma replied. "There are so many women, like Cindy Reichter, who died so quickly after their surgeries. I'm just grateful to be here."

"Excuse me." An older man approached the couple.

Russell and Emma turned to the man as he stepped closer. Emma remembered seeing him in the hospital elevator, the sadness present in his eyes the same as it was that day.

Dale extended his hand to Russell. "I'm Dale Reichter."

"Nice to put a face to the voice," Russell said. "You've done a great job here."

"Yes," Emma said. "What a great turnout."

"My girls worked very hard," Dale said with pride.

"Can we get a couple of shots of the three of you talking?" Alyson asked.

Russell and Emma, now used to having their pictures taken, continued talking to Dale. They'd become the face of the national anti-morcellation debate. Dale, on the other hand, was clearly uncomfortable posing and had to stop talking while the camera clicked.

"The race will start in fifteen minutes!" Gail shouted into the megaphone.

"We should get our numbers," Emma suggested. "It was really nice to meet you, Dale. Thanks again for putting this together."

"You can thank my daughter at registration," he said. "She was the ɔrains behind all this. Good luck in your recovery. I'm sorry you have to deal with this."

Emma offered a smile and pushed the stroller toward the line of people under the white tent. On the registration table sat a large picture of Cindy Reichter. Seeing it gave both Russell and Emma pause.

Cindy, as with the other images Russell had seen of victims of morcellation, was young and full of life. Her smile told of better times. Her absence, the grim reality of neglectful medical professionals.

RICHARD

"The race is today," Elaine said to Richard over breakfast. "It's a beautiful day. You should think about going."

Richard laughed. "Those people hate me."

"I doubt they hate you. They're mad at the hospital."

"I represent the hospital, more specifically the surgical department."

"It might be good to go, help change their minds about you."

"These people have lost loved ones. It's not the place for me."

Elaine sighed. "If you say so."

"I say so," Richard replied.

"Madeline said she'd go with me if you didn't want to."

"No," Richard said sternly. "You don't belong there."

"Maybe we all do," Elaine shot back. "If your mother died of cancer, our boys' grandmother, we should do something for cancer research."

"Why do you care so much?" Richard asked.

"Why don't you care at all?"

The question took Richard by surprise. He did care that his mother died of cancer. She was his mother. He did care that the disease that took his mother decades ago still didn't have a cure. But he was a surgeon, not an oncologist. He chose surgery so he could fix things. Oncology was often a futile specialty.

"I'll make a donation," he replied after a moment of thought. "Send it in anonymously."

"Because throwing money at the problem is the same as showing up."

"It's what I'm comfortable with," he replied.

"We wouldn't want to take you out of your comfort zone," Elaine said.

"If you want to go to the race, *GO!*" Richard barked. "I'm not going."

Elaine stormed out of the room. She'd been bluffing and Richard knew it. She wasn't going to go without Richard. There was no way Elaine and Madeline would make it past the first kilometer before searching for the closest Starbucks and abandoning the race route.

As much as he didn't want to admit it, Elaine's words struck a chord. Richard rose from the table, picked the paper off the counter and brought it into his home office off the den. He opened *The Times* and saw the write-up on the Run for Cindy, a race to raise money and awareness for leiomyosarcoma.

Richard fingered through the hanging files in the bottom drawer of his desk until he found the black folder. It was stuffed in the back, the second to last file in the drawer, marked *Misc. of Misc.* He knew a folder marked *MOM* would have been too hard for Elaine to ignore. He opened it slowly, as though something inside waited to jump at him.

The contents were the same as the day he'd put them in the folder and locked them away. Letters from his mother as her health deteriorated, apologies for missing out on the achievements she'd knew he'd come to have and words of encouragement for the times when life brought him the unexpected. Richard never read them all, only skimmed them when his father had given him an envelope with his name on it.

Underneath the letters was a picture of Richard and his mother when he was a baby. The caption on the back identified him as three months old. Richard had been a pudgy baby and his mother couldn't have appeared any more in love with her round baby. Richard picked up the picture and compared it to the only other picture in the folder. The picture of Richard, in hospital scrubs, holding an equally fat baby. The caption on the back, written in Janine's perfect penmanship read *Daddy and his Addy (3months).*

A lump formed in Richard's throat and anger swelled at the same time. He'd suppressed his mother's illness and untimely death, pushing it like the file folder, to the recesses of his memory. He'd done the same with Addison and Janine.

All it took was an obnoxious doctor to start a national campaign and here he was looking at his past. He should've been a better son to his ailing mother and grieving father. He should've done more cancer research. He should've been a better father, a better man. He was a coward hiding behind intelligence and a fancy title. What did any of that mean at the end of the day?

Richard opened the middle drawer of the desk and took out his checkbook. He wrote out check number five hundred and thirty-seven to Race for Cindy in the amount of ten thousand dollars.

THE RACE

"Are you sure you can handle this?" Keith asked Addison as they walked across the open field.

"It's been six weeks since my surgery," Addison said. "Besides, by insisting my mother come I have no choice but to walk."

Keith laughed.

"Mrs. Jones!" Addison heard a familiar voice yell from behind her. She turned around to find Suzy Polar standing with her father.

"Hi Suzy," Addison said.

"You came!" Suzy exclaimed.

"Of course I did," Addison said with a smile. "I wouldn't miss this for the world. Everything looks amazing! Did you help with these balloons?" Suzy smiled and nodded. Addison turned to Suzy's father. "I'm sorry for your loss."

"Thank you," he replied. "Cindy was a great woman."

"Mom," Suzy squealed. "Look, it's Mrs. Jones. I told you she was coming."

"Thank you for coming," Rebecca said to Addison. "It means so much to Suzy. She really enjoys having you as her teacher."

Addison blushed. "Of course. I enjoy having her as a student. I was really sorry to hear about your mom."

"Thank you," Rebecca said.

"Racers, take your mark!" Gail's husband hollered into the megaphone.

Rebecca excused herself and made her way to the starting line as it filled. Adults, kids, strollers, even a couple of dogs lined up with their owners. Gail, Rebecca and Carmen took their places at the front. Three minutes later the bullhorn sounded and the runners were off.

Dale watched as the racers took off down the path, into the woods. The girls, with their bibs marked numbers two, three and four, led the way. Their husbands stayed behind to man their stations. He looked down at the bib Gail had pinned to his chest marked number one. "You were always number one," he said, looking at the picture of his wife on the registration table.

"You going to walk the route?" Joel, Carmen's husband, asked. "We put a memoriam marker at each kilometer with the picture of a woman affected by LMS."

"Carmen told me," Dale replied. "I think I'll sit this one out."

He pulled up a chair and took a seat next to the poster of his wife. The pain in his chest was real. He could feel his heart crack seeing Cindy's beautiful smile. There were some women who smiled just for the sake of the picture being taken. Cindy always smiled because she loved life.

Russell and Emma walked the path, enjoying the day and the weather. They took their time, stopping at each kilometer, reading the background of each woman remembered along the way. Emma clutched Russell's right hand tightly with her left.

"It's going to be fine," he said. "Tomorrow is going to be another beautiful day and the day after that and the day after that. You're going to be fine."

They hadn't walked half a mile before Janine started on about why the race had to be five kilometers instead of three miles.

"It just makes no sense," she said. "We don't measure the highways in kilometers or speed in kilometers."

Addison and Keith laughed as she nattered on.

Dale clapped when the first runner crossed the finish line. He wondered how far back his girls were. "They did such an amazing job, Cin," he said. The tightness compressed his chest. He missed her so much. Three more runners crossed the finish line to more cheering from the crowd of supporters. The nausea set in as another wave of applause signaled more runners returning.

"Mommy!" Dale heard Suzy exclaim.

He looked across the field to see Rebecca taking long strides toward the finish line. When she was about fifty feet out, she slowed her pace until Gail caught up. They slowed even more for Carmen. The crowd, seeing the sisters unite so that they could cross the finish line together, erupted in applause.

"I'm good now," Dale said, feeling his breath get short. "They've got each other, Cin. I need you."

EPILOGUE

I'm not going to lie. The thought of not being alive for Kaitlin's tenth birthday terrified me. It kept me awake at night, scared and angry at the thought of missing my firstborn's first double-digit birthday. But as my scans showed no evidence of disease, my hopes were replaced with an almost-confidence that I would be here to celebrate with her. That was before today.

Today I discovered a lump in my groin. For many lucky women my age, a pain in the groin might not be something to worry about, a pulled muscle. However, for me, it is all I can worry about. For me, the first thought is always recurrence. Always. I've been feeling what I can only describe as a pull in my left groin for a couple of weeks now. I haven't mentioned it because I didn't want to upset Russell unnecessarily. Part of me also didn't want to acknowledge what I fear most.

I don't know if my disease has returned and if it has, how quickly it will spread. I pray that I can see Kaitlin blow her candles out and make a wish. I pray this journal entry can be discarded. But I have to be honest. I want to write my thoughts as they formulate in my head. I never had the time to journal. Now it's all I have until I don't. Is this the beginning of the end?

AUTHOR'S NOTES

While this story is fiction, leiomyosarcoma is all too real. It is rare and aggressive, making it one of the most lethal illnesses to develop. To date, there is no cure and it does not respond well to standard cancer treatment regimens. To learn more about LMS and how you can help raise awareness and funding, please visit www.slaysarcoma.com.

ACKNOWLEDGEMENTS

This book wouldn't have been possible without the courageous work of my sister, Amy. Your unwavering strength will never be forgotten. And to Hooman, thank you for loving my sister unconditionally, dancing with her until the end.

To my mom, JoAnn, and siblings Amy, Alison, Andrea, Sarah and Dan, your continued support and input means the world to me. Lindsay and Ivana, thank you for your critiques and encouragement along the way, and at all times across different time zones. To my husband, Chuck, you have been my pillar of strength through this all. I love you. Thank you, everyone, for believing in me and this book.

To Allison Williams, The Unkind Editor, your edits and advice continue to help me improve as an author.

And last but definitely not least, to all of the women and families affected by uterine leiomyosarcoma. It is my hope that one day there will be a cure. Together, we will fight this disease.

ABOUT THE AUTHOR

A native of Pennsylvania, A.K. Mills gave up a job in Information Systems to pursue her dream of becoming an author. *The Snow White Effect* is her third novel. When not writing, she enjoys spending time with her family and two dogs.

Other works by A.K. Mills:

The Parts I Remember

The Parts That Followed

References

* Sugarbaker, P., Ihemelandu, C. & Bijelic, L. Ann Surg Oncol (2016) 23: 1501. doi:10.1245/s10434-015-4960-y

* FDA.(2014). *Laparoscopic Uterine Power Morcellation in Hysterectomy and Myomectomy: FDA Safety Communication.* Silver Spring, MD: U.S. Department of Health and Human Services.

* Institute of Medicine. (2011). *Medical Devices and the Public's Health The FDA 510(k) Clearance Process at 35 Years.* Washington, D.C.: The National Academy of Science

CPSIA information can be obtained
at www.ICGtesting.com
Printed in the USA
BVOW09s0915120418
513153BV00003B/7/P